"Do you think I did it?

Do you?" Veronica asked. Her voice sounded cold, and hurt kindled in her eyes.

"No," Nathan said. "I don't."

Relief flickered briefly across her face. "Then why go behind my back?"

"I want to find out what's going on here. If one of your clients isn't responsible, it must have to do with your past. I don't know much about amnesia— I hoped your doctor could help me understand it."

She shivered. Nathan warmed her hands between his, then drew her into his arms.

"Nathan—it's important to me that you believe me."

"Shh," he said. He cupped her face in the palms of his hands, his mouth a whisper away. "I do believe you. We're going to solve this together." Lowering his head softly, he pressed his lips onto the soft edges of her mouth. "You're not alone, Veronica. Not anymore."

RITA HERRON

Award-winning author Rita Herron wrote her first book when she was twelve, but didn't think real people grew up to be writers. Now she writes so she doesn't have to get a real job. A former kindergarten teacher and workshop leader, she traded her storytelling for kids for romance, and writes romantic comedies and romantic suspense. She lives in Georgia with her own romance hero and three kids. She loves to hear from readers so please write her at P.O. Box 921225, Norcross, GA 30092-1225, or visit her Web site at www.ritaherron.com.

Rita Herron
Send Me a Hero

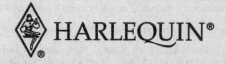

TORONTO • NEW YORK • LONDON
AMSTERDAM • PARIS • SYDNEY • HAMBURG
STOCKHOLM • ATHENS • TOKYO • MILAN • MADRID
PRAGUE • WARSAW • BUDAPEST • AUCKLAND

ISBN 0-373-36013-4

SEND ME A HERO

Copyright © 1998 by Rita B. Herron

www.eHarlequin.com

Printed in U.S.A.

With thanks to:

Bonnie Crisalli, who first encouraged me to write
for Intrigue, Julianne Moore for her suggestions
and for buying this story, and Natashya Wilson for
giving it a title and seeing it through to the end

and with love to

Lee, my husband and very own hero

Chapter One

Darkness hung in Veronica's bedroom like a cold black cloud. She awoke with a start, her heart pounding. The light she kept burning in the bathroom had gone out—or had someone turned it off? She froze, momentarily paralyzed with fear. Someone was in her apartment. She could feel his presence.

Her chest constricted so tightly she couldn't breathe. She strained to hear, praying she was just imagining the intruder, but a creaking sound echoed through the eerie quiet. Footsteps padded across the carpet. Terror rippled through her as she frantically scanned the room. A whisper of someone's breath penetrated the silence. As her eyes grew accustomed to the gloom, she spotted a shadow silhouetted against the far wall near the door, but it disappeared so quickly she wasn't sure it had really been there.

Was she having another nightmare? The shadow moved, appearing ominous in the dimness of the room. The silver glint of a knife flickered in a ray of moonlight trickling through the venetian blinds. A chill slithered up her spine. Someone stood, hovering in the doorway, staring at her. And she had no place to run. Trembling, she scooted back on the bed and reached for the phone.

Just as her fingers closed around the handset, the dark shadow lunged over her bed and straddled her. The phone fell off the hook. The sound of the dial tone rang through the room. She flung her hands at the man and kicked wildly, but his heavy weight settled against her body, pressing her into the mattress. He snapped her hands above her head in one fluid motion. The scent of cheap cologne and stale tobacco wafted around her, turning her stomach sour. His hot breath scorched her neck, and she tried to scream, but he pressed a pillow firmly over her face, muffling the sound. The heat of his sweating body seeped into hers. Something sharp pricked her upper arm. Then her hands were free and the point of the knife jabbed into the soft skin at the base of her throat. She was too petrified to cry out.

Determination and anger replaced her fear. She would not just lie here and let someone kill her.

Shoving with all her might, she bucked upward, twisting sideways in an attempt to dislodge him. Then she swung her fists wildly and slammed against his body, managing to knock the pillow away. She grabbed his arm and wrestled for the knife. The blade sliced into her wrist, but she barely noticed the pain as she fought for her life. With one last desperate effort, she managed to knee him, causing him to fall to the floor. The knife dropped onto her bed. She grabbed it and lunged for the man as he reached for her again. A loud groan escaped him, and she thought she'd stabbed him. He jerked backward and stumbled against the wall, then knocked over her lamp with a loud crash, shattering it into tiny pieces.

Gasping for air, she stared in horror at the blood-covered knife in her hands. Blood seeped from her arm and trickled onto her bedclothes. Her gaze swept the room again for her attacker. Had she mortally wounded him?

Panic raced through her. She needed to run. To scream. But her limbs felt like lead pillars, and her vocal cords had snapped shut. The man's heavy breathing rattled through the room. The stink of death permeated the air like the last burning embers of a fire. Veronica tried to shout for help, but the wretched sound she made came out as a whisper.

Her attacker groaned. Staggered. Collapsed against the plush carpeting in the doorway. Veronica's breath came out in shaky distorted pants. She grabbed the phone from the floor and pressed the button down for the dial tone, then punched 911. Dizzy with fear, she closed her eyes in an attempt to regain her balance. This time the police would have to believe her. They couldn't laugh her away as a paranoid, helpless woman like the last time she'd called. After all, an unconscious—perhaps dead—man lay sprawled on her bedroom floor. That was all the evidence they would need.

Another wave of dizziness assaulted her. Veronica fought the nausea, fought the exhaustion, but lost. Clutching the phone in one hand, she closed her eyes and mumbled for help, but the light slowly faded around her and she drifted into a sea of darkness.

DETECTIVE NATHAN DAWSON heard the police call come in over the radio dispatch, quickly dropped his soggy hamburger into its paper wrappings and picked up the receiver. "Dawson and Ford here."

"Ten-thirty. Intruder. Possible homicide. Caller is in the vicinity of Green and Washburn."

"We're in the area," Nathan said. "Specifics?"

"Address—apartment J-5, Bainbridge Apartment complex. Report came in from a woman," the dispatch officer said. "Not sure if the perp is still in the apartment."

Nathan glanced at his partner. Ford arched his bushy eyebrow and continued to chow down on his thick hamburger, using his tongue to lick the mustard dribbling down his pointed chin. The man was disgusting. Nathan already sensed tension between them. He wasn't sure why, but Ford had made it clear he didn't want a partner—especially him. He had to admit the feeling was mutual.

"Got a name?" Nathan asked.

"Not yet. Running the address through the computer now," the dispatch officer said.

"Caller still on the line?" Nathan had already turned the car around and was heading in the direction of the complex.

The officer on the other end sighed. "No. I've already radioed the paramedics. She sounded out of it, like she might have been on drugs. Only thing she said was, 'Help me, I think I've killed someone.' Then she must have passed out or…''

The officer didn't have to finish the sentence. Nathan knew what the *or* meant. She might be hurt, she might be dead. Or the whole thing might be nothing. As a policeman, he never knew what he was going to walk in on. Always be prepared— it was the motto a policeman lived by—either that or die. ''We'll be there in five. Over.'' Nathan flipped on the police siren and headed down Main Street, passing idle motorists and slipping through traffic with practiced ease.

Ford shook his head in disgust. ''Can't even finish a damn hamburger without some ruckus going on at that apartment complex. Fourth call we've had this week.''

''I'm surprised. Seems like a classy place.''

Ford spoke through a mouthful of food. ''Some nutcase has been calling in. Hope to hell this ain't her. Might have us a repeated homicide caller.''

Nathan kept his eyes trained on the road ignoring Ford's blasé attitude. He hoped Ford proved to be a responsible partner; he was cautious about who he trusted to cover his back. A blue-and-white pulled up just as he swerved into the parking lot. His hand automatically checked his gun as he climbed out. ''Check the exterior of the complex,'' he told the uniformed officers.

The man-woman team nodded. Each apartment had its own outside door and private entrance. Nathan and Ford moved silently to the one marked J-5.

The apartment was dark, the door unlocked. Ford maneuvered the flashlight inside the doorway and rolled it around the room, sweeping it with a dim stream of light. Weapon ready, Nathan slowly entered the apartment, his ears pricked, his gaze penetrating the darkness and scanning the den. Sofa, chairs, entertainment center, fairly empty room. Ford checked the small white kitchen, gave him a nod, and Nathan checked the outer bath. Small, but neat. Even in the dim light he could tell the front living area hadn't been disturbed.

A slight moan rumbled from the back. He and Ford exchanged glances and crept to the door. Nathan eased it open, his .38 poised. Tiny rays of moonlight sliced the darkness, and he spotted a figure lying in the rumpled bed. Broken glass lay shattered on the floor. Pillows and magazines were scattered around, a pair of black heels tossed in separate directions. Another groan pierced the air. Nathan moved closer to the figure.

"If there was an intruder, he's not here," Ford said.

Nathan stood beside the bed, quickly assessing the situation. The woman groaned as if she was frightened or in pain. Drops of blood were splattered all over the bedclothes and she held a bloody knife clutched in one hand. Blood oozed from an open wound in her right wrist, and a tiny droplet lingered on her throat. "Get me some towels from the bathroom," he ordered Ford.

First he had to remove the weapon, in case she woke up and tried to use it on him. He replaced his gun in its holster, slipped the knife from her fingers, jerked a plastic bag from his pocket and dropped it inside. Ford tossed some towels his way. Nathan slowly lowered himself beside the woman and wrapped one around her wrist tightly, then pressed another on top to stop the bleeding.

"She gonna make it?" Ford asked, walking around the room.

"Yeah. But she's lost some blood." Nathan noted the pale color of her creamy skin against her long dark hair and his heart thudded. "Miss, miss, can you hear me?" he asked, gently shaking her.

"She's a looker, ain't she?" Ford moved up beside him.

Nathan glared at his partner. "Hit the lights and bring the team in to start looking for traceables." Ford leered at him but left the room.

The woman's dark eyelashes fluttered, and her soft pink lips quivered as she tried to speak. She had a small frame, almost lost in the blood-splattered white cotton gown, high cheekbones, and dainty fingers that were well manicured but devoid of nail polish. He quickly inventoried her body to see if there were other wounds. Her skin was flawless, her legs long and slender. There didn't appear to be any other cuts, except a point where it looked like the knife had pricked the skin at the base of her throat. Bruises marked her other wrist and slender thighs.

He heard the wail of the siren and breathed a sigh of relief. The paramedics would arrive soon. She was much too beautiful to die.

"I KILLED HIM, NO…NO," Veronica mumbled. She kicked at the tangled bedcovers in an attempt to escape the horrible nightmare.

A hand gripped her arm, and she threw up her other hand in defense and screamed. Thank God the sound came out. Maybe this time someone would hear her before he killed her.

"Miss, it's okay. I'm Detective Nathan Dawson, Oakland County Police Department."

Veronica drew back and clenched the sheet to her chest. Trembling, she forced herself to open her eyes, expecting to see the shadow from her nightmare.

The man sitting beside her flashed his badge. "Can you tell me your name?"

Veronica nodded numbly. "Veronica…Miller."

The detective offered a smile. "Lie back and relax, Ms. Miller. Then tell me exactly what happened."

Still disoriented, Veronica stared at the handsome detective as he propped a pillow behind her back. He wasn't wearing a uniform, but the badge seemed real. She felt unsteady and confused, and so weak she thought she might faint. How had this man gotten into her apartment?

"The paramedics will be here any second. I have to keep pressure on your wrist wound."

Dazed, Veronica glanced down and saw the bloodstained towel he'd wrapped around her arm. The horror and reality of what had happened seeped in, and she trembled.

"It's okay, now. We're going to take care of you." The

man's deep, husky voice soothed her nerves. A calmness enveloped her. Finally someone was going to listen to her.

"You told the 911 operator that you'd killed somebody." The detective stretched one long leg out in front of him.

"What?" Veronica swallowed. She didn't remember making the phone call. She especially didn't remember admitting to murder.

She started to push her tangled hair away from her face, but realized her fingers were covered in a red sticky substance. Blood. Her stomach roiled. Visions of the attack flashed through her mind. The detective wiped her palms with a towel, then pressed a clean cloth to the cut on her arm.

Veronica bit her lip. This couldn't be happening—not again.

"Once again, miss, you said you killed someone." Detective Dawson gave her a concerned look. "Can you tell me exactly what happened? Was someone in your apartment?"

Veronica glanced around the room, searching for the shadow of the body she'd seen collapse on her floor. Nothing. "I don't understand. He was right there." She pointed to the floor beside the venetian blinds. Blue lights swirled and flashed outside her window. An approaching siren wailed loudly. Her stomach turned again.

"He put a pillow on my face. He tried to smother me. I couldn't breathe." She pressed her hand to her throat, gasping for air as she relived the horror of the attack. "I fought him, knocked the knife out of his hand. But the room was dark, so dark, and I tried to call for help, but I felt dizzy."

"You're okay now, Ms. Miller," the deep voice said softly. "Try to relax. Take a deep breath."

Veronica's gaze swept the room. Panic crawled through her. It hadn't been a dream. She hadn't imagined the stranger in her apartment. But where was his body? "He attacked me. He was going to kill me. What happened to him?"

Pieces of her shattered lamp littered the floor, pillows had been tossed around the room, her makeup and perfume bottles were overturned on her dresser. Her breathing came out in sharp pants. "I…where is he?" She searched the detective's face but saw nothing except questions in his troubled expression.

"That's what I need you to tell me, miss. You were alone when we got here. You'd passed out. The phone was off the hook and the door was unlocked."

"No," Veronica said vehemently. "I always lock my door. Always. And the windows, too."

Detective Dawson nodded. Another man entered the room, taking big, lumbering steps toward Veronica. His rough appearance and chilly expression made Veronica shiver.

"This is Detective Ford," Dawson said.

The man scrubbed his hand over his bristly red beard. "Dawson, we didn't find anyone here. Dead or alive." He stared at Veronica. Wariness settled over her. She'd dealt with skepticism all her life. This man didn't believe her. His glowering look said everything. Coming back to her hometown had been a mistake. Her grandmother had always told her to stay away, but her grandmother's death had prompted the return of her childhood nightmares, and she'd felt compelled to come back.

Ford must have recognized her name from when she'd called in before. He probably thought she was a psychotic, paranoid woman. Veronica forced back a sob and searched her mind for an explanation, aware Dawson was studying her. "There has to be a body. He fell. He collapsed right in front of me." But then she'd collapsed, too. Her head still ached. And why was her mind so foggy? She felt as if she'd been asleep for days.

The two detectives exchanged looks. "No sign of forced entry," Ford said. "No footprints outside the window."

"The knife you had, was it yours?" Detective Dawson asked.

Veronica nodded. "It…it looks like one from my kitchen."

"Dust everything," Dawson said. "And have Handley canvass the adjacent apartments—see if they saw or heard anything."

"Will do." Ford cast Veronica another smug look and

headed toward a uniformed policeman standing in the doorway.

"Check the carpet for hair fibers, too," Dawson said.

"I'm on it," Ford said, smirking at him.

Dawson raked a hand through his sandy, unkempt hair. Veronica rocked herself back and forth, striving for calm.

"Can you give us a description of the intruder?" Dawson's voice sounded deep and husky, and Veronica's anxiety mellowed slightly.

"I didn't see his face. He was just…big." She tugged the sheet tighter around herself, and suddenly realized she wasn't wearing anything but a skimpy cotton gown. And it had drops of blood all over it.

"Think, Ms. Miller. You might have seen something that could help us. Did he have a limp? A scar? Did he say anything?"

Veronica shook her head, realizing how little she really had seen. She noticed the strong chiseled jaw, the small cleft in Detective Dawson's chin, the bronze tones of his skin. She forced herself to try to remember details about the other man. "He had on a mask or something. Maybe a stocking. And he wasn't quite as tall as you."

Detective Dawson scribbled in his small notepad.

"And he smelled…"

"Smelled like what?" Dawson asked.

Veronica closed her eyes. "Like sweat and some kind of cologne."

"Did you recognize the cologne?"

Veronica shook her head. "I don't think so. But there was something else." Her mind was still foggy, and the more she tried to remember, the more her head ached. "I can't remember."

Dawson nodded. "It may come back to you. If you remember anything, today or tomorrow or anytime, let me know."

"I will," Veronica said, tightening her fingers around the sheet.

Ford came back in, a scowl on his face. He'd obviously

heard her comment. He lumbered over and planted one beefy leg on her cream-colored ottoman. "The neighbors say they didn't hear anything unusual," Ford said. "Are you sure you weren't entertaining and things just…well, got a little out of hand?" Ford raised his eyebrows suggestively.

Fury churned through Veronica. "How dare you insinuate such a thing. I thought you were supposed to be a policeman— here to help protect the citizens." She squared her shoulders and tried to sit up as she leveled a cold look at Ford, but fell exhausted back against the sheets. She was unaware the movement caused the bedding to fall to her waist until she caught the nicer detective staring at her and realized she'd exposed her gown. A blush crept up her neck and she reached for the blanket.

Detective Dawson handed her a bathrobe from the chair beside the bed. He made certain the towel was secure around her wrist. "Put this on. And try to stay calm, miss."

"Did you have company?" Ford asked again. His persistence annoyed her, but she decided to play it cool.

Veronica belted the robe tightly and sat on the edge of the bed. "No, I was alone all evening." Detective Dawson's body felt hot next to her. His eyes were like liquid pools of scotch whiskey, tame and wild at the same time. They reflected none of his thoughts, but if she wasn't mistaken they hinted at a burning desire she recognized as male interest.

She didn't have time for male interest. She needed this detective to find out if someone was trying to kill her. Or maybe he knew her history and had already decided she was a flake.

She'd endured skepticism before. She didn't know if she could endure it again.

"You have to believe me," she said, panic lacing her voice. "There was someone here. He tried to kill me." She covered her face with her hands as the memory flashed through her mind.

Detective Dawson patted her shoulder in a comforting gesture. "Relax, miss, it's over now."

Ford wasn't so kind. He narrowed his eyes at her, reminding

Veronica of a mean old bulldog, then held up an empty wineglass. "Ms. Miller, were you drinking last night?"

Veronica hesitated. She knew where this line of questioning was headed, and she didn't like it. Not one little bit.

"I had one glass of wine," Veronica said through clenched teeth. "It wasn't even full."

Ford rattled a prescription pill bottle in front of her. "And these? Did you take some before you went to sleep?"

Veronica closed her eyes and grimaced inwardly. "I…I've had trouble sleeping. The doctor recommended them. But I didn't take one last night."

Ford held the bottle up to the light. "Sleeping pills? Hmm." A smug expression crossed his weathered face. "You know, mixing alcohol and drugs can cause hallucinations."

"That's not what happened. I told you—someone attacked me."

Nathan Dawson's warm, strong hand covered hers. "Relax, Ms. Miller. We're dusting for fingerprints." He gestured to where two officers searched for clues. "You said you fought him. Do you think you injured him?"

Veronica struggled to remember. "I…I thought I stabbed him, but I'm not sure."

"Where?" The detective pointed to his chest, then each of his limbs in turn as he spoke. "Left side? Right? His arm?"

"His right arm," Veronica said. "He grunted and moved off of me then."

Dawson smiled. "Good, that'll help us. We'll have the blood sample from the knife analyzed to see if there are two blood types on it. If something happened here, I'll get to the bottom of it. It could have been a robbery attempt."

Ford cleared his throat. "Listen, Dawson, there's something you ought to know."

Dawson gave Ford a warning look. "Later, Ford. Right now, we have a crime scene to investigate. Now get busy." Ford sighed disgustedly and left the room.

"I've been getting hang-up calls," Veronica said, hoping to tell her side of things before Ford had a chance to muddy

Dawson's impression. "And I've been hearing noises as if someone's been hanging around outside my apartment. I told the police, but they haven't done anything."

"I'll check into it," Dawson said.

"Thank you, Detective." Veronica twisted her fingers together as she forced herself to meet his intense gaze.

Nathan Dawson didn't move. His amber eyes turned from a light brown to a darker shade streaked with gold. Veronica's entire body tingled with awareness. But she reminded herself her reaction was simply because he was being nice to her. He was going to help her.

She had to make him believe her. She wasn't crazy. Reporters and people who knew of her background would disagree, but she knew differently. She'd actually lived a mundane, quiet life for the past few years in Fort Lauderdale. Then she'd moved back to Oakland, a suburb of Atlanta, her hometown, and strange things had started happening. She'd been a frightened and withdrawn little girl when she'd left Oakland. But she wasn't a little girl anymore. And she was tired of running scared. She'd been running her whole life.

But not this time. This time she intended to get to the bottom of things.

The paramedics rushed in, accompanied by Ford. "I'll let them see to you now." Nathan rose from the bed as one of the paramedics took his place. "We'll talk some more later."

He felt in his pocket for his cigarettes, then remembered he'd quit six months ago, the day he'd walked out of the hospital and realized he had a second chance at life. Literally. The accident had almost stolen his future, and he'd decided he wouldn't finish the job with nicotine.

But damn, he missed the buzz. Especially now. Hot on a case. And the woman? Hell, he couldn't remember the last time he'd felt such a jolt of heat slide into his gut. A good, long smoke always cleared his head, something he desperately needed.

He stepped outside with Ford, but felt like he was abandoning Veronica. Something about her tugged at him. Maybe those enormous dark eyes. Or those high, sculpted cheekbones. Or that jet-black hair that streamed down her back like reams of silk.

Mentally shaking himself, he forced his mind to forget the physical attraction he felt for her. It had no business in his job. Besides, the woman was scared out of her mind. She claimed someone had tried to kill her, and it was his job to find out who attacked her. He knew real fear when he saw it, and this woman had been terrified.

"Listen, Dawson," Ford said as soon as he made it to the front stoop. "I don't think anyone tried to kill this broad."

Dawson gritted his teeth. "She is not a broad. She's a woman—a citizen who has requested our help."

Ford slammed his fist against the rail. He made no attempt to lower his voice. "You've been suckered in by those pretty looks. Don't you know who she is?"

Dawson chewed the inside of his cheek. "Should I? Is she someone famous?"

"Not the way you mean." Ford sighed audibly. "She's a kook."

"What?" Dawson tried to hold on to his patience. "If you've got something to say, Ford, spit it out."

Ford scratched his beard. "We've gotten a couple of calls from her before."

Nathan eyed Ford with curiosity. "Yeah, she told me that. Why didn't someone follow up on it?"

Ford grunted in obvious disgust. "'Cause she's a flake. Two weeks ago she said someone was lurking outside her apartment."

"And?"

"Turned out to be a stray cat. I told you, she's a nut." Ford's big belly shook as he let out a harsh breath.

Nathan frowned, still unconvinced the woman wasn't in danger. "There could have been someone there."

"She called again last week. Said someone had been in her office."

"Yeah? What did you find?" Nathan arched an eyebrow.

"Nobody but a cleaning service. Said she's been getting hang-up calls, too, and some pretty weird messages."

In spite of himself, Nathan was growing more and more curious, not just about Veronica, but about this case. "What kind of messages?"

Ford shrugged. "Don't know. When she brought in the tape, it had been erased." He shifted to his left foot and rubbed his thigh. "My guess is, she made it all up. Trying to get attention."

"Yeah? What makes you think that? Her injuries look pretty damned real to me."

"Well, she's weird. Everyone who grew up around these parts knows about her."

"And why is that?" Nathan asked, growing tired of Ford's cat-and-mouse game.

"'Cause of what happened to her folks years ago."

Nathan leaned against the porch railing. "What about her parents?"

Ford pulled out a wad of chewing tobacco and stuffed it in his mouth. "That's the interesting part. Veronica Miller grew up around here, but she moved to Florida to live with her grandmother."

Nathan knew there was more. Ford was obviously enjoying dragging the story out, adding suspense. "Okay, I'll bite. Tell me the rest."

Ford grinned. "Veronica Miller's parents died right here in this town. Same time of year as this. Police called it a murder-suicide. Father killed the mom, then killed himself."

Nathan swallowed, feeling the cold bite of winter all the way down to his toes. Through the glass door, he saw the paramedic helping Veronica through the hallway. She looked pale and fragile. Then she glanced up and met his gaze, and the corners of her mouth lifted in a slight smile of relief. His gut tightened.

"They say Veronica witnessed the whole thing, but she doesn't remember it," Ford continued.

A drop of sweat rolled down Nathan's neck. "How old was she?"

"Seven." Ford paused. "There's more. Reporters went nuts over the story. The girl had to see a shrink." Ford spat a blob of tobacco juice off the porch edge. "Sounds to me like she still may be crazy. You know they say kids never get over traumatic things like that. Makes some of 'em pure schizo." He studied the toe of his battered boot. "There were rumors she might even have killed her parents herself."

"It's hard to believe a seven-year-old would be strong enough to kill two adults," Nathan said. "Any evidence to support that theory?"

Ford scratched his beard. "Just the fact she was holding the murder weapon when the police arrived."

Nathan adapted his poker face. "Let me guess. The parents were killed with a knife."

Ford grinned. "Yep. A kitchen one. Kind of like the one she had when we got here. And she kept muttering that it was her fault. Some said her grandma whisked her away to cover it up."

A sigh of frustration escaped Nathan. He looked out over the small landing of her apartment complex. The outside lights shone brightly, and pansies filled the flower beds. What a beautiful little complex, and what a sad story.

Veronica and the paramedic came to the door. She seemed vulnerable and troubled and she'd called him for help. As an officer of the law, he had to protect her. But what exactly was he protecting her from? From some weirdo or from herself? She could be telling the truth. But if Ford was right and Veronica was unstable, perhaps she hadn't been attacked at all.

A rancid taste filled his mouth. He wanted to believe her, but he had to check out all angles. And knowing about Veronica's past shed a whole different light on the situation.

Chapter Two

A dozen questions tumbled through Veronica's head.

"We'll have this arm stitched up in a minute," the doctor said. "You were mighty lucky. Another quarter of an inch and your main artery would have been severed." Arlene Baits reminded Veronica more of her grandmother than a physician. She'd been especially tender and kind while she'd cleaned Veronica's wound, chatting to distract her from the unpleasant chore.

But the past few hours kept replaying themselves in Veronica's head like an old horror show. The only halfway bright spot had been meeting Detective Dawson. He hadn't looked at her as if she were nuts like so many people in the past. But she'd seen him talking to Ford, whispering and glancing back and forth at her. Something was up. Either they'd found evidence in her apartment they didn't want to tell her about or they didn't believe her. She knew what Ford thought. But she couldn't read the other detective. He'd been kind and concerned and performed all the seemingly appropriate police tasks. But he kept staring at her as if he could see into her soul.

No man had ever looked at her that way. She shivered, then flinched as the doctor dabbed antiseptic over the small nick on her throat.

"All done. How did you say this happened?" the doctor asked again.

"Someone broke into my apartment and attacked me," Veronica said for what she felt like was the umpteenth time. At least she hadn't implied she'd tried to commit suicide like the paramedics.

The elderly woman clucked her tongue. "Can't be too safe these days. I keep a dead bolt. And my puppy dog, Randall, barks at anything that gets near me."

Veronica smiled. Maybe she needed to get a dog.

"What'd you say your name was, dear?"

"Veronica Miller."

"Oh." Dr. Baits tilted her head sideways as if in thought. "I knew of some Millers a long time ago." Her eyes widened, then narrowed again. She suddenly pressed her lips tightly together. Her hands trembled as she helped Veronica down from the examining table.

Veronica wondered at the woman's strange reaction. The doctor was old enough to have known about her parents. And their murder. Maybe she remembered them. Maybe she had an idea who had killed them.

"You can go now," Dr. Baits said, her face pale.

Veronica started to question her, but Dr. Baits quickly opened the door. "That detective said he's waiting to drive you home." The woman forced a smile, but Veronica recognized the lackluster quality. "Handsome young fella. Better not keep him waitin'."

Handsome didn't matter, Veronica told herself. Just as long as he could do his job.

"Thanks for everything, Dr. Baits." Veronica felt weak. Perhaps she'd return when she felt better to question the woman. She wobbled on unsteady feet but managed to make it to the waiting room without collapsing. All she wanted was a nice warm bed and some sleep. Then she remembered what had happened in her bedroom, and knew she couldn't sleep there tonight.

"Are you all right?" Detective Dawson rose from the stiff-looking vinyl chair and rushed instantly to her side. His arm curved around her elbow in support. Veronica was immediately grateful she'd changed from her thin cotton gown into a pair of jeans and a sweatshirt.

"I'm fine," Veronica lied. "Just exhausted."

The detective nodded. "You want to go home? Or do you have some family—" an odd expression crossed his face "—or do you want to go to a friend's house?"

Veronica froze, her gaze colliding with his. She read understanding and something else she couldn't identify. His eyebrows furrowed, and once again that strange probing look darkened his eyes, making her wonder what he had on his mind or how much he knew about her. Questions lingered in his expression. He seemed to have as many as she did.

"No friends," Veronica said as he walked her to the car. She thought of Eli, her parents' friend who lived only a few miles away. He was also her godfather, but she didn't feel comfortable horning in on his family. "I just moved here a couple of months ago," Veronica said, deciding not to go into a long explanation.

"From Florida?"

"Yes, but I was born here," Veronica said. Maybe she should tell the detective bits of her past before he heard the distorted version from someone else. "My parents died when I was a child so I moved away with my grandmother."

"What brought you back to Oakland?" Dawson asked.

"I'm a tax attorney. After my grandmother died, I didn't have any real ties to Florida. When Abe Walsh retired, I took over his practice."

"I remember Walsh," Dawson said. "Decided to travel the world. Must have retired with a hefty chunk of change."

Veronica remained silent, her thoughts scattered. She'd had to return to this town. Back in Fort Lauderdale, her boyfriend, Ron had pushed for more commitment, but she'd been leery. Her childhood nightmares had returned, occasionally a flash of something from her youth seeping in. Eli had contacted her, too, wanting to see her—it seemed like everything had come together at once, bringing her here. She'd decided if she finally put all her ghosts to rest, maybe she could move on with her life.

"You want to go back to your apartment?"

An image of yellow police tape, shattered glass and dark shadows filled her mind. Veronica shook her head. "No, a hotel would be nice. I'd like to stop by and pack a bag though."

He opened the car door. "Sure. You should have dead bolts installed tomorrow."

"I will."

Dawson made his way to the driver's side and climbed in. "Which hotel?"

"One of the busy ones in town," Veronica said automatically. *One where no one will know me.* She wrapped her arms around herself in a protective gesture. "Maybe I can lose myself in the crowd."

AFTER NATHAN MADE SURE Veronica was settled into the hotel room, he headed to the station. If Veronica thought she could ever be lost in a crowd, she was wrong. The ridiculous thought made him chuckle. She was the most beautiful woman he'd ever seen. And he realized when she'd made the statement that she didn't have a clue how men saw her.

Or had her statement meant something else? Had she wanted to lose herself as in *commit suicide?* He'd considered the possibility as soon as he'd seen the wrist wound. The paramedic had immediately asked her the same question. Her big dark eyes had turned to the young man in disbelief, as if she couldn't fathom why he would ask such a thing. Considering her confused state, the combination of alcohol and possibly sleeping pills along with her troubled past, the assumption seemed logical.

But still, something bothered him about the incident. He didn't know what had happened at her apartment, but he didn't think she'd tried to take her own life.

"Stop thinking with your hormones and use your brain," he muttered to himself as he turned into the precinct. It might be 2:00 a.m., but he intended to start his investigation of Veronica immediately. He only hoped she didn't turn out to be nuttier than his Aunt Willemena's fruitcake.

An hour later, his eyes blurring, he slurped down the dregs of his third cup of coffee and choked down a stale bear claw. The files on the Miller family lay before him. There appeared to be enough for the beginnings of a novel.

Good heavens, the woman was a legend. Or at least the news of the Miller murder-suicide had been highlighted in Atlanta newspapers for months after her parents' deaths. He stared at the yellowed edges of the old newspaper article, and his heart twisted at the sad expression on Veronica's face—a seven-year-old girl with the weight of her mother's and father's deaths on her mind. Her big, dark eyes glistened with pain and turmoil, and a single lone tear streaked her cheek as she clutched an elderly woman's hand.

They stood beside a gravestone, Veronica with a small bunch of fresh daisies almost crushed to pieces in her tiny hand. A few mourners hunched in the wind on the dark, dreary day, a day much like this one had been. Police and reporters had been present, too. The poor child hadn't been able to grieve without being hounded by the press. Or the police. What kind of effect had the gossip and media attention had on her?

He leaned back in his chair, studying a picture of her folks when they were alive. The hot coffee burned his throat as he gazed at a tiny Veronica being cuddled by her father. It was the only picture where she was smiling. He realized it wasn't the color of her eyes, but the deep sadness that had drawn him to believe her.

Annoyed with himself, he stood and paced across the room. Why was this story getting to him? He balled up several pieces of paper and spiked them toward the trash can. She was a grown woman now, not a child. An independent adult—a respected tax attorney. He had to remain uninvolved.

Maybe his recent stay in the hospital had something to do with his reactions. Months of lying in bed and going to rehab to regain the use of his leg, reliving the moment the bullet had pierced the lining near his heart—a near-death experience did something to a man. And losing his partner—he would never forget the devastation he'd felt when he'd awoken to find Reid gone. He'd died because he trusted the wrong person. Nathan had come as close to dying himself as he'd ever come. In those dreadful months of recovery, he'd realized something. There wasn't a person in the world who cared about him. Not one.

His family had all been gone for years, and he'd never let anyone get close to him. For the first time in his life, he'd begun to think about his future. Not just his future as a detective, but his future…alone. But this wasn't the time to pursue a relationship. And work definitely wasn't the place.

He slam-dunked another piece of paper into the trash can and sank back in his chair. His stint in the hospital had obviously turned him into a melancholy wimp. Police work and marriage didn't mix. He'd seen dozens of marriages fall apart because wives couldn't stand the hours, the danger and fear of losing their husbands. And the combination of a policeman getting involved with a victim was lethal. He had a job to do and he intended to do it.

He shuffled the papers and zeroed in on a column a few weeks after the reported murder-suicide. The journalist suggested that Veronica had suffered severe trauma from the incident. The psychiatrist treating her had released very little information, except that she had repressed the horrible memories of that fatal night. And that she might never remember the details. Serious long-term effects might reveal themselves in her later years. Schizophrenic behavior often resulted from childhood trauma. So did paranoia. Illusions of someone threatening the person were common. Suicide in cases like this was prevalent, most likely in the teens or early twenties. He couldn't ignore the facts: Veronica fit the profile, even her age, which was twenty-seven.

Nathan scrubbed his hands over his eyes, and leaned on his palms. Things were not looking good for Veronica's case. He had to admit Ford might be right. He couldn't do anything else tonight. The lab wouldn't be open until morning. It would take time to study the evidence and match blood types.

If Veronica had stabbed someone with that knife, the person's blood should show up. And if they couldn't find any evidence to support her claim, well, he'd discover the truth about her, too. He stood and dragged his weary body toward the door. He might as well get some sleep. Tomorrow he had work to do. And he had to forget about the alluring Veronica Miller as a woman. Whether she was delusional or someone was threatening her life, she obviously had personal problems.

And that was looking on the bright side. After all, she just might be a lunatic.

VERONICA BRUSHED DOWN her straight black skirt and smoothed her teal silk blouse over her bandaged arm, grateful the blouse's collar hid the small cut on her neck. She walked into her office, hesitating momentarily as she always did when she entered the huge Victorian house that had been her father's office years ago. Of course, it had undergone major renovations, but she'd hoped being in his work space might jog her memories. So far it hadn't.

A yawn escaped her. Last night she'd barely slept. She'd tossed and turned in the hotel bed, wondering why someone would attack her. It had never happened before. So why now? Could it have been a simple robbery attempt?

In the wee hours of the morning, she'd slipped into a fretful sleep, and she'd awoken at dawn, still unrested. But she had to come to work today. Although she'd always been a failure with people, especially men, she was a whiz at numbers—a skill and service her clients paid prime money for. Work was her salvation.

"Ms. Miller, Wayne Barrett is waiting for you in your office." Veronica's secretary, Louise Falk, gave her a sympathetic smile as she stopped to check her messages. "He's on the rampage this morning."

Veronica smiled. "I expect so. He not only received my

bill, but he just learned he owes the government a huge sum of money.''

Louise sipped her coffee. The woman was tall and skinny and could drink five pots of coffee a day without getting jittery. Veronica envied her that. She and caffeine did not agree. She fixed herself some decaf tea and hoped she could enjoy it before Barrett exploded.

''You want me to call 911 if he starts shouting?'' Louise licked the sticky icing from a Danish.

''I think I can handle him.'' Veronica's fingers tightened around her leather attaché case. ''By the way, did you find the Avondale file?''

Louise gave her an odd look. ''You filed it yesterday before you left. Don't you remember?''

Veronica chewed her bottom lip. ''Oh, yes, that's right.'' Massaging her temple, she searched her memory. She didn't remember filing it. What was wrong with her? Normally she was organized, but lately she'd been misplacing things. First she thought she'd lost her keys, then she'd found them in her office desk. And now a file.

''Well, good luck with Barrett,'' Louise said, turning back to the computer.

Veronica mumbled thanks, squared her shoulders, reminded herself of the assertiveness training classes she'd taken and strode toward her office.

Wayne Barrett, big-time entrepreneur, offered a perfunctory greeting as she entered. He sat gripping a mug of coffee, tugging at his waxed mustache. A designer suit, red power tie, Gucci shoes—the man had money and liked to flaunt it. He even had his nails manicured. He said he could enjoy his wealth better if he held it with polished hands. She'd disliked the man the moment she'd met him.

''Hi, Mr. Barrett.'' Veronica placed her tea and briefcase on her desk, snapped open the sleek Italian case and pulled out a file. ''I assume this is what you came to discuss.''

Barrett perched in the red leather chair nearest her desk, crossed one leg over the other and leaned forward, Veronica was sure, to intimidate her. "Of course. You knew it wasn't what I was expecting." The anger in his deep baritone jostled her already taut nerves.

But she refused to show it.

Instead she met his cool gaze and calculating eyes with a confident smile. "I know. But when you withheld information about those bonds from me and your wife—"

"My ex-wife," Barrett clarified hastily.

Veronica nodded, although she knew the divorce hadn't been officially granted yet. "Yes, your ex-wife notified the courts of this money, and the government had to be informed. I'm sorry it worked out like this, but my hands are tied."

Barrett's nostrils flared with anger. He stood and glared into her eyes. "I paid you to work this out. Walsh always took care of me."

Veronica leaned back in her chair, putting some distance between them. This man smelled like whiskey and it was only 8:00 a.m. He had the nerve to blame her for his loss, when he'd withheld pertinent information about his earnings from the government.

"I found you every loophole available—within the law." Veronica punctuated the last words, simultaneously tapping her pen on the desk for emphasis.

"You know this will cost me two million," Barrett said. "I thought you were the best tax attorney around. Walsh even recommended you."

Veronica refused to let him faze her. "I am a good attorney, but I'm also honest. I won't go to jail to hide your earnings, Mr. Barrett. Or to save you from having to pay your wife and the government what you lawfully owe them."

A vein bulged in Barrett's pale forehead. "Sometimes, Ms. Miller, there are worse things than going to jail. Remember, I know where you live." He jerked his own briefcase from the floor and stormed from her office.

Veronica exhaled a shaky breath at his implied threat. Could Barrett have attacked her the night before?

The phone jangled, catching her off guard, and she almost

jumped out of the chair. Forcing herself to steady her voice, she picked up the receiver. "Hello, Veronica Miller speaking."

"Veronica, this is Eli."

Veronica relaxed, grateful for the comfort of her godfather's voice. She'd missed talking with him lately.

"How are you, dear?"

"I'm fine. Just got rid of a nasty client, but what's new?"

Eli laughed. His voice was rusty, and she realized age had crept up on him while they'd lost touch. "Tomorrow night we're having a reception in honor of my son Gerald."

"Oh. What's the occasion?" Veronica asked. Although she didn't remember Gerald, Eli had kept her informed of all his son's political activities through his letters.

"It's a kickoff for his campaign," Eli said, pride evident in his voice.

"Like father like son, huh?" Veronica said.

Eli laughed. "Yeah, but he's not stopping at senator. He wants to run for president."

"Wow." Veronica was mildly impressed. "What time is the party?"

"Seven o'clock. And bring a date if you want."

Veronica laughed silently. She hadn't been in town long enough to meet anyone she wanted to date. She'd spent the first few weeks getting settled and reviewing a few of the accounts she inherited from Walsh. "Sounds great," Veronica said. "I'll be there." She was tempted to tell Eli about her midnight visitor, but he sounded weary himself, and with Gerald's decision to run for election and Eli's own commitments to several state departments, he obviously had his plate full. Besides, living on her own had taught her to be independent. Eli had his own family and life to deal with.

"See you then." Eli coughed, then hung up.

Hmm. Eli still hadn't shaken the cold he'd had when she'd had lunch with him. Veronica reached for the stack of files on her desk. Paperwork should take her mind off her problems.

Later that afternoon a light knock sounded at the door. Louise poked her head in. "This package arrived for you."

Veronica squinted in confusion at the brightly wrapped package. "For me?" Who would be sending her a gift?

Louise placed the small package on the desk. "Maybe it's from a secret admirer," she said, slipping out the door.

Veronica removed the small card and read it silently. "Something to remember me by. See you soon."

It had to be from Ron. But what did he mean he would see her soon? She'd told him she wanted time and space. For heaven's sake, she'd moved to Oakland to get away from him.

She examined the package. Pale blue paper with roses on it. Her hand trembled. Something about the wrapping seemed familiar, but she couldn't place it. She silently chastised herself for being so jittery. She'd probably bought similar paper and wrapped a gift with it for someone else.

She must be getting paranoid from lack of sleep and nerves. Gingerly, she fingered the delicate baby pink bow and finally lifted it from the gift. The paper came away easily. She slowly opened the container and took out a beautiful music box in the shape of a hot air balloon. It was lovely. The familiar characters from *The Wizard of Oz* danced in the basket. Again, something about the gift tugged at the corners of her memory, but nothing materialized.

Ron hadn't sent the gift. She was sure of it. He was the most practical man she'd ever known, he would never have sent her something this frivolous. But if he hadn't sent it, who had?

As she stared at the little scarecrow and cowardly lion, the image of Dorothy in her red slippers appeared in her head. Dorothy tapping her ruby red slippers together chanting, "There's no place like home. There's no place like home." A vague memory floated through her mind; her mother had read her the story as a child. She'd had the music from the movie. A chill slithered up her spine. Why did the childlike story make her feel so frightened? Had she been listening to the song the night her parents were killed?

With shaking fingers, she slowly wound the music box and listened as it played. She hummed along in a low voice. "Somewhere over the rainbow…"

An image of Dorothy being chased by the bad witch and the horrid monkeys took her breath. Her hands shook so violently she dropped the music box onto the desk with a thud. The song droned on. "Why, oh, why, can't I?" Veronica covered her ears to drown out the sound. Why, oh, why, couldn't she remember what happened that night?

As the music continued to play, she could almost hear her mother's soft voice singing the words. Her mother had given her a music box just like this one for her seventh birthday, only a few days before her death. She hadn't seen the music box in years. And nobody had known about it except her parents.

NATHAN STOOD in the open doorway of Veronica's office, one hand gripping the shiny doorknob, the other shoved in his pocket, and watched silently as Veronica stared at the small music box. She mumbled something about monkeys.

"The monkeys, they're after me." Panic tinged her voice, and her eyes were glazed and haunted with shadows.

"What's wrong with her?" he asked the tall, lanky secretary. She'd opened the door for him when Veronica had refused to answer her buzzer.

"I don't know," she said, her voice filled with concern. "She's been acting a little strange lately, forgetting things. A messenger delivered a present for her a few minutes ago." Louise pointed to the torn wrapping paper. "It must have been that music box. I've never seen it before."

Nathan closed the distance between himself and Veronica in a few quick strides. "Why would it cause her to react this way?"

"I have no idea," Louise said, wide-eyed.

"I didn't mean to do it," Veronica whimpered in a tiny voice that jabbed at Nathan like razor-sharp scissors. He didn't have a clue what she meant or even if she knew, but he needed to snap her out of this delusional state. He lowered himself beside her.

"Ms. Miller," he said, gently nudging her shoulder, "Ms. Miller, can you hear me?"

An almost childlike cry escaped her. Although he told himself this was strictly business, that this woman might be psychotic, his heart wrenched. All he could see in his mind was a picture of a sad little girl with a handful of crushed daisies standing beside her parents' grave. Lost and alone.

"Ms. Miller…Veronica, can you hear me? It's Detective Dawson." He took her icy hands in his and turned her to face him. Gently he stroked some warmth into her chilled fingers and watched as her breathing began to steady. "Veronica, tell me what happened. I'm here to help you. You have to talk to me."

"I'll get some water," Louise said, dashing from the office.

"Veronica, look at me." He framed her face with his hands and forced her to meet his gaze. Although her eyes still seemed slightly glazed, her pupils weren't as dilated as when he'd first arrived, and she focused on him. He kept talking in a soft, comforting voice. "I came by to see how you're doing today. Everything's going to be all right."

Veronica's limp body sagged against her chair. She glanced around her office, her desk, then back to him, still in a state of confusion.

"Veronica, will you talk to me now?"

"What…how long have you been standing there?" Her voice sounded weak and distant.

"Not long." Nathan replayed the details of her file in his head. The lack of evidence from the night before complicated things even more. He needed more details from Veronica. "We need to talk."

Louise rushed in and thrust a glass of water in Veronica's hands. "Are you okay, Veronica?" Louise rubbed a hand over her own forehead and made a futile attempt to tuck the loose strands of her auburn topknot back into place. "You scared me to death."

Veronica looked at her in confusion, then seemed to visibly shake herself. "I'm fine." She stared at Nathan, a dazed look on her face. "What did you say you were doing here?"

"I came by to ask you some more questions. Who sent the gift?"

"I don't know," Veronica said in a listless voice. "The card didn't say."

"You shouldn't have opened a strange package after what happened last night." Nathan turned to Louise. "What did the messenger look like? Was it a courier service?"

Louise bit her lip. "I…I didn't see them. I went to the rest room and found it on my desk when I returned."

"What time is it?" Veronica asked, looking more and more confused.

Louise and Nathan exchanged concerned looks. "It's about four-thirty," Nathan said.

"Why don't you go on home?" Louise suggested. "You don't have any more appointments today. I'll answer the phone and lock up." Veronica nodded, and Louise made a hasty exit.

Nathan quickly took the initiative. "We're through with your apartment, Ms. Miller. Why don't you call a service to clean up while you and I go someplace to talk?"

Veronica's dark eyebrows arched in surprise.

"About your case," Nathan clarified. "We need to discuss what we found at your apartment." That would be the hard part, Nathan thought morosely. He had no idea how she would react to his report.

Veronica nodded and stood. Nathan noticed her trembling hands, the way she almost collapsed against her desk as she tried to stand. "Are you okay?"

A sudden bout of determination filled her eyes. "I will be," she said simply. She buzzed Louise, asked her to call her usual cleaning service to clean her apartment, then grabbed her brief-case and purse and headed toward the door. "Let's go to the café around the corner, Detective Dawson."

Nathan watched the way her curvaceous backside swayed

in her short black skirt as she disappeared out the door. The woman definitely had a figure. Subtle round curves. Just enough breasts to fill a man's hands. Gorgeous long legs.

And she carried herself like she had all the confidence in the world. But he knew her bravado was a sham. When he'd witnessed her unveiled fear only moments earlier, he'd had to order himself not to wrap her in his arms and comfort her. Worse, he'd had to remind himself he was a professional, a detective, not the woman's boyfriend or lover. *Veronica Miller's lover.* Just the thought made his groin ache. But a personal entanglement with this woman would be a mistake.

Business, buddy, strictly business, he reminded himself as he followed her to the elevator. Maybe if he told himself that fact often enough he would believe it.

Chapter Three

Several minutes later, Veronica seated herself at a small table in the corner of the café with Detective Dawson. She liked doing business, enjoyed working with facts and numbers, but she'd always had trouble dealing with people. Give her a calculator and a computer any day. They didn't talk or expect anything. She couldn't fail them, she couldn't cause them to die.

What did Detective Dawson know? Had he discovered the truth about her?

Her stomach knotted with dread as he sat at the secluded table she'd chosen in the corner. Did he know who'd broken into her apartment? Had he come here to ask her to go to the police station to identify her attacker? A part of her desperately wanted that to happen, while another part of her wasn't quite ready to face the truth.

She slipped her hair from its clasp and finger combed through it, letting the strands float around her shoulders. Somehow the simple act helped her to relax.

Hadn't that been her problem her whole life? She couldn't remember who'd killed her parents because she couldn't face the truth. That was what the psychiatrist had told her grandmother. She could understand as a child not being able to remember, but was the truth too horrible for her to accept even now?

Her stomach turned as the waiter placed glasses of club soda in front of them. Veronica brought her glass to her mouth merely to have something to do with her hands. She barely felt the cold liquid brush her lips before she set it back down and twined her fingers in her lap. Taking a deep breath, she looked the detective square in the eye.

"Ms. Miller—Veronica, may I call you that?"

Veronica nodded.

Dawson stretched out his long legs, brushing his knee against hers. She wondered if it was accidental. She'd been too frightened the night before to notice this man's powerful masculinity. His broad shoulders and muscular body filled out his cream-colored polo shirt to perfection. He had a hard, chiseled face with high cheekbones and a small cleft in his chin, and sandy blond-brown hair that was so thick she briefly considered sinking her fingers into it.

"You look better," Dawson said with a slight smile.

"Thanks. I feel a little better." Veronica shifted, uncomfortable. The way his deep, husky voice murmured her name sent a shiver up her spine. It was too personal. And his amber-colored eyes gazed at her with such sincerity she wanted to confide in him, to tell him the whole, sordid truth. But if she did, would he help her?

"Okay, Detective Dawson, what did you want to discuss?" Always get to the point, Veronica had learned. Take charge of the meeting. Don't let the other person intimidate you.

The detective's mouth curved into a smile as if he knew exactly what she was doing. She shifted again, this time brushing her leg against his. The soft fabric of his khakis felt warm against her stockinged thigh. He smiled again.

"Detective?" She raised her glass for another sip of her club soda.

His gaze followed the movement, then suddenly, as if he

realized what he was doing, he straightened in his chair and assumed a more businesslike pose. His smile faded, and a serious expression darkened his eyes.

Veronica decided she preferred him the other way.

"Like I said, the police finished combing your place."

"And?" Veronica's pulse jumped.

"They didn't find anything to indicate an intruder."

Veronica's hands tightened around the glass. "How about the blood on the knife?"

The detective sipped his drink, then set his glass down with a thud. "The tests aren't finished yet. There weren't any fingerprints though. Except yours, of course." He paused as if he was waiting for her reaction. "If someone was there, they wiped their prints and blood off the knife after you passed out."

Veronica leaned back and closed her eyes momentarily. Could she have imagined the whole thing? As a child, she had such vivid nightmares that she swore they were real. Could it be happening all over again? When she opened her eyes, Detective Dawson was watching her.

"You want to tell me about the music box? Why did it set you off like that?"

Veronica swallowed, tried to lift the glass for another drink, but her sore arm ached and she spilled the cold liquid down the front of her blouse. Dawson calmly handed his napkin to her, his intense gaze unnerving her even more. He stared at her arm where she'd been wounded the night before. She was grateful the long sleeve of her blouse covered the bandage, although the imprint of it could be seen through the sheer material.

"Tell me about it, Veronica."

Deep down inside, Veronica's heart twisted. How she wished she could tell someone the awful haunting secrets she kept buried inside. For some reason, it seemed especially important that she make this man believe her.

But when she opened up to people, they thought she was nuts. She'd only shared her fears and details of her past with a couple of men in her life, and they'd turned away from her. She couldn't bear to open herself up to that kind of pain again.

Dawson folded his hands on the table. "Veronica, I can't help you if you don't talk to me."

She laid the soggy napkins on the table and met his gaze. "It was nothing. It just reminded me of the movie."

"Yeah. Almost everyone's seen *The Wizard of Oz,* but most people don't freak out when they hear the theme song."

Veronica squelched the retort on the tip of her tongue. She might as well tell him as much of the truth as possible. He would probably find out everything about her when he checked into her past. "My mom used to sing me that song before she died."

Dawson rubbed his thumb over his chin. "I can understand how that would upset you. But you don't know who sent it?"

Veronica shook her head. "I told you in my office, I have no idea."

"Maybe someone in the family?"

"I don't have any family." Veronica's hands squeezed her glass. "I'm sure you've discovered that by now."

Dawson's brief nod told her all she needed to know. Of course he'd read her history. Was he here just to satisfy his curiosity or did he really want to help her?

"And you live alone? Not even a pet? Cat or dog?"

Veronica shook her head. "No. I don't like cats. I'm thinking about getting a dog, though."

Dawson downed the rest of his drink. "Hmm. There were cat hairs in your apartment."

Veronica glanced up, her eyes wide. "Cat hairs. Then that proves it, someone must have been there."

"That proves a cat might have wandered in sometime when you left the door open. It doesn't prove a person was there."

Veronica frowned.

"Okay, let's get back to the music box. Why did it upset you so much?" Dawson asked softly.

Veronica hesitated, cupping her empty glass in her hand and swirling the ice cubes around. "My mother gave me a music box that played the song for my seventh birthday. It was a few days before she died. No one knew about it except my grandmother.'' Veronica sighed. ''And my grandmother is dead.''

Dawson nodded, his expression unreadable. ''What about a housekeeper?''

''We didn't have a housekeeper. And the strange thing is that I think it's the same music box.''

Dawson drummed his fingers on the table. ''What makes you think that?''

Veronica chewed her lip. ''I'd forgotten about it until I saw it. Then my memory came flooding back. It had this little crack in the bottom left corner where I dropped it, but Daddy glued it back together.''

''And this one has a chip in the same place?''

''Yes.'' Veronica was quiet. ''I haven't seen that box in years. I didn't even remember it existed, much less know what happened to it years ago.''

Dawson made a mumbling sound. ''Okay, let's assume someone found it and sent it to you. When your grandmother passed away, maybe she'd kept it with some of her things. Did she leave you anything valuable? Money, property, jewelry?''

Veronica wrinkled her forehead in thought. ''Why do you ask?''

''I'm looking for an angle. I thought if she did, perhaps there's another family member out there who wants the inheritance, too. It might explain the attack. Has anything like this happened before?''

''No.'' Veronica mulled over the possibilities. ''And there wasn't any other family that I'm aware of. Besides, my grandmother didn't have much financially. Just a small house, a few personal things. We weren't wealthy by any means.''

''What happened to the house?''

''I sold it,'' Veronica said. ''I couldn't stay there without her.''

Dawson ran a hand through his thick hair. ''Do you know

anyone who would want to hurt you? Any enemies? Someone who might have a vendetta against you? Co-workers or clients you've made angry in the past?''

Veronica shifted uneasily as Wayne Barrett's arrogant face flashed before her, his threat echoing in her ears. He had lost two million dollars. Still, she hated to accuse him of trying to hurt her when she had no proof.

Detective Dawson covered her hand with his. ''If you want me to help you, you have to trust me.''

Veronica's jaw ached from clenching it. Trust. The seventy-five-million-dollar word. She'd never totally trusted anybody, not even Ron. It had eventually destroyed their relationship.

''Come on, Veronica. These are routine questions any detective would ask. We can go down to the station to finish this if you'd rather, but I thought you'd feel more comfortable here.''

''All right,'' she began. ''In my business, I've made a few clients angry, usually by not saving them as much money as they want.''

''Lost any cases recently? Had to turn anyone in to the IRS?''

Veronica smiled. ''I don't lose, Mr. Dawson.''

''Nathan.''

''What?''

''If we're going to be working together, I'd just as soon you call me by my first name.''

''Is that normal?''

Nathan grinned. ''It is for me.''

Veronica couldn't resist a smile. The man could probably charm Uncle Sam out of an audit.

''I'd like you to get me a list of all your clients. Highlight any who haven't been pleased with their settlement.''

Veronica nodded, and glanced up at the waiter. ''Would you like to order dinner?'' he asked.

As if on cue, Veronica's stomach growled. ''Sure. I skipped lunch. I'll have a salad and quiche.''

''Real men don't eat quiche,'' Nathan muttered. Veronica

smothered a laugh. His mouth quirked into a smile as he met her gaze. "You're beautiful when you smile." He handed her the bread basket and she blushed. "Bring me the ribs."

Veronica laughed again, this time unable to smother the sound. "A real macho man, huh? I suppose you want your meat bleeding?"

"Sure, it's juicy and tender that way," Nathan said with a grin.

As the waiter placed their orders, Nathan turned back to Veronica. "So you may have a disgruntled client in the wake. How about boyfriends? Any lovers or ex-ones we should worry about?"

Veronica tensed and tore her roll in half. How in the world could she answer that?

"Are there, Veronica?" Nathan's husky voice made her squirm. "Are you involved with anyone I should know about?"

She slathered butter haphazardly all over her roll. "No," she said softly. "No one you should know about."

THERE WASN'T A MAN in her life. A ridiculous sense of relief filled Nathan. After following Veronica home and making sure her apartment was secure, he headed to the station.

Veronica's lack of a boyfriend eliminated the possibility of an ex-lover trying to hurt her, but he had a disturbing feeling that wasn't the reason he felt relieved. Damn. He couldn't do this. He could not get involved with her. He could not be suckered in by her big doelike eyes or that lyrical voice of hers. He could not care about Veronica Miller.

She was just a case. Just a strange, bizarre, fascinating case. And the first person to make him feel really alive since his accident. Since he'd come back to work, he'd mostly stuck to routine investigations. Now, he'd finally been handed something interesting. Only it wasn't just the case fascinating him. It was the woman herself. She was beautiful and enticing, although quite possibly a mental case.

But for some reason he believed her.

He parked at the station, climbed out and hurried to his desk. Ford was perched on top, one leg swinging against the metal frame, his hand around a mug of coffee. Or what the precinct called coffee. It tasted more like bitter chunks of sludge, but it usually did the job—it kept you awake when duty called. And right now, duty had his number.

"Okay, Ford, what did you find out?" Nathan relaxed into his chair, refusing to let Ford see his irritation. He knew Ford thought he was too young to be a detective, and Nathan intended to prove the man wrong. He also understood Ford's skepticism about Veronica, and Ford had a right to his doubts. Shoot, even *he* had doubts.

Ford pointed to a file on his desk. "Got some background on the Miller woman. She moved here from Fort Lauderdale a couple of months ago. Left a booming practice to branch out on her own."

"Any problems with co-workers there?"

"Naw. Her boss said she was a brilliant attorney. Said she kept to herself, didn't socialize much. Thought she was a little weird, but didn't say anything specific."

Nathan opened the file. Somehow he felt guilty, as if he was violating Veronica's privacy. He'd never felt that way before. Investigating people was his job. "Did he know why she decided to leave the practice?"

Ford slurped his coffee. "No. Her boss seemed shocked, said her announcement came out of the blue. He even offered her a partnership, but she refused."

Nathan tapped his fingers on the file. Why had she left such a good position to move back here? To the town where her parents were killed—a place that must hold haunting memories for her? Was she running from someone or something back in Florida?

"Oh, her secretary did say she thought she was seeing a counselor. Said the move might have had something to do with her boyfriend, too. They had a big fight before she left."

Nathan glanced up at Ford.

"Said his name was Ron Cox. Sent a return plane ticket to her office the day she left."

Nathan swallowed, angry with himself for being so gullible. Veronica had told him there was no man in her life. If she'd lied about having a boyfriend, what else had she hidden?

VERONICA WAS MESMERIZED momentarily by the opulence of Eli's mansion. She'd never known anything like it. The three-story Georgian home and estate had been featured in a magazine once, so she knew it had been designed with ornate Ionic columns, imported marble and tile, elaborate decorative moldings, and its extensive gardens featured statues, topiary and fountains. It certainly didn't look like anyone's home. Taking a calming breath, she opened her car door, made her way up the cobblestone walkway and rang the brass doorbell. A butler answered.

"Eli, it's so good to see you." Veronica waved to her godfather as he crossed the marble floor of his elegant foyer and approached her. A brilliant smile spread across his face, and Veronica was grateful to see his coloring had improved from the week before.

Dressed in a tuxedo, starched white ruffled shirt, and shiny Italian shoes, he looked distinguished and evermore the politician as he gracefully executed his way past staunch supporters and fans of his own days as senator.

"It's good to see you, dear." Eli kissed her on the cheek and extended his arm to escort her into the enormous main dining room. A crowd of sleekly dressed guests were chatting and sipping champagne, or nibbling at the array of hors d'oeuvres situated artfully on white linen-covered tables. A massive crystal chandelier sparkled above the candlelit room, and additional silver trays filled with food and drinks were being passed around by waiters dressed in black.

An uneasy feeling flitted over Veronica as she joined the party. Tension crackled through the air. Hushed murmurs and curious stares met her appearance.

Someone was watching her. She'd had the same feeling

before—twice when she'd gone walking around her apartment complex, and once on the ride to work. She'd considered reporting her fears, but she had no proof. And she knew the police wouldn't believe her.

"Relax, dear, they won't bite," Eli whispered in her ear.

Veronica laughed softly. Even in Eli's letters, he'd had a sense of humor. "I'm really not much of a party person." Veronica spotted a woman watching her from across the room. She recognized Eli's wife, Barbara, from pictures she'd seen in the paper. Barbara wore a long black velvet dress that flattered her figure. Veronica smiled as Barbara approached, but the smile Barbara returned lacked warmth. "I hope your family didn't mind me coming."

Eli shook his head, his thinning dark hair lacquered in place. "Nonsense, of course not. This is a party for my son. I've wanted you to meet my family for a long time."

"Veronica, it's nice to meet you," Barbara said in a formal tone.

"Thanks for inviting me," Veronica said, curious at Barbara's coldness. "This is a lovely party."

"And you look lovely yourself." Barbara raked her gaze over Veronica. Her gray eyes reminded Veronica of a stray cat's, beady and glittering as if she were preparing for an attack.

Veronica suddenly felt self-conscious. She'd dressed in a short black evening dress she'd worn to dozens of other business functions. It was modest but well fitting, slightly curved off the shoulders but certainly not revealing. But Barbara seemed to disapprove. Or maybe it wasn't the dress, maybe it was just her.

"Hi there, Eli. Things are going well." A small, white-haired lady wearing spectacles ambled up and slipped her arm around Eli's waist. A sleeping, white long-haired cat nestled under her arm, and she seemed oblivious to the fact that her turquoise silk dress was covered in feline hairs. Eli grinned and patted her back. A pudgy older man, mostly bald, strolled up beside her.

"Mom, this is Veronica Miller. You remember my god-daughter." Eli swept a hand toward Veronica. "Veronica, this is my mother, Alma. And this is Daryl Scroggins. He used to be the police chief around here years ago."

The old woman's pale coloring turned a pasty white. "Yes, I remember something about her," the woman said in a low voice, peering at her over her glasses. "Nice to see you, Miss Miller. Amazing how much you look like your mother."

"Yes, it is," Barbara said in a clipped tone.

Eli's mother hurried away, making Veronica wonder if she'd somehow caused the woman to be uncomfortable. Daryl Scroggins gave her an assessing look, his right eye twitching nervously. "So you're the little Miller girl all grown-up?"

Veronica's fingernails bit into the palms of her hands. She didn't think a reply was necessary.

"Bad thing about your folks." Scroggins shook his head. "Wish I could have done more back then."

"Thank you." The quiet that descended on the room made Veronica's chest ache. She heard several people whispering about the murder-suicide. She'd never believed the story, but neither could she remember the truth about what had happened. If she had, she could have convinced the police to investigate further. Her grandmother had repeatedly complained that the police hadn't done everything they could have to solve her parents' case. On the other hand, she had discouraged Veronica from returning to Oakland.

Eli stroked her arm. "Come on, Veronica. I want to introduce you to some friends."

Veronica tried to relax, but she felt like an unwelcome outsider. When Eli briefly introduced her to his guests, she sensed tension in their tight smiles and nods. They knew who she was, knew of her past. Some of the people had probably known her parents.

Coming back to her hometown had been a huge mistake. She'd wanted to remember, but could she really deal with all the gossip and curious stares directed her way?

She gazed into the crowd as Eli chatted with an old friend.

A familiar face wedged its way into the sea of people. Detective Dawson. What was he doing here?

"You know that man?" Veronica asked.

Eli nodded. "Of course. I know almost everyone in town."

Veronica couldn't take her eyes off the detective. He turned and spotted her from across the room. Their gazes locked. She could feel his heated look burn into her skin. Where he'd looked handsome in casual clothes, he looked absolutely devastating in a tux and tie. The black color and fit of his jacket made his shoulders look even broader, and the dim lights gave his bronze tones a tint that radiated sex appeal. She smiled shyly. He smiled, but his jaw tightened and he gave her a short nod. Still, as she walked away, she felt his gaze searing into her.

"How's your practice?" Eli asked.

"Growing," Veronica said, trying to tear her gaze from the detective. "My calendar's almost booked. Being this close to Atlanta really helps."

Eli's face reddened and he broke into a coughing spell.

"Are you all right, Eli?"

He nodded, wiping his mouth with the corner of his napkin. "Fine."

Veronica sighed in relief. She hadn't been around Eli much while she was growing up, but he'd always sent birthday cards and called regularly. And he was her last link to her parents. Eli had been their best friend. She'd had the foolish notion that if she lived close by, his family might welcome her. But so far, his mother and wife hadn't exactly been warm.

"I guess you've been working so hard you haven't had time to get married?"

Veronica took a glass of club soda from a waiter, surprised at the question. "No. I'm not sure marriage is for me."

"Why do you say that, dear?" Eli asked. Veronica noticed the age spots on his hands and realized he was getting older. If her father were still alive, they'd be almost the same age. Although he'd been dead twenty years, she still missed him.

"I guess I'm just a loner," Veronica said. "But I don't

mind. I'm independent, have my own business, friends.'' She squirmed, hating herself for lying to Eli.

"You've already made friends here? Anybody I might know?''

Veronica assumed Detective Dawson didn't count. Or her secretary. "Well, not yet. I've only been here a short while.''

"Well, I'd like to be the lady's friend.''

Veronica jumped at the sound of the deep voice behind her.

"Gerald!'' Eli turned and grinned broadly as a tall, medium-built, dark-haired man slapped him on the back.

"The party's great, Dad,'' Gerald said with enthusiasm. "And who's this beautiful woman on your arm?'' Gerald's wide grin showed off a set of perfectly straight polished teeth. A politician's smile, if she'd ever seen one.

"This is Veronica Miller,'' Eli said, grinning.

Gerald's smile widened. "It is a pleasure, Ms. Miller. Welcome to our home.''

Veronica smiled, a shiver slithering up her back as Gerald took her hand and kissed it. When she glanced up, she saw Detective Dawson watching her, his face impassive.

"My pleasure, too.'' Veronica studied Gerald. He was handsome in a polished sort of way—smooth, soft-looking skin; neat clipped nails; small, stylish, round glasses; not a hair out of place. Still, she felt uneasy with him.

"Father says you're new to Oakland. A tax attorney?''

"Yes,'' Veronica said. "I was working in Fort Lauderdale but I decided to branch out on my own.''

"Atlanta certainly can use you.'' Gerald grinned flirtatiously. "Perhaps I can show you the city sometime and we can have dinner?''

"Perhaps,'' Veronica said. She noticed the detective easing near her.

Eli frowned. "I thought you didn't have time for a social life.''

Veronica shifted and squeezed her hands around her glass at Eli's disapproving tone. "I haven't. But maybe sometime I will.''

"Excuse us for a minute," Eli said, deftly guiding Gerald away.

"I'll definitely see you later, Veronica," Gerald said, giving her a wink.

Veronica felt a presence behind her.

"Hi," Detective Dawson said softly. "I didn't realize you knew the former senator."

Veronica faced him and sipped her drink. "He's my godfather. He was a friend of my parents."

Dawson leveled her with a probing gaze. "So, you're friendly with the family?"

Veronica laughed nervously. "Hardly. Eli's kept in touch with letters and cards. I just met Gerald." Besides, I don't remember the others, she added silently.

"I see." Dawson downed a swig of his champagne. "Gerald has his eyes out for you. You looking for a new boyfriend?"

"What are you talking about?" Veronica asked, her nerves on edge.

"Why didn't you tell me about Ron?" Nathan asked.

Veronica glanced at her hands. "There's nothing to tell."

"Listen, Veronica. I'm trying to help. But how can I investigate your story if you don't tell me the truth?" Nathan asked. "A lover—"

"Nathan." A woman called, flitting toward them.

Nathan frowned. "We'll finish this discussion later." He motioned to a woman a few years older than Veronica with dark red hair swept up in a fashionable chignon and glittery combs on both sides. "You know Tessa?"

Veronica shook her head. She knew Tessa was Eli's daughter from a previous marriage, but they'd never met. At least not that she remembered. Tessa must be close to forty. She was wearing blue spiked heels and a royal blue dress that hugged her curves and dipped to expose her ample cleavage. She sauntered toward them, confidence radiating from her every pore. "Nice looking," Veronica said, wondering if in spite of the age difference, the detective had dated her.

"Yes," Dawson said in a low voice, "she is."

Their gazes locked again. Once again the tension radiating between them was palpable.

Tessa maneuvered her way between Veronica and Nathan. "Hi, Nathan. Good to see you again."

"You, too," Nathan said. Veronica tensed and watched Tessa give Nathan an appreciative look.

"Hi, Tessa." Veronica extended her hand. "I'm Veronica Miller. Your dad and I—"

"I know who you are," Tessa said in a sweet voice. But oddly, her blue eyes reminded Veronica of cold, crystal ice chips. "My father told us you were coming. Maybe we can go shopping together some time," Tessa suggested.

"Sure," Veronica said, confused about the mixed signals emanating from Tessa.

Daryl Scroggins, the former police chief, joined them, introducing her to his wife. "Welcome to Oakland, Miss Miller," the middle-aged woman said. "Eli talks about you all the time. Did you really set up your office in the converted house where your father worked?"

"Yes," Veronica said. "It's a lovely office and a great location."

"I don't mean to be rude, dear, but you're not living in that…that other house, are you?" the woman asked, fingering a gold broach pinned to the lapel of her organdy suit.

Veronica stiffened. "You mean my parents' house?"

"Yes," the woman said.

Tessa's long, red fingernails tapped up and down Detective Dawson's sleeve. "That would be so spooky."

"No," Veronica said. "I'm not staying there. I have an apartment."

"You know they never sold the place," Scroggins commented, taking a long draw of beer.

Another elderly woman joined them. "I've been selling real estate around here for years. Tried for a while to sell the house, but no one would buy it."

"'Fraid it might be haunted," Scroggins said. "You haven't been out there have you, Miss Miller?"

Veronica shook her head. "Not yet."

A sudden hush fell over the crowd at her statement. It was as if a cold wind had blown into the room, absorbing all the warmth. Nathan's expression was unreadable.

"Well…" Scroggins said. "Let me know if you decide to go. House has been sitting there empty for years. Might not be safe. We've had some vandalism from time to time, but old Mr. Parker who lives near there keeps an eye on the place."

"Thank you." Veronica shivered as images of empty, cold, dark rooms, rotten boards covered in cobwebs and scampering, hungry mice came to mind.

"I wouldn't go out there for anything in the world," the nosy old real estate lady said. "Spooky the way it happened. Your dad was a good attorney. Then one day—"

"Vera, let's get another drink," her husband said, and steered his wife away.

"Come have some finger food with me," Tessa purred into Nathan's ear.

"Why don't you get us a plate?" Nathan suggested, capturing Veronica's gaze.

Veronica swallowed, trying to block out the old woman's words and keep her emotions at bay.

Tessa's ruby red lips formed a perfect pout. "Okay. I'll bring you some champagne, too," she said. Eli's daughter sauntered away, flirting with every man in sight. Before Veronica had a chance to speak, Eli approached with a younger version of himself. It had to be his youngest son, Sonny. He was only two years older than Veronica. Staggering slightly, he steadied himself and flashed her a grin. Veronica cringed. He appeared to be drunk. Drunk and leering.

"This is Sonny," Eli said. "Sonny—"

"I know who this is," Sonny said with a slight slur. "I've been dying to meet her all night."

Detective Dawson's posture straightened. The older police chief, Scroggins, engaged Eli in a conversation.

Veronica offered her hand to Sonny. He grabbed it and planted a sloppy kiss on the top. "Pleased to meet you, V."

"It's Veronica," she said through clenched teeth.

"Dad said you used to live around here when you were little."

Veronica nodded. An older couple approached, staring at her as if they'd seen a ghost. "That's right."

"How about you and me painting the town?" Sonny grabbed another glass of champagne from a waiter who whizzed by.

"I don't think so," Veronica said. "I'm busy with my new practice."

Tessa sauntered up and handed the detective a tray of goodies. She stared at Veronica, then Sonny.

"Why not? Got to have fun sometime," Sonny said, leaning so close Veronica could smell his strong cologne. The odor mixed with his breath and seeped into her nostrils, almost making her ill.

"I don't have time," Veronica said, backing away.

Sonny reached for her arm, his mouth turning down. "I'm a lot of fun."

Veronica felt the detective watching her. He was going to interfere. She didn't want to make a scene. "I'm really tired. I think I'm going home." Veronica pried Sonny's fingers away and made a hasty retreat toward Eli to say good-night, ignoring the angry look Sonny shot her. Two more couples stopped her to welcome her to town, one a potential client, the other old friends of Eli's who remembered her parents.

"We sure were sorry to hear about them," the thin man said sympathetically. "Mighty fine people. Your dad was a good lawyer."

Veronica nodded, unable to speak past the lump in her throat.

"We're glad you came back," the woman added, patting a

hand over her gray curls. "You were so little. I know you missed growing up without your folks."

"Yes," Veronica said. "But I had my grandmother." And Eli's letters, she added silently. Their conversation ended when a man walked up onto a platform and silenced the crowd. He introduced himself as Gerald's campaign manager, then broke into a speech about Gerald. Veronica rubbed at her temple where a headache was starting to form, and headed to the door. She couldn't get her parents out of her mind.

As she neared the door to the hallway, she was surprised to see her secretary chatting quietly in a corner with Gerald. She hadn't realized Louise knew him. She started toward them, but changed her mind and decided she really was ready to leave.

She caught Eli and he walked her to the door. "I hope it wasn't a strain for you to come here tonight," Eli said.

Veronica kissed him on the cheek. "Of course not. Thanks for having me, Eli." Then she hurried to the car, trying desperately to put her parents' deaths out of her mind. But as she drove down the long driveway and pulled onto the highway, she thought she saw a car pull out behind her. Was someone following her?

AFTER VERONICA LEFT, Nathan quickly extricated himself from Tessa's clutches, bade good-night to Eli and hurried to his car. He was going to find out the truth. Knowing Veronica had lied about her boyfriend had eaten at him all day. If he didn't talk to her about it tonight, he'd never get any sleep. He'd looked over her client list, and a few names had drawn his eye as possible troublemakers. And what the hell had been going on at that party? The tension had been as thick as a desert dust storm.

He parked in front of Veronica's apartment, surprised to see he'd beaten her home. He flipped off his lights and waited. Maybe she'd gone to a friend's, or was driving around for a while. Seconds later her black Acura streaked by. She practically jumped from her car and tore up the path to her apartment, glancing over her shoulder as if she was looking for someone. Either something had upset her, or she was in a huge hurry.

He slammed his car door and rushed after her, determined to find out the truth if he had to drag it out of her. He caught her just as she made it to the stoop.

"Ms. Miller," he said, grabbing her arm. She shrieked and spun around, her eyes wide with fright, her skin glowing alabaster in the harsh glow of the streetlight.

"I'm sorry. I didn't mean to scare you."

She winced and rubbed her bandaged arm.

"I'm sorry," Nathan said. "I forgot about your injury. I never meant to hurt you."

Her jaw clenched and shadows darkened her eyes. He instinctively knew something had happened.

"What's wrong?" he asked, inhaling the soft scent of her perfume. She smelled faintly like roses.

Veronica shook her head, her keys jangling in her trembling hands. He took the keys and opened the door, and they walked into her apartment in silence. He reached for the light switch, but she flipped it on, dropped her purse and darted to her bedroom.

"Veronica, can we talk?" he called.

"In a minute." She closed the door, effectively shutting him out.

Her voice sounded shaky. Why wouldn't she talk to him? Was she planning more lies? Maybe she was taking a pill or getting a drink to calm herself.

He studied her den, hoping to learn more about her. A simple beige leather sofa faced a natural wood entertainment unit with a small TV and stereo. Two navy wing chairs flanked a stone fireplace. The room was sleek and neat but devoid of color. Unlike most feminine rooms, it lacked fluffy pillows and tons of knickknacks. Unpacked boxes were pushed into the corner. She had a small collection of mystery novels stacked on a table and an assortment of tax- and financial-related books filled a bookcase. A big book sticking out from under a stack of magazines drew his eye. He lifted the magazine and read the title. *The Psychotic Mind of a Killer*. Hmm. Interesting.

Her walls were bare of pictures and he saw no photographs of family or friends anywhere. Odd. Then he remembered his apartment was similar. Was Veronica as lonely as he was?

The door squeaked open, and she came in wearing jeans and a pale pink T-shirt that molded her rounded breasts. She'd scrubbed her face free of makeup and had shed her shoes. He didn't know why he found her being barefoot so sexy, but he did. He shifted in his seat, reminding himself of the reason for his visit. He couldn't trust her or give in to this crazy attraction.

He decided to cut to the chase. "Why didn't you tell me about Ron? And that you knew the senator?" He wondered why her connection to a notable figure had been absent from her file.

Veronica walked across the room, putting some distance between them. "I told you, there's nothing to tell."

Nathan couldn't prevent the expletive that tore from his mouth. "Listen, Veronica, you called the police because you said someone attacked you—"

"Someone did attack me," Veronica said, anger coloring her cheeks.

"Then you have to help me. I'm trying to find out who it is, and I don't have time for these games."

"I'm not the one playing games, Mr. Dawson."

"You had a lover in Fort Lauderdale but you left out that tiny detail. You said you didn't have a boyfriend."

"I didn't think it was any of your business," Veronica snapped. "We broke up."

"Everything about you is my business," Nathan said, softly.

"Well, you don't have to worry about Ron. We dated, Detective. That's it."

Nathan glared at her. "He wanted more?"

Veronica paused. "Yes. But I didn't. I moved. End of story." She exhaled. "Besides, Ron's not dangerous."

A long silence stretched between them. Nathan wasn't so sure. He'd been a cop too long. A scorned lover or boyfriend could mean trouble. Men had killed for less. He would investigate Ron Cox whether Veronica believed him dangerous or not. Her earlier comment reverberated in his head. "What did you mean—you weren't the one playing games?"

Veronica hugged her arms around her in a protective gesture. "I think someone's trying to drive me crazy."

Nathan narrowed his eyes. "First someone is trying to kill you. Now they're trying to drive you crazy. Which is it, Veronica?"

"I don't know," she said, her voice breaking. "Maybe both."

"Did something happen on the way over?"

Veronica hesitated, avoiding his gaze. "I'm not sure. I thought someone might have been following me, so I kept driving, but then they disappeared."

Nathan cleared his throat. "Did you get a look at the car?"

Veronica crossed the room and peeked through the blinds. "No, it was too dark. It looked like some kind of Jeep but I couldn't tell for sure."

Nathan paused. He remembered her strange reaction to the music box, the animosity at the party, the conversation he'd overheard about her family. And when she'd fled the house, he'd seen the former senator's pale face.

"Did something happen at the party you're not telling me about?" Nathan asked.

Veronica shook her head. The doorbell rang, and she went to get it. Nathan was right behind her.

"Who is it?" she asked, her hand on the doorknob.

"Florist delivery service," a young male voice answered.

Nathan peeked through the blinds. When he saw the truck with the familiar flower logo on it under the streetlight, he nodded for her to open the door.

The young man was wearing a yellow paper hat with the

words, Fancy Flowers, printed on the front. He held up a long white box with a yellow ribbon tied around it. "Your lucky day, er, night," he said, grinning.

"Thank you." Veronica took the box and smiled.

"Sure thing." The teenager waved and almost tripped over his feet to get back to the van after Nathan handed him a sizable tip.

She carried the box to the kitchen counter. "It's probably from Eli," Veronica said. "A welcoming gift. He used to send me flowers for my birthday."

Nathan followed her to the kitchen. "Let me check it first."

Veronica glanced into his eyes. "You think—"

"I don't know," Nathan said. "But it's better to be careful."

"There isn't a card," she said, looking over the box.

Nathan carefully examined the package, then slowly untied the ribbon. When he lifted the lid, she gasped. He swallowed hard and glanced at her pale face. Tears pooled in the corners of her huge eyes. "Oh, my God," Veronica whispered. "Who would do such a thing?"

Nathan gritted his teeth. The box was filled with crushed daisies, like the ones Veronica had held in the picture by her parents' grave.

She dropped her head into her hands and shook her head back and forth, her voice desolate. "Everything was fine until I moved back here. Why is this happening to me? Why?"

Nathan heard the frustration in her voice, the fear, the agony. He couldn't stand it any longer. The smart thing to do was not to get involved. But then again, he didn't always do the smart thing. Sometimes he just went on gut instincts. And right now his gut instincts were screaming at him to comfort her. Ignoring the branding heat of the police badge in his breast pocket, he took her in his arms and held her while she cried.

Chapter Four

Veronica tried to shove away her lingering fear, but her body trembled and her mind raced with unanswered questions. Had someone been following her when she'd left Eli's house? And if so, whom?

And who could have been so cruel as to have sent a box of crushed daisies?

While Nathan's arms tightened around her and he stroked the long column of her spine with his wide palm, she sagged against him, her heart racing, her mind ordering her to extricate herself from his comfort. Her body adamantly refused.

"I don't know what's going on, but we'll get to the bottom of it," Nathan said in a quiet voice. He gently traced his thumb along her chin and tilted her face to gaze into her eyes.

Embarrassed at her loss of composure, she brushed the damp tears from her cheeks and inhaled a calming breath. But being held in Nathan Dawson's arms was definitely not calming, and inhaling the deep musky scent of his body and cologne was intoxicating. A danger in itself. Although his jaw was taut, heat flared in his eyes. His gentle touch and powerful, protective arms made her sway.

"Veronica?"

Desire laced his husky voice, his lips a mere whisper away, his breath hot on her skin. Veronica's breasts pressed against the hard wall of his chest. Heat skittered up her spine, and the rough texture of his stubbled jaw on her cheek sent a shaft of white-hot need darting through her.

"Tell me not to do this," he whispered as his lips grazed her hair.

"Nathan, I—" Veronica's unspoken argument died when his warm mouth descended on hers in a bold motion, sending a rush of pleasure and passion though her that was almost frightening in its intensity. His mouth devoured hers, his lips daring and forceful as he claimed the tender recesses of her mouth with his plunging tongue. Veronica's body reacted to his need by molding to his hard masculinity, and a low moan escaped her when his lips moved to the delicate skin beneath her jaw. Quivering now from his touch instead of fear, she felt his hands press her intimately against him, and she muttered a raspy sigh that was partly a plea to stop, partly a plea not to.

Nathan suddenly gentled his hands and loosened his fierce hold on her, letting his hands linger at her waist as he touched his forehead to hers and exhaled loudly. His words came out on a ragged breath. "I'm sorry."

Veronica tensed immediately and flexed the palms of her hands against his chest to push him away, his apology shredding her fragile pride. Instead of releasing her, Nathan continued to stroke her back as he had before, slowly allowing the tension to ease from both their heated bodies. When he finally looked at her, she saw a mixture of the passion they'd ignited along with a strong sense of regret, but he still didn't let her go.

"I shouldn't have done that, because I'm working on your case," he said in a husky voice. "Not because it wasn't good."

Veronica felt her anger slip and toyed with the pleats of his cummerbund. Beneath her thin T-shirt, her nipples stood erect against the soft cotton, and her breasts ached for Nathan's touch, a realization that shocked her. She had her own policies about not getting involved with people she worked with, and she desperately needed his help as a detective.

"Veronica?"

Why had her reaction to his touch been so volatile? Ron had barely excited her. "You're right," she finally said, pulling away.

Nathan gave her a hard, assessing look, then dropped his hands to his side. "Do you have some coffee?"

Veronica wrung her hands. "I'm not a coffee drinker. But I'll make you some."

"Don't go to any trouble."

"No, it's okay. It's instant. I keep it for…just in case." She darted to the door, biting her tongue. She'd almost told him she kept it for Ron, but she'd been here several weeks and hadn't invited him for a visit. In fact, she hadn't even considered the idea. She'd simply bought the coffee out of habit.

Still shaken from the passionate kiss, she willed her hands to be steady while she made tea and coffee. Nathan's scent wafted into the kitchen, and she felt his penetrating stare on her back and heard his steady breathing in the strained silence of the room.

"How long have you been here?" Nathan asked, glancing around the tidy kitchen when she handed him the steaming coffee mug.

Veronica stirred sweetener into her tea and sat down at the oak table and chairs that had belonged to her grandmother. The kitchen was clean but bare—white cabinets and countertops, a small kitchen island, beige tile floors, nothing impressive. But then she'd never gone in for frivolous things or decorating. Nathan sprawled his long legs out beside her and sipped his coffee, obviously waiting for her answer.

"I moved here about eight weeks ago."

"Did you inherit a lot of Walsh's clients?"

Veronica warmed her hands by cupping them around her mug. "A few."

"Bring any with you from Florida?"

Veronica sipped her tea. "A couple of entrepreneurs who travel worldwide, live by their fax machines. And I represent a few of my grandmother's friends. They live in a retirement community in Fort Lauderdale. With their limited pension plans and social security, they need all the breaks they can get.''

Nathan nodded and stared, his gaze unnerving her. She suddenly wished she'd thrown a heavy sweatshirt on over her thin cotton T-shirt. The memory of his heated kiss and her own response lingered between them, causing the air to crackle with tension.

Nathan swirled the dark coffee around in his mug. ''How did your firm feel about your leaving? Any hard feelings?''

Veronica shook her head. ''Not that I know of. They seemed amicable. My boss told me if I ever wanted to come back to let him know.''

Nathan took a long sip of coffee and frowned. ''How about the businessmen you mentioned? Must have been some major-league clients. Were the partners upset when you took their business?''

Veronica tucked a strand of hair behind her ear. ''One of them made a big deal out of it. But the boss said I'd earned the clients. Neither one resided in Florida anyway. Besides, my contract specified I couldn't practice within a ten-mile radius and—''

''And you're well out of that range,'' Nathan finished for her.

''Exactly.''

''Smart businesswoman,'' Nathan said, nodding his approval.

Veronica smiled. ''I like my work.'' *It's not threatening, like you.*

''Did you work up a client list for me?''

Veronica sighed. ''No, but I will tomorrow.''

''Good. Include the names of the people you worked with in Florida.''

''I really don't think—''

''Veronica, it's my job to investigate all angles.'' He drummed his fingers on the table. ''I'd like to talk to your old boyfriend, too.''

Veronica gritted her teeth. "Is that really necessary? I told you Ron isn't dangerous."

"I'll be the judge of that. Besides, it's routine."

Veronica rose, her nerves on edge at the thought of Nathan talking to Ron.

"Is there some other reason you don't want me to contact him?" Nathan asked.

"I…I don't want him to worry about me," Veronica said quietly. "Or come here."

"Does he know where you are?"

"Of course. I didn't just run away."

Nathan was silent for a moment. Tension radiated between them. "You think he'll show up here out of concern?"

"I don't know." She turned to face him. "He doesn't know about my past, though, and I'd like to keep it that way."

Nathan arched an eyebrow. Veronica realized he expected her to tell him more, but she sipped her tea instead.

He finished his coffee, leaned back in his chair and folded his arms. "Why? Don't you think he could accept it?"

A sliver of apprehension knotted Veronica's stomach. She'd suffered every imaginable kind of reaction to her past, from disgust to morbid curiosity to rejection. She had no idea how Ron would have reacted if she'd told him. But she assumed he'd have insisted she forget her need to reconcile herself with her past.

She had no intention of doing that.

"None of the people I worked with in Florida know. I didn't think it was any of their business," Veronica said, rubbing her hands up and down her arms. "Besides, I told you my relationship with Ron is over."

She refused to squirm when he studied her with his dark probing eyes. The memory of the kiss taunted her. Had Nathan already forgotten it? Probably. He was a sexy, virile man. He probably had dozens of women.

Whereas she was sexually inept, a freak—at least that was what one college boyfriend had told her. He'd attributed her ineptitude to her traumatic past.

Nathan stood, pushed his chair back from the table and placed his empty cup in the sink. "Thanks for the coffee. I'll come by your office tomorrow for that list."

Veronica nodded. "And what about Ron?"

He hesitated. "I have to check him out."

Veronica sighed.

"I'll be discreet." He closed the distance between them and covered her small hand with his own. "Trust me, Veronica."

Then he squeezed her hand and walked out the door.

She watched the door close and touched her hand to her cheek where he had offered her comfort. *Trust me, Veronica.*

If only she could. Her heart squeezed at his husky plea, and the words rang over and over in her head like the beckoning sound of church bells drawing one into its welcoming sanctuary. But trust didn't come easily for her. Too many memories, too much pain and gossip in the past, and too few friends. His kiss had been passionate, his touch warm and hungry and perhaps sincere.

But she wasn't sure she could ever trust again.

THE NEXT MORNING Nathan showered and washed his face, trying to wipe away the memory of the heated kiss he'd shared with Veronica. He'd wanted her to trust him, but how could he ask her to do that if he couldn't trust himself around her?

And why had he kissed her? It was totally against his beliefs to get involved with her. But the memory burned in his mind like the hot coals of an open fire and he was afraid he already had become involved with her. No amount of scrubbing could wipe the sweet touch of her lips from his mouth or banish the memory of her fiery response.

Damn. He had work to do. And Veronica Miller was right at the heart of it.

And worming her way into his heart—against his will.

Slinging on an oxford shirt, jeans and boots, he grabbed his badge and gun, then headed toward his car. Forget breakfast. His appetite could only be satisfied by finishing what he'd started with Veronica—and that was impossible.

He might as well work on her case. The sooner he got to the bottom of the mystery surrounding her, the sooner he could put her warm, delicate body and baby doelike eyes out of his mind. The sooner he could forget that she tasted as fresh as a mint julep on a hot summer day.

At the office fifteen minutes later, he tapped into the precinct's computer to begin his investigation of Ron Cox. It wasn't because the guy had been involved with Veronica personally, he told himself, but because it was the logical place to start the investigation. Perhaps the Florida police department had dealt with the man in some form other than his capacity as a lawyer. Sometimes lawyers were like bad cops—it was too easy to find loopholes and too tempting to cross the line.

"Hey, Dawson." Ford leaned over his shoulder, his breath heavy with cigar smoke. "What the hell you doing?"

Nathan read the information coming in over the transit. "Checking out a lead."

"The Bailey robbery?"

"No, the Miller case." Nathan skimmed the lines of text, searching for anything he could find on Cox. If he had any kind of record, he would have had to be fingerprinted. The FBI would have a file on him.

The chair beside Nathan squeaked and protested as Ford lowered his heavy bulk into it. "Why are you wasting the taxpayers' time? I told you she's a nutcase."

Nathan gritted his teeth. "I have to check it out." He narrowed his eyes at Ford. "Then *I'll* decide."

"You're crazy yourself," Ford said in a disgusted voice. "Wait till the lieutenant hears about this."

Nathan slammed his hand on the table. "I'll handle Stevens. Why don't you get to work?"

"You expect me to help you?"

"You're my partner, aren't you?"

Ford's fat cheeks ballooned out in anger. "Not by choice."

"Well, it certainly wasn't my choice, either," Nathan snapped. A buzz of voices sounded in the hallway. The other detectives and cops strolled in. Nathan and Ford glared at each other.

"I'll check the background on the Bailey case," Ford finally said, heading to his own desk.

"Fine. By dividing up, we can get the legwork done on both cases. Then we'll meet up." Nathan turned his gaze back to the screen, his eyes widening as the data kicked in. Cox had been fingerprinted and he had a record, a misdemeanor for vandalizing as a teen, but nonetheless a record.

Nathan studied the data. Hmm. Interesting.

Ron Cox was five foot eleven, 170 pounds.

Scrawny.

First wife—deceased at age twenty-five. Cox had been questioned about the murder, but released, citing lack of evidence. No mention of cause of death. Worth checking into, Nathan noted to himself. No children. Lawyer with Hepplewhite and Sutton, handles investments, been with the firm for four years, being considered for partner. Annual income $110,000.

Then he realized Veronica's salary probably tripled his own, also. Not that it mattered, but it was a real ego buster. Shaking away the thought, he turned back to the information and scanned for details on the man's arrest. Zilch. He wondered if it could have been a substantially more serious charge and he'd pleaded down to the misdemeanor.

He would check the Internet for any news articles about Cox's arrest and investments. A few minutes later he hit the jackpot. There wasn't just one, but several articles about Ron Cox. He was one of Florida's leading attorneys specializing in land investments, and Florida was booming with investors. A whole series of stories had been written about tourism and the economy. The price of land had skyrocketed for condos and town homes near the coast. As he skimmed the articles, he understood how Cox earned such a hefty salary. His specific knowledge was valued by proprietors of several major companies who were expanding and building entire vacation resorts catering to the wealthy.

Then one article drew his eye. A small subsidiary of one of

the companies had accused Cox of embezzling funds and taking money from elderly people. The case had gotten local media attention, but suddenly the news had ceased. He skimmed the next few editions of the paper and discovered a small section explaining that the company had reached a settlement and the charges had been dropped. Hadn't Veronica mentioned helping some older groups?

Nathan ran a hand through his hair and leaned back in his chair, placing his booted feet on his desk while he considered the possibilities. Did Veronica know about Cox's past?

Surely she knew. The stories had appeared in the paper only six months ago—she was still living in Florida at the time.

Perhaps Veronica had discovered something about Cox's business by mistake. Cox might be worried about her coming forth with the information. If his career was at stake, he had a viable motive—men had killed before for money. It was a theory worth investigating.

He checked his watch, then stretched and ignored the hum of the other computers and officers in the room as he strode toward the door. The flower shop would be open by now. He planned to go by and see if he could learn who'd sent Veronica the crushed daisies before he picked up her client list. Maybe the florist would solve the little mystery for him and he could wrap up this case. Then he could forget Veronica Miller.

VERONICA TRIED to concentrate on her agenda for the day as she took her morning run, but images of Nathan Dawson kept popping into her head. At least his image was more pleasing than the dead flowers she'd received and much less upsetting than the music box. Well, upsetting in a different way, she conceded.

After lying awake half the night trying to figure out the odd circumstances surrounding her arrival in Georgia, she'd finally fallen into a fitful sleep and dreamed that she was being chased by a madman, the same one who'd killed her parents, and she'd gone running off a cliff. She'd been falling, falling, falling into empty air with nothing but jagged rocks below to break her fall—her fall to death.

Picking up her running pace, she pumped her legs and turned the corner near her apartment complex, then slowed as she noticed a man wearing a dark coat walk past her car. What was he doing?

She jogged the trail that went around the parking lot and watched the man, but the hood of an all-weather coat hid his face.

Then the man was gone. Disappeared right before her eyes.

She followed the path bordering the building and searched to see if he'd run around the back, but she saw nothing except a couple of teenagers embracing on the park bench. Circling back, she scanned the parking lot to make sure he wasn't hiding behind a bush, but again she saw nothing out of the ordinary. Was she just being paranoid?

Building up speed, she jogged around the building again, once more searching for any signs of the man. A young mother pushing a stroller passed her and waved.

She veered toward her apartment, certain she was just imagining things, when she saw a hooded figure dash from her apartment door. Freezing momentarily, she forgot to breathe. Then the figure disappeared and anger replaced her fear. She charged up the steps, expecting to find her door ajar and her things scattered, but her door was locked and a newspaper lay on the stoop. She picked it up and wondered if the man was the new delivery guy. Reaching inside her pocket and retrieving the mace she carried when she jogged, she held it in one hand and rolled the paper up with the other hand so she could use it as a weapon if she needed. Then she crept inside her apartment. But once again, nothing was amiss

Hands trembling, she poured herself a glass of water then went to stand on her deck. Was she going crazy? She scanned the parking lot and play area and saw nothing but the mother and the small children. A black Land Cruiser left the parking lot, and old man Perkins meandered out for his morning paper.

Good grief. Had she been frightened over a paperboy?

She chastised herself a thousand times while she showered and dressed for work. "Now where's that red blazer?" she mumbled searching through her closet.

A few minutes later she gave up the search and pulled on a black jacket, then left for work. Maybe today Detective Dawson would show up with some answers. Once she sorted out her past, her life could get back to normal.

NATHAN FELT LIKE A THORN in a rose garden as he stepped inside the pale pink walls of the florist's shop and noticed the delicate arrangements of fragile flowers in glass showcases. A tinkling bell chimed above and a small gray-haired woman wearing an apron over stretch knit pants greeted him with a kind smile.

"What can I do for you, young man?" She wiped her hands on her apron, her eyes twinkling. "Looking for something for that special someone?"

Nathan stilled, realizing her assumption. He hadn't been called *young* in a long time; all the more reason he should avoid getting personally involved with Veronica. "No, ma'am. I need some information."

"Okay. Are you looking for something indoor or outdoor?"

Nathan shook his head and produced his badge. The woman swallowed a small gasp as her eyes widened. "I'd like to find out who sent some flowers to a woman last night."

"Why? Was something wrong with the arrangement?"

Nathan's jaw tightened as he fought frustration. "I need to know who sent them, ma'am. It's police business."

The woman squared her shoulders and ambled toward a small round table where she produced a ledger.

"Tell me who they were sent to."

"Veronica Miller. Apartment J-5, Bainbridge Apartments. They arrived last night about ten."

The woman propped a pair of wire-rimmed spectacles on her nose, then scanned the ledger. "Daisies?"

"Yes."

The woman peered over her glasses. "I thought that was odd."

Nathan cleared his throat. Now they were getting somewhere. "What was odd, ma'am?"

"Well, the daisies were already wilting. I was about to throw them out but the customer insisted on them. Paid for them in cash."

"And who was the customer?" Nathan asked impatiently.

The woman tapped her forehead in thought. "She was wearing a red jacket with a pin on it." She tapped the ledger. "I remember the pin sparkled in the sunlight—some kind of bird. A swan, peacock, pelican maybe." Then she described the customer and Nathan strode from the store.

He had to see Veronica.

VERONICA RUSHED into her front office, poured herself some tea and waved to Louise who was busy on the phone verifying appointments for later in the week. Sailing past the coatrack, she noticed her red jacket.

"Well, I'll be darned," she muttered as she grabbed it and carried it to her office. She didn't remember leaving it at work. In fact, she usually kept her jacket over her chair so she wouldn't forget it.

Deciding it wasn't important, she opened her briefcase and spread the files she'd meant to study the night before on her desk. Pouring over endless paperwork would no doubt take her mind off the handsome detective and his kiss—and the haunting memories of her early-morning nightmare. She wasn't sure which disturbed her more.

An hour later she'd compiled the client list for Nathan and set it aside. She was engrossed in one of her client's financial plans when the phone rang.

"Veronica Miller speaking."

"Veronica, it's Eli. I wanted to make sure you were all right."

Veronica's fingers tightened around the handset as the memories of the crushed flowers blurred her vision. "Of course I'm all right, why wouldn't I be?"

Eli hesitated. "Well, you seemed tense at the party. You're my goddaughter, and now that you're in town, I intend to make sure you're taken care of."

Veronica fiddled with her ballpoint pen and smiled. "I'm fine, Eli. You're really sweet to ask." She'd fretted about the flowers all night and decided there had to be a logical explanation. Perhaps Eli had ordered them and the florist had made a mistake. "Eli, you didn't send me flowers last night, did you?"

"Why, no." He chuckled. "But I wish I'd thought of it. You must have a secret admirer."

"Some admirer," Veronica mumbled as the line broke up with static.

"What? You'll have to speak up, dear. I'm on the cell phone."

"Nothing." Veronica thought quickly. "It was probably a business acquaintance, and they forgot to put in the card."

"Probably so. Listen, I'd like to have lunch later in the week. How about Friday?"

"Sure." Veronica penciled in Friday and said goodbye. She turned back to her file but a familiar scent wafted into the room and she felt someone's presence. When she glanced up, Nathan was standing in the doorway. He'd been devastatingly handsome in the tux, but even in his faded jeans and the blue oxford shirt, he looked sexy as sin.

"Hi." She fumbled with her pen and dropped it on the floor. "I guess you came by for that client list."

Nathan nodded and moved in the doorway. Veronica couldn't read his expression, but the smile she'd seen last night when he'd asked her to trust him was absent from his eyes.

"Do you have it ready?"

Veronica handed the list to him. "There are several sheets. I made notations by the ones who are no longer with me. The red asterisks indicate clients who weren't happy with their settlements, but I still don't think any of them are dangerous."

Nathan scanned the paper. "Thanks. I'll look into it."

An uneasy feeling swept over Veronica at Nathan's cold, formal tone. Where was the man who'd been so sensitive last night? The man who'd kissed her and awakened needs she hadn't even realized she'd had.

Nathan paused by the chair where she'd draped her red jacket. An odd expression drew his eyebrows together, and when he looked at her, then back at the coat, a chill slithered up her spine.

"Whose jacket is this?" he asked.

Veronica swallowed, reminding herself she had no reason to be afraid of Nathan Dawson. He was here to help her. "It's mine."

Nathan's unreadable expression turned into a puzzled frown. His long fingers stroked the colorful pelican pin on the lapel. "That pin belonged to my grandmother," she said. "There are only a few like it in the world."

Nathan's jaw hardened and Veronica tensed, her shoulders rigid. "What's wrong, Detective?"

When he spoke, his voice sounded harsh. "I went by the florist on the way over here. He said the person who ordered those flowers was a woman."

Veronica's pulse jumped. "You know who sent them?"

"The florist said the woman had long dark hair, dark eyes." He touched the pin again and stared into her eyes. Veronica could have sworn he was looking straight into her soul.

"In fact, she said the woman was wearing a red jacket with a pin on the lapel...sounded just like this one."

Chapter Five

Nathan steeled himself against Veronica's reaction. Her soft gasp and wide-eyed stare was almost convincing, and when she sagged into the chair with a dazed expression on her face, he fought the urge to comfort her. Instead he cursed himself for allowing her to get to him the day before, and he let his anger churn. He wouldn't be a sucker for anyone—not even a dark-eyed, dark-haired beauty like Veronica.

Had she ordered the flowers for herself, then pretended to be upset? Could Ford be right? Could she be mentally disturbed? With her history, it was entirely possible.

His former partner had let his personal feelings interfere with an investigation and it had cost him his life. And Nathan had almost died, too. He couldn't afford to take any chances.

"You think I sent them to myself?" Veronica finally asked in a dull voice.

He chewed his bottom lip and said nothing. The disappointment in her eyes almost softened his resolve, but he knew now he had to solve this case. Even if it meant discovering she was a pathological liar.

"That's what you think, isn't it?" The color returned to her face in a splash of angry crimson. "You're just like everybody else. Once you heard about my past, you decided I was crazy."

"I don't know what I think," Nathan finally said. "But I want to find out the truth."

"I'm sure hundreds of women own red jackets. As far as the pin, I don't know." Veronica's dark eyes blazed with fury. "Yesterday you asked me to trust you, and today you accuse me of sending myself a box of dead flowers. You don't know the truth when it's looking straight at you."

Nathan closed the distance between them and glared at her. "I'm not accusing you of anything. I'm just doing my job."

Veronica's fingers curled around the mahogany desktop. "Fine. That's what I want you to do—your job. Find out who's doing these things to me."

Nathan leaned forward and met her angry gaze. Her sultry peach scent enveloped him. For a moment he considered reaching out and stroking her, trying to calm her. But that would only draw him in more, and if she was lying, he'd become a bigger pawn in her psychotic game. Instead, he clutched the papers she'd given him and forced his voice to be level. "I intend to find out who's behind all these things, Ms. Miller."

"Good, because I want them to stop. I have work to do."

"So do I."

"Good."

"Fine."

Several tense seconds stretched between them. Finally, Nathan lowered his voice. "I checked into your boyfriend."

"My *ex*-boyfriend."

Nathan nodded. "Did you know he had a record?"

Veronica's head snapped up. "What for?"

"A misdemeanor for breaking and entering."

He watched Veronica strain to control her reaction. "Anything else?"

"He was questioned about his first wife's death."

Shock rode across Veronica's face.

"You didn't know about that, did you?" When Veronica didn't answer, he continued. "Did you know about the charges for embezzlement?"

"Those were dropped," Veronica said tightly. "Ron was cleared."

Nathan studied her. Was she defending the man because she still cared for him? Or could she be hiding something else?

"Besides, that happened in Florida. I don't see how that can possibly be related to what's going on here."

Nathan fisted his hands by his sides. "Did you and Ron ever discuss business?"

Veronica's tone was sarcastic. "Not confidential matters if that's what you're implying."

"Bear with me for a minute, Veronica." Nathan reined in his temper. "If Ron was involved in something illegal, and you inadvertently got privy to inside information, Cox would have a motive to come after you."

Veronica mulled over the possibility, her tone softening. "I suppose it's possible, but I don't remember anything. The only thing Ron told me about were a few investments."

"Land investments?"

"Yes, but I don't remember the details." Veronica shuffled the papers on her desk and shrugged. "Just bits and pieces here and there. Nothing you couldn't find out on your own if you were interested."

"Give it some thought. A name, place, anything could be important."

Veronica nodded. "Anything else?"

Nathan gritted his teeth. Yes, he wanted to kiss her rosy lips and taste the fire in her body. But that was impossible. He didn't even know if she was telling him the truth.

"You don't believe me, do you?" she said, folding her arms across her chest.

He arched an eyebrow, wondering how she'd come so close to reading his thoughts.

She lowered her gaze and shuffled through her papers again, stacking them in neat, organized piles. "I have work to do."

His chest squeezed tightly at the hurt in her voice. The image of her as a child, her parents murdered in front of her eyes flashed before him. The loneliness and desolation in her expression as she'd stood over her parents' graves holding those daisies. Damn. He wished he'd never seen that picture.

"Don't you have to go back to work, too?" Veronica asked in a clipped tone.

He finally found his voice. "I am working. You said you'd gotten some strange messages? When did they start?"

"Right after I moved here."

"I'd like to put a tracer on your home and office phones."

"Fine."

"Okay, good."

Veronica angled her pen above her paperwork. "Then that's that."

"Look, Veronica—" A knock at the door halted his words. A good thing, he thought, before he made a fool out of himself.

Louise poked her head in. "A gentleman's here to see you, Ms. Miller." She grinned and escorted Gerald Jones in. "It's our next senator—maybe our future president."

Nathan clenched his jaw at the smile the politician gave Veronica. And when she returned it with a warm one of her own, he strode out the door without saying goodbye.

VERONICA TRIED to shove thoughts of the irritating detective from her mind while Gerald surveyed her office. It shouldn't matter if Nathan believed her, as long as he found the person harassing her, but it did matter. For some odd reason she cared what he thought more than she'd cared about anyone in a long time. Disgusted with herself, she tried to resurrect the walls she'd built around herself. Hadn't she learned from experience that caring could destroy a person?

"This is pretty nice, Ms. Miller. Simple, but nice." Gerald ran his finger along the wooden statue of a seagull she'd purchased at an art show in Florida.

"Thanks," Veronica said, unsure whether his comment was really a compliment or just his way of flirting.

Gerald leaned casually against the cherry bookcase beside the door, his hands in his designer trouser pockets, his smile a showcase of polished manners. "I was in the area and dropped by, hoping to take you to lunch."

Veronica folded her hands across the top of her desk. "I really have a lot of work to do."

Gerald grinned and sauntered toward her, then offered his hand. "Well, you have to eat. It might as well be with me."

Veronica smiled. "Shouldn't you be someplace shaking hands or kissing babies?"

Gerald's rich laughter filled the room. "I don't think it'll hurt my image to be seen with a beautiful woman, especially one of Atlanta's finest attorneys."

"I see." Veronica smiled in spite of his remark. "So you wanted to talk business?"

"No, I want to relax and enjoy myself, get to know you better." Gerald led her toward the door. "After all, you're Dad's goddaughter. That must make us…godsiblings or something."

Veronica had always wondered how Eli's children would feel about her. He'd kept her abreast of their education and careers, but she'd worried they wouldn't welcome her into their family. Maybe she was wrong.

The thought of refusing Gerald's invitation struck Veronica as a good idea, but she'd promised herself she would associate with the people from her past. Perhaps Gerald had heard Eli talk about her parents, and she could learn something that would trigger a memory.

"I'll be back in about an hour," Veronica told Louise as Gerald walked her to the door.

"Take your time," Louise said, waving her off.

"Very impressive," she said as she climbed into Gerald's sleek black Cadillac and sank into the plush leather seats.

"Father bought it for me as a kick-off campaign present. Thought it would make a better image than my Porsche."

Veronica laughed. "He's got a point. Impressions are important."

"Yes, they are," Gerald said, some of the zip leaving his smile. "As Dad always reminds me." He quickly maneuvered the car onto the road, and a few minutes later they were settled at a table in a small Italian restaurant.

"This is great," Veronica said, admiring the lacy curtains and antique paintings. Soft piano music provided a perfect accent to the dimly lit atmosphere. "I've heard about this place, but I've never been here."

"They have great pasta, and the bread is just like in Italy." Gerald raised his wineglass. "A toast to us getting to know each other better."

Veronica raised her water glass and clinked it with his. "Why don't you start by telling me about yourself?"

Gerald grinned. "My life's an open book—I'm sure you've read the papers."

Veronica nodded. "Yes, but tell me about growing up. Are you and Eli close?"

Gerald's smile faded slightly. "As close as a father and son can be. There's always that parent-child thing."

Veronica studied his face, wishing she understood the parent-child thing.

"Oh, I'm sorry." Gerald looked contrite. "That was insensitive of me. Father said you don't remember your childhood."

A wave of apprehension rippled through Veronica. "That's right. At least not the first seven years."

Gerald pushed his stylish glasses up on his nose. "Is that why you came back here? Hoping to remember?"

Veronica picked at her food, hedging. "That's part of it. I hoped moving here would bring back memories, but so far it hasn't."

"Well, perhaps it still might. Dad said you're using your father's old office space."

"That's right. The real estate agent said the house has changed a lot, though. It was an insurance office for a while."

Gerald smiled at her over his glass. "And after that, an architectural designer rented the space."

"You know, I've been thinking," Veronica said. "I know my father's files were lost in a fire, but I wondered if he might have made backup copies. Could the police have confiscated them before they were burned? It would be interesting to look over some of his old work."

Gerald arched an eyebrow. "I assumed they all burned." Gerald's comment seemed innocent enough, but his tone indicated he was more curious than he let on.

Of course, he could just be curious like some of the other people she'd met before—wanting to find out for themselves if she really did have amnesia. Another self-appointed shrink.

"I have some old boxes of memorabilia," Veronica said. "Maybe I'll look in those." Or perhaps the police had the files, she thought. She would ask Nathan.

"Hmm." Gerald chewed the thick bread. "Do you think it's a good idea for you to pursue all this? I mean, what possible reason would you have to look into your father's old files—the cases would all be outdated by now."

Veronica sipped her water and decided she'd said enough. "I suppose. Anyway, maybe I'll talk to Eli about it. He might know."

A muscle tightened in Gerald's jaw. "I doubt Father would remember. He's getting up there in age now, you know."

"Yes, I know," Veronica said, thinking of her own father and the years they'd missed together.

"And Father is rather busy," Gerald said. "Between Mother, handling his finances and overseeing my campaign, I'm not sure he has time for anything else right now."

Gerald's barrage of excuses made Veronica uncomfortable. She got the distinct impression he didn't want her bothering Eli. Maybe she wasn't welcome into the family after all.

"Tell you what, if I get a chance, I'll mention it to him and let you know," Gerald said, patting her hand in a patronizing gesture.

She studied his easy smile, and her nerves jangled with the strange feeling Gerald was putting her off. She checked her watch. "I need to get back to the office. I have an appointment at two."

Gerald paid the check, and Veronica stiffened when he placed his hand at the small of her back and guided her to the car. When he dropped her at her office, she watched him drive away and wondered about their luncheon. Once the politician, always the politician. Had she really gotten to know Gerald better or had she seen only the side he wanted her to see?

NATHAN DROVE down the winding driveway to Barrett Pharmaceuticals. Although Veronica had insisted she had no enemies, after studying her client list, he'd noted a couple of possibilities. Wayne Barrett topped the list. The other one, a man named Paul Merino, had suffered a stroke and lay immobile in a nursing home.

He parked his Honda in the circular drive, noting the landscape crew working on the property by the lake. Barrett had a fortune.

But he'd lost a small fortune when Veronica had filed his taxes.

More than likely, he hadn't been very happy about that. Barrett was a shrewd, cutthroat businessman. He had stock in several other companies and a lawsuit for insider trading. And he'd recently filed for divorce. Had his financial loss triggered the divorce? Even if it hadn't, it had certainly complicated matters for Barrett. Another motivation for him to harass Veronica.

Nathan entered the modern building, scanning the various security cameras as he walked to the front desk.

"I'd like to see Mr. Barrett, please," Nathan said.

A young secretary wearing a short skirt looked up at him and smiled. "I'm afraid that's not possible."

Nathan flashed his badge, almost laughing at the surprised expression on the young girl's face. "Now, can you get me in?"

"It's still not possible." The woman straightened her shoulders. "Mr. Barrett isn't here."

Nathan fought the frustration building in his chest. "Do you know where he went or when he'll be back?"

Soft blond curls bounced around her face as she shook her head. "He's taken an extended leave of absence."

A tall man wearing an impeccably fashionable suit stepped up behind the woman. "Is there a problem, Charlene?"

The girl smiled. "This man is a detective. He's looking for Mr. Barrett."

"Good." The man extended his hand. "I'm Dwain Rogers, vice president of the company. I'm glad you're already on the case."

"What do you mean?" Nathan asked.

"I called the police as soon as I discovered the discrepancy in accounting. This weekend Barrett left with a sizable portion of the company's money."

"Do you know how I can reach him?" Nathan asked. "Or do you have any idea where he might go?"

"Not a clue," Rogers said, frowning. "But when you find him, I want to have a word with him myself."

"I'll send a team out to search the building and interview all the employees," Nathan said. "I'd like to take a look at his office."

"Fine." Rogers led the way down a plush rose carpeted hallway and into an office the size of a hotel suite. "Let me know if you need assistance." Rogers disappeared across the hall.

Nathan glanced around the office. It was furnished with expensive cherry wood furniture and dark green sofas. A fully stocked wet bar stood in the corner. He examined the man's desk, skimmed the papers on top, searched through his files, then rummaged through the top drawer. Finally he pulled out a date book and studied the dates. Barrett had had several appointments with Veronica, one the day she had been attacked in her apartment, another the following day. Then he turned the page and noted red stars punctuating certain dates. What did they mean? As he closed the book, a piece of paper slipped to the floor—a familiar newsclipping about Veronica's past. Her home address was scribbled in red ink across the top.

He stuffed the date book in his pocket, muttered a silent curse and hurried to the car. Within seconds, he'd ordered an APB on Barrett.

Then he decided to see if Veronica knew anything about

Barrett's disappearance. Maybe he'd been wrong to suspect she had done these things to herself. Both her prior boyfriend and Barrett had possible motives to harm her.

And if they succeeded, he'd never forgive himself.

AFTER VERONICA FINISHED with her last client, she released her hair from the brass clip and ran her fingers through it.

"I'm leaving now," Louise called out.

"Fine, see you tomorrow." Veronica pulled her drawer open and fished out the small photo book she kept with her at the office. She stared at the pictures of her parents, of herself as a baby in their arms, and later as a toddler. Her grandmother had made the scrapbook for her, and she'd always valued it.

Then her gaze rested on a photo of her and her parents. She was six, wearing a ruffly church dress, standing in between her parents. Her mother wore a red dress with the pelican pin stuck high on the right side of her big white collar, and her father wore a dark suit and tie. His black hair had started to recede slightly, but he looked handsome and happy to be with her.

Her parents had loved her. Her grandmother had told her repeatedly how much they'd cared for her, how her mother used to sing her to sleep at night and her father used to bring her treats. Why couldn't she remember them?

She massaged her temple, feeling the slight beginnings of a headache as she often did when she attempted to force her memory.

"Veronica?"

She recognized the deep husky resonance of Nathan's voice immediately. It sounded so different from Ron's wimpy voice, and much sexier and more masculine than Gerald's polished speech. She closed her eyes, trying to tamp her emotions.

"Are you all right?"

"I'm fine." Veronica glanced at him in his jeans and worn shirt and knew she would never ask Ron to come for a visit. After meeting a virile man like Nathan, how could she ever consider being with a dud like Ron? Shaking off the impossible thought of a relationship with Nathan, she closed her photo book and secured it back in her desk drawer.

His boots pounded against the hardwood floor. "I went to see Wayne Barrett today."

"You did?"

"Yeah. Apparently he skipped town. His employees don't know where he is."

Veronica massaged her forehead. "He didn't leave an address?"

"Nope. I don't think he wants to be found."

"Why not?"

"He stole some money from the company."

Veronica blew out a breath, then rose and glanced out the window. The sunlight was quickly fading, and dusk was beginning to settle above the willow trees outside. How could the sky be so beautiful and the world so ugly?

"I talked to the vice president, then to my lieutenant. We put out an APB on him." Nathan pulled the scrap of paper from his pocket. "And I found this in his desk."

Veronica took the note and saw her name and home address. She stared at Nathan in confusion. Then he handed her the article, and she clutched her stomach as it roiled.

"He knew about my past."

"That's right. About your parents…and your amnesia."

"You think he's the one who's been taunting me?"

Nathan shrugged. "It's possible. I definitely want to talk to him."

"When you do, ask him about my jacket. I couldn't find it this morning, then it turned up at the office." Veronica sighed. "And…"

"And what, Veronica?"

"I thought I saw someone around my apartment this morning. But then…he disappeared."

"Can you give me a description?"

She shook her head. "No. He was wearing a raincoat. He had his head covered." She hesitated, struggling to recall more details. The telephone rang, interrupting the strained silence.

"Veronica Miller speaking." She heard deep breathing, then a fuzzy, hard voice she didn't recognize. Nathan must have read the distress on her face, because he punched the speakerphone button.

"Leave the past alone," the husky voice said.

"Who is this?" Veronica asked. Her hands trembled as she stared at the phone, then at Nathan.

"Someone who knows all about you. Someone who wants you out of town."

The phone clicked into silence. Veronica gritted her teeth. Nathan had to believe her now—he'd heard the man's voice.

"We'll find out who the caller was," Nathan said, pressing the button to show the caller's number.

As the phone number blinked before her, Veronica covered her mouth and gasped.

"Veronica, do you recognize this number?"

Veronica swallowed, her voice a choked whisper. "It's... it's mine."

Chapter Six

She raised her fear stricken face to his. "Someone's at my apartment."

Nathan cupped his hands around her arms. "Let's go."

They rushed from her office. "I can drive," Veronica said. "I don't want to leave my car."

"You're shaking too much to drive. We'll get your car later," Nathan said, ushering her into his Honda. He cranked the engine and raced out of the parking lot, then radioed for backup. He covered Veronica's hand with his. "We'll catch this bastard, don't worry."

She gave him a strange look, and he realized she hadn't expected him to believe her. She'd gone through her whole life distrusting, expecting the worst from people. As a cop he was always skeptical, but Veronica wasn't a cop. She was a soft, beautiful, sexy woman who deserved someone to trust. He wanted the same. When he'd been flat on his back after the accident, he'd realized he didn't want to be alone.

But could he be that special someone to Veronica and still do his job? If he got too involved with her, would he become sloppy?

His thoughts were so jumbled he ran through a red light. Horns blasted at him. Veronica's raspy breath broke the silence and he squeezed her hand in reassurance. He considered using the siren, but if someone was still at her place, he didn't want to warn them of his arrival. He wanted to catch the creep and make him pay for frightening Veronica.

Several minutes later, he barreled into her complex and shut off his lights. The backup hadn't arrived, but he couldn't wait. "Stay here. I'll come back after I check the apartment."

Her lower lip trembled. "Be careful."

He nodded. "I will. We'll get this guy." He paused and stroked her hair. "If you hear gunshots, radio for help."

Her big dark eyes glistened with fear. "I don't want you to get hurt."

He gave her a slow smile. "Don't worry. I'll be back." Then he ran his finger along her jaw and opened the car door. Looking around cautiously, he scanned the parking lot but saw nothing suspicious. Only a couple of teenagers necking and an old man walking his dog. He hurried up the sidewalk to Veronica's apartment and inched up the steps, his hand covering his gun, ready to draw. Darkness hovered around him, and a shadow moved. He reached for his .38 as a big dog raced from the bushes. He exhaled a harsh breath. He'd almost pulled his gun on a golden retriever.

Taking the steps two at a time, he stopped at the door to her apartment, leaned one ear against it and listened. Nothing. He jiggled the door and it swung open, the squeaking of the rusty hinges echoing in the seemingly empty apartment. Slivers of moonlight streamed through the venetian blinds, illuminating his way as he crept inside. He scanned each corner and turned as he had the first time he'd come to her apartment. Nothing. Seconds dragged into minutes as he checked the rooms.

Finally he made his way back to the den and turned on the light.

Veronica stood by the phone, her hand resting on a tape recorder.

"I thought I told you to stay in the car."

"I was worried."

He slowly moved toward her and covered her hand. "What's this?"

"It's a recorder." She sighed and looked at him with her big brown eyes. Two officers rushed in, guns drawn. Nathan held up his hand to stop them.

"The apartment's clean. Search the complex." The men rushed out to follow his orders. He punched the Play button and heard the same voice that had taunted Veronica at her office. His gut clenched.

"The tape recorder's not mine," she said on a whimper. "I swear it's not mine."

Nathan wanted to believe her. "Let me take it in and dust it for fingerprints. We can also check the voice print."

Veronica nodded, her face pale. "I don't understand why this is happening." She turned away from him, her arms hugging her middle as if she needed to support herself. "I'm…I'm going to get some water."

Nathan examined the recorder to see if it could have been programmed to go off at a certain time. He didn't find anything to indicate it had. The sound of glass shattering in the kitchen jerked his head up.

"Oh, my God," Veronica said in a strained voice.

Nathan rushed into the kitchen and saw glass slivers scattered across the floor. "What is it, Veronica?" She pointed to the front of her refrigerator where someone had taped newspaper clippings of the story about her parents' deaths. He moved forward and steadied her with his hand. "These aren't yours?"

"No," she said in a heated whisper. "Of course they aren't mine. Do you think I'd keep something like this on my refrigerator?"

Nathan was glad to see the anger flare in her eyes; it was better than the shock and desolation he'd seen a few minutes before. "No, I don't," he said honestly.

Veronica traced her thumb along the photograph of the gravestone. Her finger lingered at the headlines suggesting she might have been a child murderess. "I don't know why someone would do this," she said in a voice so soft he almost didn't hear her.

"I don't, either," he said quietly, nestling his hand under her elbow to guide her to the table. "But I intend to find out."

Veronica sat ramrod straight, her eyes glazed as he fixed her a cup of tea. He joined her, and they sipped in silence. "You don't remember anything about that night?" he finally asked.

She shook her head and pushed a strand of hair from her face. Her hair swept her shoulders, stark black against the porcelain flesh of her neck, and hung like an ebony curtain shadowing the solemn angles of her delicate cheekbones. "I wish I did. I've tried so hard to remember."

The other two officers appeared in the doorway. "We didn't find anything, sir," the youngest one said.

Nathan nodded. "I can take it from here. You two go on, but patrol this area tonight." The men agreed, then left. Nathan turned to Veronica.

"Your past may not be the reason for these tauntings, but someone is certainly using them to hurt you," Nathan said, thinking of the range of possibilities that existed.

"My past has always controlled my life." Veronica emptied her cup and put it in the sink. "I have to face it and bury it so I can go on."

"What are you talking about?" Nathan asked.

Dodging the shattered glass on the floor, she stepped forward and faced him, determination darkening her brown eyes. "I'm going to drive out to my parents' old home. Maybe seeing the house—where they died—will trigger my memory."

Nathan pushed away from the table. "You're not going out there alone."

"I need to do this," she said as she walked into the den.

Nathan grabbed her arm and swung her around. "Veronica, you're too upset to drive. Besides, even if you had your car, remember what Scroggins said about the place not being safe. No one's lived in it for twenty years."

In a defiant act that Nathan had to admire, Veronica jutted her chin out and said courageously, "I have to go."

"Okay." He released her arm and headed to the door. "But I'm going with you."

FIVE MINUTES LATER, hands entwined, her stomach aching, Veronica stared at the haze of oncoming headlights dotting the highway and gathered her courage. She had to face the past. It was the only way she could move on. After finding the newspaper clippings on her refrigerator, she knew the past was a clue to all the mysterious things happening to her.

"You said the house was on Dover Drive?" Nathan asked.

"Yes. It's at the end of the street," Veronica said, remembering what her grandmother had told her. She could hear her grandmother's sweet Southern voice: "Honey-child, you used to ride your tricycle all over the place. Drove your mama plumb crazy when you started riding a two-wheeler. You'd zoom up and down the dirt road, fly around the dead end, then screech your tires like you was hot as a fox on a road race."

Veronica smiled at the memory of her grandmother's voice. If only she could remember riding the bike, seeing her mother and father, hearing *their* voices. Sometimes she felt as if she had a big bottomless hole inside of her that would never be filled without those memories.

Then other times she trembled at the thought of recalling her parents' deaths. Did she really want to remember the horrible details?

"Veronica, are you all right?" Nathan asked, turning on the side road that led to the subdivision.

"I'm fine," she said. "Just thinking."

"About your parents?"

"Yes." Sensing his sincerity, she considered sharing her feelings, but Nathan's job stopped her. What if she remembered she had killed her parents? Could she handle knowing she had destroyed her own family? Would he arrest her?

A shiver tore through her, and Nathan glanced at her. "Cold?"

She wrapped her arms around her middle. She could hear the cold metal handcuffs clamping shut. "A little."

"This isn't much of a subdivision," he said as the road narrowed. "It's more like living in the country."

"I know. It was a long time ago. Grandmother said the houses were on half-acre lots."

Even in the dark, Veronica noticed there were only two other houses on the road. Both were old and dilapidated, barely livable. A black cat with a tiny white spot on its face darted across the road and Nathan swerved to miss it. "Geez. Crazy animal's going to get run over."

"I guess he's not used to seeing many cars out here," Veronica said.

The car hit a pothole and he steered it around another one, then slowed as they neared a dirt drive. Tall pines and spruce trees lined the road casting shadows across the dark earth while a quarter moon provided just enough light for Veronica to see the ragged condition of her childhood home. Most of the trees were bare of leaves, their branches tired and frail with winter. Her heartbeat pounded in her ears as the car crawled toward the old house. Morosely, she thought the dead-end street and deserted house symbolized her life.

What had once been a lovely white house with a front porch now looked weathered and saggy, with rotten boards, chipped paint and overgrown bushes marring the front stoop. A few of the shingles on the roof hung precariously to the side. Tree branches blown from a storm had crashed into one window, sending shards of broken glass across the wooden planks and front steps. The hedges and grass were overgrown, the yards full of weeds, and a mountain of kudzu covered a broken-down fence around the backyard. An old rusty wheelbarrow filled with pine straw lay overturned in the gravel drive.

Nathan stopped the car, flipped on the parking lights and turned off the engine. Dark clouds billowed above and thunder rumbled somewhere in the distance. A few scattered raindrops glistened on the windshield.

Veronica forced her mind back to the photographs her grandmother had shown her—her father pushing her in a homemade swing from the oak tree in the front yard, her mother planting petunias around the mailbox, Veronica running through the water hose on a scorching summer day.

She and Nathan sat in stony silence, the air between them heavy and tense with unanswered questions, the slow drizzling rain turning into a downpour. Veronica knew Nathan was watching her, waiting for any sign of her memory to return, but she tried to block out his presence and focus on the past, on remembering some detail, however small it might be. The car closed in around her, and the dreams she'd had as a child lingered in the back of her mind, teasing her fear and rattling her concentration. As in her repeated nightmares, a shadow, big and hulking, loomed before her, hands outstretched, ominous fingers reaching for her, strangling her with their bony tendrils. Thunder crackled like hungry mountain lions roaring in the night. Lightning lit the sky in jagged streaks and patches against the dark sky.

The air became still and thick and hot. Veronica suddenly couldn't breathe. Raindrops beat violently against the car, pounding relentlessly as the clouds unloaded their water onto the earth like teardrops falling from the sky. Veronica closed her eyes and dug her fingernails into the sides of the car seat, her heart racing painfully, fear pressing like a giant boulder on her chest. Her throat constricted, and perspiration trickled down her neck. The shadow's giant fingers encircled her neck. She was gasping and heaving for air, praying the shadow would leave, that it wouldn't find her, that she could run far, far away and never have to see it again.

"Veronica, Veronica, can you hear me?" Nathan was shaking her, but she couldn't respond except to go limp in his arms. "Look at me, Veronica. Are you all right?"

The car spun in crazy circles. She swayed and groped for something solid to hold on to. Then she felt Nathan's strong, powerful arms surround her, heard somewhere in the deep recesses of her consciousness his husky voice murmuring words of comfort, felt the gentle brush of his lips across her forehead, his hand stroking her hair and massaging the tension from her straining muscles. Her lungs drew in cleansing breaths as she struggled for composure. She blinked back the tears she'd tried to keep at bay all evening, but moisture trickled down her cheek, soaking his shirt.

"I can't remember," she finally said, her voice thick with emotion. "I try so hard, but I just can't."

"Shh, it's okay," Nathan said softly, tenderly combing her hair with his fingers.

"You know, I can understand why I blocked out that night," Veronica said in frustration. "But why the rest of my childhood? I don't even remember living here."

He wrapped the long ends of her hair around his fist and tightened his hold. "Maybe there's a reason you can't remember. Maybe you're not supposed to."

Because I killed my parents, I'm the reason they died.

The self-recriminations and guilt that had consumed her all her life roared through her head, and she trembled again. Nathan pressed her against his chest, his body offering the kind of solace only a man with great tenderness and unfathomable passion could give. She sagged against him and absorbed his strength, allowing his warm breath to mingle with her own and his scent to envelope her with its intoxicating, masculine aroma. His hands were hypnotic, his voice like the soothing purr of a lover's caress, his hard body a wall of strength.

"Do you want to talk about it?" he asked.

Veronica shook her head. "You'll think I'm crazy."

"Try me."

She looked into his eyes, the dark rich color of scotch drawing her in with their tenderness. "I had these nightmares as a child," she finally said. "I still have them sometimes."

"What happens in the dreams?"

Veronica hesitated, trying to gain control of her emotions. "I'm in the bedroom with my parents…but there's someone else there. I can see a shadow."

Nathan traced his finger along Veronica's hand, opened her palm and twined her fingers with his. "Then what happens?"

"I don't know." She clenched her hands in frustration. "I can't see the person's face. I try and try but I can't. It's dark and I try to scream but…but nothing comes out."

He cradled her and rocked her gently in his arms. The only comfort she remembered was her grandmother's arms. Nathan's felt stronger, more secure, as if he'd never let the shadow capture her.

"I think it's a vision of the person who was there," she continued, "but the—the doctor said it was just a figment of my imagination," Veronica finished in a low voice. "He said the shadow represented a little girl's fear or something like that."

"The police didn't find evidence of anyone else being there that night?"

"My grandmother said they didn't. That's when they ruled it—" She broke off, unable to finish the sentence.

"I know," Nathan whispered. He rubbed her shoulders and wiped the tears from her eyes with the pads of his thumbs. "Why don't you let me look into it? I'll talk to the police chief who was in charge of the investigation years ago."

She didn't know what to say. "You believe me?"

Nathan chewed his lip. "I want to help you find the truth. Isn't that what you want?"

Veronica nodded and lowered her eyes. He hadn't exactly said he believed her—only that he wanted to find the truth. She wanted desperately to find the truth, too. But the thought also terrified her. If she found out she *had* caused her parents' deaths, would she be able to live with herself?

NATHAN WRAPPED his jacket around Veronica, hugging her to him. A surge of protectiveness swelled inside him and he wanted to barricade himself around her so she would never have to feel afraid again. His body throbbed with unleashed desire as her breath whispered against his neck in tiny puffs and her fingernails dug into his chest with a kind of desperation that made his chest ache and his lower body harden with pure need. The scent of her shampoo invaded his nostrils, and his hands itched to tangle themselves in the long ebony strands of her glorious hair.

But he could not take advantage of her. She was a frightened, confused woman who needed his help and understanding. Not his body, not his lust or his potent desire.

"I'm going to take you home," he said quietly, unfolding his arms from around her and settling her back against the seat. He tried to ignore the flicker of want burning in her eyes as the moonlight illuminated her face.

Then the need was gone, and he saw the walls being resurrected around her as she clutched the jacket more tightly around her. He drove slowly and turned the radio to a soft rock station to fill the awkward silence. When they arrived at her apartment, he walked her to the door.

"I'm coming in to check the apartment."

Veronica didn't argue. She looked tired and slightly nervous as the door squeaked open, and he was certain the memory of finding the tape recorder and the newspaper articles still lingered in her mind with haunting clarity. He switched on the light and followed her as she walked through the house.

"Why don't you get some rest," he suggested, fighting the urge to take her in his arms one more time.

Veronica nodded, the pallor of her face a ghostly white in the dim light. "I think I'll take a long bath."

"Do you want me to stay?"

Her head snapped up. As she stared at him with a multitude of questions in her eyes, he instantly realized what she thought he'd implied. A big part of him wanted to let her believe that, to test her and see what her answer would be. But he still didn't know if she was doing these things to herself, and he couldn't take advantage of her.

"I meant out here—until you get through." He shifted from one foot to the other and avoided looking at the creamy base of her throat. "I thought you might feel safer that way."

A tiny smile tilted her rosy lips, and she handed him his jacket. "Thanks. I do feel safe when you're around." Then she turned and hurried into the bathroom.

He heard the water running, imagined the bath salts turning

into bubbles, Veronica stripping down to beautiful nothingness and slipping inside the tub, her rosy nipples taut and glistening with water, her bare toes dangling over the side of the tub begging for his kiss.

He muttered a curse, then settled onto the couch and dropped his head into his hands. Veronica felt safe with him. That should make him feel good—but she wasn't safe with him. Sure he wanted to protect her and comfort her, but he was a man. A simple male, who also wanted to take her to bed and show her his raging desire.

He bit his lip and listened with one ear for the water to turn off, praying silently that she'd locked the door.

VERONICA RELAXED into the sea of bubbles and stared at the unlocked door, wondering if Nathan had seen the flicker of need she'd unveiled before she'd rushed into the bathroom. She was so inexperienced and shy, too afraid to ask him to join her—too afraid he would say no.

Dribbling the warm water over her skin, she realized she hadn't been much of a sexual being at all. Not until she'd met Nathan Dawson. She'd tried with Ron, forced herself to let him touch her, but beyond the touching, which she hadn't really enjoyed, and a few pleasant kisses, their sex life had been a failure. She'd thought she might be inept. But Nathan had awakened that hidden part of her that she'd never felt, and her body tingled with anticipation at the mere thought that he was sitting on her sofa while she lay naked in her tub. What would she do if he opened the door and joined her?

She lay back and imagined him opening the door and walking in, envisioned him staring at her with raw heat and need in his eyes, then watched with her heart pounding as he stripped his clothes off and came toward her, his lips curved into a deliciously wicked smile. He was standing proud and masculine, his broad chest and body and legs covered with sandy blond hair, his sex throbbing and bold, screaming for her.

Veronica sat bolt upright and grabbed her robe, embarrassed at her errant thoughts. Thank goodness she hadn't told him to join her. The words had been on the tip of her tongue, but she hadn't said them. If he wanted her, he would make a move.

And obviously he hadn't.

As she tightened the robe around her waist and combed the tangles from her wet hair, reality crept in—he didn't want her because he thought she was crazy.

NATHAN STRODE toward the door for the tenth time, his fingers itching to turn the knob and join Veronica. His hand fingered the buttons at the top of his shirt, but warning bells sounded in his head. He wanted her with an intensity that made him question his own sanity. He had to remember why he was here—certainly not as Veronica's lover.

He was here because she might be crazy, and he needed to solve her case. And as much as he wanted to take the woman, to pour himself into her sweetness, he couldn't—not until he unraveled the truth from the mystery surrounding her.

He dropped onto the sofa, hurriedly scribbled some notes, collected the tape recorder and article, then picked up the phone and checked in with the precinct. He'd post an officer outside her door. He couldn't stay himself. He couldn't stand the temptation.

"Dawson, where the hell have you been?" Ford said, adding a few succulent curse words that Nathan tried to ignore.

"I'm still working on the Miller case. What's up with you, partner?"

Ford laughed. "I'll fill you in on that robbery if you ever come in."

Nathan gritted his teeth. "I'll meet you there in the morning." *I'm also going to make an appointment to see Scroggins, the officer who worked the Miller case years ago.*

"You know you're wasting your time with that weirdo," Ford said deadpan.

"You do your job the way you want, I'll do mine the way

I want,'' Nathan growled. ''And I want a guard outside her apartment all night.''

''Oh, God, you're hung up on her, aren't you?''

''Just do what I said and get a guard here,'' Nathan snapped, cutting Ford off. ''If there's any flack, I'll take responsibility. See you in the morning.'' Nathan paced the floor for the next thirty minutes, hoping Ford would send the guard before Veronica came out. He didn't think he could stand being alone with her and not holding her.

Finally she stepped out from the bathroom, her hair wrapped turban-style in a towel, her creamy flesh glowing in the vee at the top of her long silky robe. He swallowed a groan. ''I have to go in a few minutes. I've asked for a guard outside your door.''

Veronica toyed with the sash around her robe. ''Thanks for staying.''

He nodded, studying her. She looked more relaxed and calmer, her cheeks rosy from the warm bath. ''Do you think you can get some sleep now?'' He certainly knew he wouldn't.

''I'll try,'' Veronica said, offering him a shy smile.

''Then I'll see you tomorrow. I'll wait outside until he shows.'' He jotted his phone number on a pad next to the phone. ''Here's my number. Call me if you need me.'' Then he hurried to the door so he could escape before he touched her.

''Nathan?''

He paused and looked into her eyes. The desire he saw in her expression almost broke his good intentions, and he gazed at her for a long moment. The question lingering between the two of them crackled like static electricity. He should get out of there before he did something they both might regret. He reached for the doorknob but couldn't leave. Not without touching her one more time.

He closed the distance between them, traced one finger down her jaw, then lowered his mouth to hers. Gently, slowly, he savored the yearning he felt in her response, the soft moan that escaped as she parted her lips and teased his mouth with her tongue. She tasted sweet and needy, and his ache for her grew as he angled his head and deepened the kiss. She caressed his jaw with her soft palm, and he thought he would die from the raw need that surged through him.

A knock sounded at the door, bringing his sanity back. "That's probably him now."

"Probably," Veronica whispered.

He pulled away slightly, momentarily leaning his forehead against Veronica's to gain control. "I should go," he finally said in a low voice. "I'll talk to the guard before I leave."

Veronica nodded, her breath gently brushing against his cheek. "Thanks, Nathan."

Her whispered words brought a smile to his face. As much as he wanted her, winning her trust was more important than his own desire. He nodded, then said good-night and closed the door.

VERONICA WATCHED out the window as Nathan hurried to his car and drove away. Being alone hadn't really bothered her before, but tonight she felt bereft as he walked away from her. People were always leaving her—first her parents, then her grandmother. And when the investigation was over, Nathan would leave, too. She had to be prepared for that. He was only doing his job. She touched her finger to her lips and smiled; at least she had the memory of his kiss.

A shadow passed beneath the streetlight and Veronica locked the dead bolt. She peered out the window again, bending one blind slightly so she couldn't be seen, then searched the darkness for any sign of the shadow. A van pulled up and a group of teenagers piled out, laughing and talking.

Veronica massaged her temple and fought the panicky feeling that often came with night. Her body ached with fatigue, but she still didn't want to go to bed. Would she have the nightmare tonight? Would she imagine the screams of her parents as she often did when she closed her eyes?

She reminded herself that Nathan had posted a guard outside her apartment, then fixed herself a cup of hot tea and turned on the TV. After grabbing a crocheted afghan her grandmother had made, she curled up on the sofa to watch *Miracle on 34th Street,* hoping she might fall asleep before dawn. As she sipped her tea, her thoughts drifted to her past, to the visit to her old house, to Nathan and how she'd felt in his arms. Maybe he could help her unravel the secrets of her life, and maybe if she discovered she *was* the reason her parents had died, she would one day be able to forgive herself. And maybe he wouldn't walk out on her when this was all over.

Veronica sighed. That *would* take a miracle.

Chapter Seven

In the car, Nathan tried to distract his thoughts from the sensuous way Veronica had looked all freshly bathed, the ebony strands of her hair glistening with moisture. He had to forget the kiss. And that little throaty moan she made—

Damn. He needed to occupy his mind with work so he wouldn't have time to think of the non-work related activities he craved indulging in with the woman. Cursing his uncontrollable reaction to her, he dialed the precinct. "Sherry, this is Detective Dawson. Can you find out who handled the Miller case years ago?"

The elderly policewoman whistled into the phone. "Anything for you, hon." He waited, listening to her fingers click on the computer. Seconds later she spoke up. "Daryl Scroggins. He was the police chief back then. Retired about five years ago."

"Thanks, Sherry. You're a doll."

Sherry laughed. She was always teasing him to find a good woman and settle down. "Come by the house and I'll make you a pecan pie."

Nathan laughed. "Maybe one day soon."

Sherry chuckled. "And bring your woman by so I can meet her."

"There isn't a woman," Nathan said, although he instantly thought of Veronica. "Listen, Sherry. See what you can find out on Wayne Barrett and Barrett Pharmaceuticals."

"Sure thing."

"Thanks. I'll talk to you later." He remembered seeing Scroggins talking to Veronica at Gerald's campaign party. He hung up and dialed Scroggins.

"This is Detective Dawson," he said. "I heard you worked on the Miller murder-suicide investigation twenty years ago."

Scroggins sounded defensive. "Yeah, why do you want to know?"

"Well, I'd rather not talk about it on the phone. I'd like to come by your house."

He waited, curious at the long pause on the other end of the line. "Not tonight," Scroggins finally said. "My wife and I have company."

"Okay. How about in the morning?"

"I'm busy."

Nathan tightened his fingers around the phone, wondering again at Scroggins's reluctance. Was he really busy or just putting him off?

"You name the time, I'll be there," Nathan said, refusing to give up.

"Look, son. That case is two decades old. You ought to leave the past alone."

Nathan frowned at his last statement, then Scroggins slammed down the phone. What was it the person had said on the message to Veronica?

Leave the past alone.

VERONICA TOSSED and turned in her sleep as she wrestled with demons from her past. Flinging her hands wildly, she tried to escape the clutches of the approaching shadow. Patches of gray light enveloped her, blurring her view, and she strained to see the doorway, but air pressed around her, suffocating her, tearing the life from her lungs as someone thrust a bloody knife toward her. She opened her mouth to scream, but the sound caught in her throat and a sliver of pure terror racked her body. Her parents. They were going to die.

She reached out to save them, to run for help, but something blocked the doorway and her legs were immobilized like steel pillars, dragging her down. She crouched into a ball and hid in the darkness, biting her lip until she tasted her own blood, covering her ears to drown out the pain of her parents' cries. She closed her eyes so tightly her eyelids ached and her chest heaved with her silent sobs. She couldn't save them.

Perspiration trickled down her neck, but the room grew cold as if death had opened a door. The sharp sound of someone's shoes scraping along the floor made her flesh crawl. She'd had that feeling before. A loud thump followed. Was it her parents' bodies collapsing against the floor as the life slipped from them?

She awoke with a start at the sound of another loud thump against her front door, her body trembling from the remnants of the recurring nightmare. It took her several seconds to steady her breathing, to remind herself that she had lived through this one, just like she had lived through that night.

Her stiff muscles protesting, she jumped off the sofa, stumbling over the afghan tangled around her feet. She tried to focus and stared at the door for several seconds, straining to hear. Nothing.

She slowly padded over to the window and peeked outside. The gray fog of morning greeted her.

She opened the door slightly, retrieved the morning paper, relocked the door and carried the paper to the kitchen, hoping the local news could displace the fear lingering from her troubled sleep. Although determined to push her nightmares from her mind, she shook slightly as she made her tea. When she opened the paper, the headline shocked her: "Owner of Barrett Pharmaceuticals skips town with stockholders' money."

Hmm. Wayne Barrett was a ruthless businessman and a callous husband who'd cheated on his wife both financially and physically. As she skimmed the article, she found a list of the major stockholders. Interesting. Gerald, Eli's son, owned over forty-five percent of the company, his grandmother forty percent. Had Barrett ripped them off, too? And was Barrett the main supporter for Gerald's campaign? If so, Barrett's move could have a drastic effect on Gerald's future. Eli was wealthy, but campaigning could drain a person's wealth.

The story posed lots of questions about Barrett, and she was certain she would be hearing from Barrett's ex-wife's lawyer. She might as well shower and get to work. If she didn't, she'd probably have newspeople hounding her house. Reporters had nearly driven her crazy as a little girl. They were the last people she wanted to talk to.

As NATHAN STUDIED the files Sherry had left on his desk, he rubbed his hand along his aching neck, trying to work out the kinks he'd gotten during his tortured sleep the night before. He'd dreamt about Veronica. First he'd been holding her and giving her comfort while they searched through her parents' old house, then he'd been caressing her in the twilight with nothing but a sheet covering them. She'd been naked in his arms, and he'd made sweet love to her over and over. Her cries of pleasure had been so beautiful, and they kept replaying over and over in his head like a soft jazz song.

Both dreams taunted him. Both dreams made him want her more. In the wee hours of the morning, he'd been so tormented, he'd almost gotten up and called her just to hear her voice. Now, he was plain frustrated and felt like biting off someone's head.

He smelled Ford's smoky breath before he heard him speak. Ford would be the perfect one to vent his irritation on.

"I tied up the robbery case yesterday while you were messing around with that nutcase with the brown eyes."

"I wasn't messing around with her. I was investigating." Nathan gave him a sharp look. "Make any arrests?"

"Yep. Bunch of punk kids. Recovered all the merchandise, too." Ford lit a nonfilter cigarette and blew a stream of smoke in the air. Nathan gritted his teeth, inhaling the smoky aroma, mentally reminding himself Ford was not going to egg him into smoking again. He'd given up the habit.

If he hadn't, he'd have smoked a pack this morning when

he'd woken up with the sheets tangled around him and visions of Veronica Miller dancing around his head.

"Great," Nathan said, standing up. "I've got some legwork to do."

"We're supposed to be partners," Ford said sarcastically.

Nathan grinned. "I know. I made a list of places I'd like you to check out for me."

Ford growled. "Listen here, you can't waltz in here and tell me what to do."

"Hey, we're partners, right?" Nathan grinned and walked toward the door. He planned to be waiting on Daryl Scroggins first thing so the man couldn't put him off again. "Besides, it's official. Stevens wants us to check out Barrett Pharmaceuticals."

"At least that's a real case," Ford said. "I saw the paper this morning."

"Well, get the details," Nathan said. "It's *our* job to find out the truth, not the reporters'." He wanted to know exactly how Barrett and Gerald Jones knew each other. Especially since Gerald had been at Veronica's office only two days before.

Ford snarled and puffed his cigarette, his eyes gleaming with anger.

Nathan didn't point out that Barrett was one of his prime suspects in harassing Veronica. He laughed silently. Ford would really be pissed if he thought he was helping him with Veronica's case. After all, Ford thought Veronica was crazy.

"GOOD MORNING, Louise." Veronica stepped into her office and paused. "Eli, what are you doing here?"

Eli's warm smile wasn't as bright as usual. He gave her a hug. "I came to visit my goddaughter. Anything wrong with that?"

Veronica shook her head. "No, of course not."

She took a stack of messages from Louise. "All about Barrett?"

Louise nodded. "The phone's been ringing like mad. And it's only eight o'clock!"

Veronica laughed and opened the door, leading Eli in. He shoved his hands in his pockets. He looked tired and worried, and she suddenly felt uneasy.

"Something wrong, Eli?"

She settled at her desk and motioned toward the couch. Eli shook his head and picked up the glass paperweight her grandmother had given her when she'd graduated from law school.

"Eli?"

"Oh, yes." He placed the paperweight down, his shoulders straightening. "I came to talk to you about Gerald."

Veronica nodded, noting the newspaper he had rolled up under his arms. "This wouldn't be about Barrett Pharmaceuticals, would it?"

Eli gave her a shaky smile. "You're a smart girl, Veronica."

"I'm an attorney," she said. "And Barrett was my client. Everybody is interested in that."

"I assume you know Gerald and my mother owned stock in his company."

Veronica nodded. "Is this going to affect Gerald's campaign?"

"I believe we have that covered," Eli said. "But that's not what I want to discuss."

She arched an eyebrow, unable to read Eli's strange expression. Did he want her to handle Gerald's financial affairs with the company? "Okay, what is it then?"

He settled down in the chair, looking weary. "I know Gerald took you to lunch the other day."

"Yes."

"I'm not sure you and he…well, that you should—" Eli coughed, struggling for words.

"That we should what, Eli? Work together?"

He swallowed, and Veronica noticed the bulging vein in his throat. "That you should become involved."

Her eyes widened, her temper quickly surfacing. "Involved?'' She stood up, hands on hips, and glared at Eli. ''You're telling me you don't want me to date your son?''

''That's right,'' he said quietly. ''Gerald's in the middle of a campaign, there's enough gossip about Barrett—''

''And you think I'll have a bad effect on his reputation.'' Veronica tried to squelch the hurt building in her chest. She was his goddaughter and she'd trusted him. She thought he loved her.

But when it came to his family, she was an outsider, someone with a past that could hurt his precious son.

''Don't worry, Eli,'' she said in a hard voice. ''I don't plan to get romantically involved with Gerald.''

''Wait, Veronica,'' Eli sounded desperate. ''You don't understand.''

''Oh, I understand perfectly,'' she said, walking toward the door and opening it for him. If she'd had the slightest hope she would handle the family's business or be a part of Eli's life, the idea had just died. Being her godfather had simply been a responsibility he'd carried out for her parents' sake. No emotional ties.

Well, she could handle that. She'd never had anyone to depend on but her grandmother anyway. ''I really have work to do now, Eli.''

He frowned, his gray eyebrows knitting together. ''I'm sorry if I've offended you, dear. That wasn't my intention.''

''It's fine,'' Veronica said, forcing a smile. ''I'm glad you came by.'' *But don't bother to again.*

Eli hesitated as if he wanted to say something else, then shook his head and walked out the door.

''SCROGGINS, glad you could see me,'' Nathan said, pushing his way through Scroggins's front door.

The older man gave him a surly look and stepped into the marble entryway. ''I didn't exactly say I could see you.''

Nathan grinned. ''Well, now I'm here, I think you can make time for me. After all, you and I have a lot in common.''

''How's that?'' Scroggins asked, his frown deepening.

"We both stand for the law. I'm a detective and you were once the police chief."

Scroggins's hand shook as he rubbed his balding head.

"I'll just take a few minutes of your time, sir," Nathan said, finding his way through the house.

Scroggins followed him into a den filled with fancy furniture, but piled with magazines and ashtrays. A bulldog growled from his post in the corner near the stone fireplace. "Have a seat," Scroggins said sarcastically, pointing to the newspaper-covered sofa.

Nathan swiped a stack of papers to the side and lowered himself onto the expensive furniture, aware Scroggins wanted him to hurry. He didn't intend to.

"I thought I told you to let the past alone," Scroggins said, settling himself in a brown recliner angled toward the large-screened TV.

"Well, sir, I'd like to do that, but it seems someone else doesn't want to do that."

"What are you talking about?" Scroggins asked.

"You know Veronica Miller?"

He nodded. "Course I do. Everyone knows who she is."

Nathan winced at his snide remark. No wonder she was skeptical about people's reactions. "I'm trying to find out who's harassing her."

Scroggins frowned. "And how do you think I can help?"

Nathan explained briefly about the intruder, Veronica's call for help, the message on her machine, the newspaper articles. "Someone is either out to hurt her or—"

"Or she's doing it herself," Scroggins said.

"I was going to say 'or they're trying to drive her crazy.'"

"Why would someone want to do that?"

"I thought you could tell me," Nathan said. He steepled his fingers in front of him and leaned forward with his elbows on his knees. "Tell me about her parents and the night they died."

"I don't see how that can help." Scroggins huffed and adjusted his recliner.

"Humor me," Nathan said, aggravated at Scroggins's lack of cooperation. "You investigated the case. I suppose you knew her parents."

Scroggins nodded, closing his eyes briefly. "It was a sad thing. The Millers were nice folks. Mrs. Miller was pretty as a peach, sweet and good with the little girl."

"And the father?"

"A nice man, good lawyer. Everyone in town respected him."

"He didn't have any enemies, no cases pending or ones he'd lost that could have angered someone enough to hurt him?"

"Not that I know of."

"Did you investigate it?" Nathan asked, growing angry.

Scroggins patted his bulging belly. "Look, it was a long time ago. I did everything I could."

"What happened to Mr. Miller's files?"

Scroggins shrugged. "Burned up in a fire couple days later."

Nathan bit back an expletive. "Didn't he have any backup copies?"

Scroggins shook his head. "Look, we weren't so big in computers then, it was hard to copy and store papers. Took up too much space to keep extras."

"Didn't you think the fire was a little suspicious?"

"Maybe." Scroggins rolled a cigar between his fingers. "But there wasn't anything I could do about it. Hell, I knew everyone in town—didn't know a soul who'd hurt Miller and his wife. Had to be a murder-suicide." Scroggins heaved a breath, then continued. "At first, the grandma wanted me to keep investigating, then she changed her mind. She was glad I closed the case, said she didn't want the child dragged through any more trauma."

Nathan narrowed his eyes at Scroggins. "Look, you were a cop, for God's sakes." The man said nothing, and Nathan paused, realizing Scroggins must have a strong connection to the townspeople. Had he given up so easily because he'd been afraid he might step on someone's toes? "How about the Millers? Did they have a happy marriage?"

"Had a squabble or two like most married folks. Mostly little petty things." Scroggins paused as if remembering. "Except for that night. It was a terrible one."

"If no one was there, how did you know about the fight?" Nathan asked.

Scroggins scratched his head. "Well, Ms. Trudy, woman who lived a couple houses down, had set out to carry the Millers some fresh jelly she'd made. Drove up and heard the fight. She got scared, rushed home and called."

"Do you know what prompted the argument?"

Scroggins shook his head. "Don't know. Little girl's the only one that knows that."

Or the murderer. Veronica has amnesia. "Veronica says someone else was there. She sees a shadow in her dreams."

The old man's eyebrows arched, the wrinkles beside his eyes drawing out in thin lines. "She was just a kid, Dawson. Poor little thing was traumatized. Why, she was in shock when they carried her to the hospital. Took her a few weeks before they could even get her to talk."

Nathan's gut clenched. This was getting him nowhere. "And you called the case a murder-suicide. What did you base that on?"

"Wasn't nothing else I could do," Scroggins said, lighting his cigar and glaring at Nathan as if he dared him to argue. "Weren't no witnesses. House was a mess, furniture overturned, lamps broken. Ms. Trudy claimed she heard the Millers screaming at each other. By the time we got there, they were both dead."

"And Veronica?"

"She was sitting 'side the bodies. Covered in blood. Had the danged bloody knife in her hands."

Exactly the way he'd seen her the first time. Nathan chewed his lip in thought. "I read the articles. Someone suggested Veronica might have murdered her parents?"

"Yeah, but I couldn't go with that. She was just a little bitty thing. I don't think she could have done it."

Nathan agreed. But still…if someone was there and she'd seen them, and that person knew she was a witness… "Was there a suicide note?"

"Nope. That worried me." Scroggins blew out a puff of smoke. "I figured it must have been a crime of passion. Man stabbed the woman in anger, then couldn't stand himself for killing his wife so he killed himself."

"Makes sense," Nathan said, knowing it was possible. Domestic violence cases were more frequent than he'd ever dreamed.

"Would you mind if I looked over your file on the case?"

Scroggins snapped his head up. "What you want that for?"

"I wanted to do some checking on my own." Maybe he would find out why Scroggins was so reluctant to help him, too.

"Look, Dawson. I know you want to protect the Miller woman. But have you considered the fact she's doing all this to get attention?" Scroggins scraped his fingernails up and down the chair. "It was common knowledge she had some emotional problems after her parents died. Her grandmother took her away, but I heard she had to see one of them psychiatrists. Even heard one time she tried to commit suicide when she was a teenager. Took some sleeping pills or something."

Nathan hadn't heard that. He remembered her wrist wound and hearing the paramedics asking her if she'd cut herself on purpose. Then he remembered how vulnerable and afraid she'd looked the night she'd called them, and he couldn't bring himself to believe she'd done that to herself. But if it were true, he would find out.

And if Scroggins was holding something back, he would find that out, too. "Thanks for your time," he said in a clipped voice. Then he strode out the door, slamming it behind him.

Back in his car, he headed toward the precinct. Maybe Ford

had something on Barrett. He picked up the phone and dialed Sherry. "Hey, Sherry. It's Nathan."

"Hey, sugar. What's up?"

"Got anything on that voice print on the Miller tape?"

"Yeah, but we couldn't tell if it was a man or a woman's. It was computerized."

"How about the results from that knife?"

Sherry paused. He knew she was consulting the computer database. "Only one blood type identified. Ms. Miller's. Oh, and there was evidence of a sleep-inducing drug in her system."

"Hell." Nathan stopped at a red light and tapped his hand impatiently on the steering wheel. "No other blood? DNA?"

He heard Sherry snap a piece of gum in her mouth. "DNA tests indicate the possibility of another person's blood on the knife, but the tests are inconclusive."

Nathan silently cursed, contemplating his next move. Veronica had been certain she'd cut the intruder's arm. Back to square one. "I need you to run another check for me."

"Okay, what is it this time?"

"I'd like a list of all the townspeople who lived in Oakland at the time of the Miller murder-suicide."

"That'll take some time."

"I know, but it could be important." Nathan hesitated, a frisson of guilt shivering up his spine. "Pull up anything you can find on Veronica Miller. I need to know everything about her life after she moved to Florida with her grandmother." He paused again. "And, Sherry, she's had some…some emotional problems. Find out the names of any psychiatrists she's seen over the years."

As he hung up, a knot of apprehension tightened his stomach. Veronica's face flashed into his mind. He wanted her, and he wanted to believe her. But he had a job to do. And he had to know the truth, even if it killed him.

AFTER AVOIDING the media all day and finishing her paperwork, Veronica hurried home, needing to be in the sanctuary of her own apartment where she was safe from the questions and phone calls about Barrett. And where she could nurse her hurt over Eli's rejection.

Working all day was really a blessing—she'd been too busy to think about Nathan Dawson and the strange feelings he evoked in her. She'd been too busy to worry about the threatening phone call the day before. She was grateful she'd had Louise call a locksmith to have the locks changed for her. She kicked off her shoes as she entered and started undoing her blouse, peeling the silky fabric away as she made her way to her bedroom. A jog would help ease her tension.

Maybe four or five miles.

She would jog until she dropped from exhaustion, both physically and mentally. The faint scent of a man's cologne made her pause but she dismissed it, thinking it must be the potpourri she'd put in the bathroom. Or maybe Nathan's lingering scent. She tossed her blouse onto the bed, shimmied out of her skirt and dropped it to the floor, then reached for her hose. But out of the corner of her eye, she spotted something odd. Slowly she glanced up, caught sight of the mirror and gasped.

Someone had been in her apartment. Again. And this time they'd written all over her mirror in bright red lipstick:

"Leave the past alone. Bury it or *you'll* be buried alive."

Veronica's legs wobbled as she sank onto the bed and reached for the phone. She considered dialing 911, but instead grabbed Nathan's card off her dresser and punched in his number.

"Hello?" His husky voice calmed her immediately.

"Nathan, this is Veronica."

"Yeah?"

She heard her own shaky breath and tried to find her voice.

"Veronica, what's wrong?"

She shuddered. "Someone…someone broke in…can you—"

"I'll be right there, Veronica. And don't touch anything. I'm on my way."

Seconds dragged into torturous minutes as she waited for Nathan to arrive. Veronica twined her hands and rocked herself back and forth, then jumped when a pounding sounded at the door. Wrapping her robe tightly around her, she stumbled to answer it.

"Veronica, it's me. Open up!" Nathan yelled.

She swung open the door and stared at him, her heart pounding at the look of concern on his face.

"Are you okay?" he asked, gripping her by the arms and checking her all over.

"I am now," she whispered. Then she fell into his arms and sank against him.

Chapter Eight

With one arm still around Veronica, Nathan closed the door. "Shh, it's okay," he muttered softly as he stroked her trembling body and felt her chest heave against his. His own breathing was erratic, his pulse racing, his mind still trying to erase the fear that had jolted through him when she'd called. On the way over to her apartment, he'd envisioned a number of disturbing scenarios, and to see her now and know she was all right sent a wave of relief rushing through him.

She was a gutsy woman or she could never have become an attorney, but she felt small and fragile in his arms, and anger burned through his veins at the thought of someone terrifying her. In the back of his mind, the evidence was piling up. Scroggins's information taunted him—as a child she'd had to see a psychiatrist; as a teenager, she'd taken sleeping pills and tried to commit suicide; then when the blood tests came back on the bloody knife from the attack, there had been a sleep-inducing drug in her system.

Damn. She didn't look emotionally disturbed. She looked beautiful and sexy as hell. Her long ebony hair fell in silky strands that tempted him beyond reason. She smelled like peaches and soap, and some womanly scent all her own that was as intoxicating as an aphrodisiac.

Questions needled him. He could be wrong about her. But he shoved the thought aside. It felt too right to hold her, too perfect to have her snuggle against him as if he were her savior. *You couldn't save your partner, and he died because he trusted the wrong person. And you almost died trying to help him. What if you can't save her? Your heart is at stake here. Will you die trying?*

He loosened his hold and rubbed his hands up and down her arms, hoping to soothe the tension from her stiff muscles and get his own irrational emotions under control. Her body felt so welcoming and his own reacted as a man to a lover's, not as a cop to a woman in distress.

And if you're sloppy because you're involved with her and someone is trying to hurt her, you could cost her her life. The thought sobered him immediately.

"Thanks for coming," Veronica said softly, raising her dark eyes to look into his. The fear and vulnerability trapped him, held him hostage, and he watched with admiration as she made a valiant attempt to gather her own composure. He wanted to make love to her. Now, more than ever. Not because she was afraid, but because she didn't want him to see it.

Instead he reminded himself that if he finished this case, he would be done with Veronica. And more than likely she wouldn't want anything to do with him. They'd met under such stressful circumstances that they'd connected. But could it last?

He tilted her chin up and stroked her jaw with the pad of his thumb. "You want to show me what they did this time?"

The slight nod of her head was her only answer. He released her and took a deep, calming breath while she led him to her bedroom to see the violence someone had inflicted upon her—the most primal part of him wished she were leading him to her bed instead. The soft sway of her curves beneath the satin robe drew his eye, but he forced himself to scan the room, his gaze finally resting murderously on the message written on her mirror.

"Son of a—" he muttered, striding over to examine the lipstick-scrawled words.

"I don't know how they got in," Veronica said, hugging her arms around her. "I had the locks changed today."

When he glanced at her, an unsettling thought hit him in the gut. He'd never seen a more innocent-looking face. But as he studied the writing, something nagged at him. He'd seen Veronica's signature on her client list. The person who wrote the damning message dotted their *i*s with an open circle just like Veronica.

She smiled slightly and lowered her hands by her sides. He jerked his gaze away. "Who changed the locks?"

"I don't know. I had my secretary call and set it up."

"Louise, the woman I met?"

"Yes," Veronica said. "I was in a meeting all afternoon. She met the locksmith, then brought me the new keys."

Nathan frowned and pointed to the mirror. "You didn't touch it?"

Veronica shook her head. "No, I went straight to the phone and called you."

He met her gaze and saw his own need and desire reflected in her turbulent eyes. She ran her tongue over her lips and combed her fingers through her hair. Her hand was trembling.

He turned away and picked up the phone. "Ford, I need some assistance." He briefly explained about the threatening message.

"You want us to do what?" Ford growled.

"Fingerprint Ms. Miller's apartment."

"The woman probably wrote the threat herself," Ford said. "You're wasting the department's time. When are you going to quit thinking with your hormones?"

Nathan reined in the curse word on the tip of his tongue. Hadn't he told his former partner, Rick, the same thing? But Rick hadn't listened. And now he understood why. Rick had been just as mesmerized by that girl, Melissa, as he was by Veronica. Rick had made a fatal mistake in trusting a suspect. Was he falling into the same trap?

And whether he liked it or not, somehow he and Ford had to learn to work together.

"You know if you'd stop running every time that woman called, she'd quit pulling these pranks," Ford said snidely.

"Just do it," Nathan snapped. "And don't take all day about getting here." He slammed down the phone, then glanced up and saw Veronica watching him, her expression unreadable.

"Thank you for checking into this," she said quietly.

"I'm going to find out who's doing this," Nathan said. *Even if it's you.*

But deep down, he couldn't believe it was. Then he thought about Scroggins and what he'd said about Veronica's father's files being burned after his death. The coincidence was too neat and tidy to be a coincidence. And he already had two suspects with motives to threaten her—Veronica's old boyfriend and Wayne Barrett. Maybe she was an innocent pawn in someone else's twisted game. Maybe she really did need his protection. He'd be a fool not to listen to his own instincts.

"I'd like to talk to your secretary," he said, hesitating.

"Sure." Veronica dialed Louise's home phone and explained about the break-in.

Nathan heard Louise's shriek.

"I'm fine," Veronica said. "But Detective Dawson wants to ask you about the locksmith."

He didn't hear Louise's reply, but Veronica handed him the handset. "Ms. Falk, which locksmith company did you use?"

"Rogers Locksmith," she said. "Why, good gracious, I can't believe this has happened. I watched him change the locks myself."

"And it was just the two of you?" Nathan asked.

"Well…" Louise hedged. "I mean there are other people who work for the man's company, but he was by himself at Veronica's."

"It's strange," Nathan said. "Veronica's apartment has been broken into twice, and there was no sign of forced entry. It's almost as if the intruder had a key."

"I don't know anything about that," Louise said, sounding slightly defensive. "I only phoned the man, Mr. Dawson."

Nathan paused at her haughty tone. Could Louise be involved? What motive would she possibly have? He shook himself from his thoughts, remembering how upset Louise had been when Veronica had received the music box. He heard the doorbell and hung up. Veronica let Ford and a young, uniformed officer in. He saw the wide frown Ford gave Veronica and noticed her posture go rigid in defense. He wondered what kind of lawyer she was, probably pretty forbidding if her dark eyes were angry instead of frightened. When she met his gaze, he almost smiled at the display of bravado she showed his partner. She was used to dealing with people like Ford. She wasn't going to let him intimidate her. Good.

"Make it quick," he heard Ford tell the young officer as he began dusting the mirror. Ford put on his own gloves and began combing the place. "Is there anything missing, Ms. Miller?"

"I don't think so."

"Why don't you look around?" Nathan suggested.

Veronica started to pick up some books off the table.

"Don't touch anything, just check and see if anything's been stolen," Ford said.

Nathan glared at Ford. "I'll walk with you, Veronica."

She nodded and walked through the kitchen, then the bathroom and the den. Her gaze rested on an antique mahogany desk in the corner. "It looks like someone's been through my desk."

Nathan studied the sleek wood and the modern computer, the closed drawers. It looked neat to him, definitely not as if it had been ransacked. "Why do you think that?"

"My disks have been moved," she said. "I keep them in alphabetical order." She pointed to the file box. Some of the disks were upside down and they definitely weren't in any order.

"They're also color coded according to the files I'm working on at the present—completed files, cases pending. See, they're all jumbled."

Nathan motioned to Ford. "Dust this case inside and out. If there's anybody else's fingerprints on them, I want to know."

Ford grumbled but followed his instructions. Nathan noticed Veronica's pale face. She looked tired and weary, and suddenly he wanted to see her away from this apartment, and away from her office, where she wouldn't be so strained. "How about we go get a bite to eat? Chinese sound good?"

A look of surprise crossed her face as her eyes met his.

"There's something I want to talk to you about," he said, realizing he was making up an excuse to spend more time with her.

"The case?"

Nathan nodded. Oh, well, he thought as she went to change clothes, the case was as good an excuse as any.

"I NEED TO STOP by my place and get my wallet," Nathan said when they were in the car. Veronica nodded, and he drove the short distance in silence. "Come on in. I want to check my messages."

As soon as they entered, Nathan regretted the decision to invite her in. His place was a mess. His black lab greeted them by thumping his tail on the floor and whining for food. "Hey, there, Chocolate," he said, stroking his head.

"Pretty dog," Veronica said, petting his back. The dog nuzzled her hand, flopped onto the floor and rolled over with his legs sprawled.

"He wants you to scratch his belly," Nathan said.

She laughed and knelt down, then rubbed Chocolate's stomach. His tail thumped in response.

"Sorry the place is such a mess. I haven't been here much lately." He grabbed clothes and newspapers and shoved aside an empty can of dog food as he tried to clear a path to the sofa.

He saw Veronica take in the sparse furnishings, the tattered, out-of-date sofa, the socks balled up on the floor. "Looks like you need a housekeeper," she said.

Their gazes locked. Nathan grinned. "I need more than that."

He saw the hesitation in her eyes and wished he could retract his statement. "I'll check my messages and get my wallet," he said quickly, and left the room. He returned to find Veronica staring at a photo of his parents.

"They died a few years ago," he said quietly. "A car wreck."

"No brothers or sisters?"

"Nope, just me."

She placed the photo back on the scarred-pine end table. "I'm sorry. I know how that can be."

Feeling uneasy at the sympathy brimming in her eyes, he motioned her to the door. "Come on, let's go eat."

As they drove to the restaurant, Veronica watched the buzz of cars rush by, heard the sound of horns and engines. She imagined what her life would be like without the chaos she'd encountered since she'd arrived in Oakland. In Florida, she'd felt some semblance of being a normal, respected attorney. There, no one knew about her past.

Here, she felt like one of the yellow traffic lights that were now blinking and blowing in the wind, warning people to approach with caution. Perhaps she should forget her search into her past. Perhaps she should go back to Florida.

And to Ron. Where everything was safe.

She stared at Nathan's strong, chiseled profile, and a sliver of desire curled low in her belly. She could still feel the imprint of his touch when he'd held her. His strong masculine scent invaded her senses, reminding her that he was a man of action and power, not one who wanted to impress people. An honest man, one who protected and served the people, one who put his own life on the line for the sake of the town.

How could she ever go back to Ron after knowing Nathan? And how could she leave Oakland without confronting the very past she'd been running from all her life?

"I hope you like spicy food," Nathan said, pulling into the parking lot. "The Kung Pau chicken is delicious."

"Sounds great." Veronica wet her lips with her tongue, a shiver of excitement skittering up her spine as she noticed him watch the movement. He put the car in Park and turned to her, his silent perusal straining her already-taut nerves.

"What?" she finally asked.

He shook his head. The look of need she'd seen a few minutes earlier disappeared, and she wondered if she'd imagined it. "Nothing. Let's go."

A few minutes later they were seated in the dimly lit oriental parlor where Chinese lanterns and fans adorned the walls. A huge aquarium filled with colorful fish kept small children entertained while they waited for their food, and soft oriental music played in the background. Veronica relaxed and studied the menu.

"Let's share a couple of entrées," Nathan said.

Let's share more. She bit her lip, shocked at her own thoughts. "Sure. The Kung Pau chicken and what else?"

"You choose."

Veronica smiled. "Snow pea shrimp."

Nathan closed the menu. "Sounds great." The waiter approached to take their order.

"Egg rolls?" he asked.

"Of course," Veronica said. "And sweet and sour soup."

"Egg drop soup for me," Nathan said.

"Wine, sir?"

Nathan arched an eyebrow.

"I'd like a glass of Chablis," Veronica said.

"The same for me." He grinned. "Well, it seems we have compatible appetites."

"Looks that way." She patted her stomach. "And I'm starving."

Nathan's gaze raked over her attire, lingering for a long moment on her casual silk T-shirt, then sweeping up her neck to focus on her mouth.

Veronica cleared her throat, a blush creeping up her cheeks. "I meant I was hungry for food."

He leaned back in the chair and broke into laughter. The rich, deep sound filled Veronica with a heady sense of power. He covered her hand with his, and she stared at the rough, callused skin and golden hair covering his knuckles, then glanced back up at his face. His laughter died, but a slow lopsided smile curved on his lips that was so sexy she was tempted to reach out and trace his mouth with her fingers. Instead, he turned her hand over so he could look at her palm.

"Tell me about yourself," he said quietly.

Veronica tensed, and he gently traced circles in the center of her palm with his finger. "You already know everything."

He paused, tilted her face to his and smiled with a gentleness that contrasted sharply with his hard features. The tender gleam in his eyes filled her heart with mushy thoughts she knew she shouldn't be thinking.

"I know some of your past," he said in a low voice. "But tell me about living with your grandmother. Tell me about school and why you decided to be an attorney. Tell me what you like to do—besides work."

"Oh."

"Relax, Veronica. This isn't an inquisition." He squeezed her hand. The warm sincerity in his touch only heated her desire for more. "I'd like to know you—the Veronica that isn't being taunted by some lunatic."

She forced a smile, grateful the waiter interrupted with wine and their egg rolls and soup. Reluctantly she pulled out of Nathan's hand to take a sip of her wine.

"Well, my grandmother was a sweet woman, a little old-fashioned."

"That must have made it hard when you were a teenager?"

"What?" Veronica suddenly wondered if this *was* an inquisition. She had too many secrets to hide, too many things she wasn't proud of.

"I figured she was strict, you know, about dating."

"Oh, yeah. She was. But she was fair."

"She was good to you?" He wiped a drop of soup from the corner of his mouth, and Veronica shuddered inside.

"Yes, she was great. She encouraged me to…to see a counselor when I was little."

Nathan paused, his spoon near his mouth. "Did that help?"

She avoided his probing stare. "Some, I guess. The nightmares went away for a while. Then I got involved in school activities and things were better."

"Let me guess—cheerleader?"

Veronica laughed. "Hardly. I was on the swim team."

"Wow, I'm impressed."

"You should be. I beat Ray Winterbottom every time."

"Who was he? Your boyfriend?"

"No way. He was a computer genius." She smiled and sipped some more wine. "Probably a millionaire by now."

Nathan grew silent and Veronica wondered if she'd said something wrong.

"And what about law school?"

"Easy," she said. "I wanted to be like my dad."

The sudden silence between them was filled with tension. "I can't get away from it," Veronica finally said. "I have to face it so I can go on."

"Is that why you came back to Oakland?"

"Yes. I've always had the nightmares. But when my grandmother died, it was like it was all happening again. That feeling of losing someone—I had to come back."

The waiter interrupted and brought their entrées. Nathan took a bite, then sighed. "I talked to Scroggins, the officer in charge of your parents' case."

Her fingers tightened on her fork. "What did he say?"

"Not much." Nathan chewed another biteful of food. "I wondered if all this might be connected to your father's death. Perhaps a case he'd worked on. So I asked him about your dad's files. There weren't any backups."

"I figured as much." Veronica's mind started spinning. "Do you really think all this might be connected to one of Dad's cases?"

Nathan shrugged. "I don't know. So far, none of your cases from Florida show anything suspicious. I'd say right now we've got three possibilities. Your old boyfriend—"

"It's not Ron," Veronica said matter-of-factly.

Nathan arched an eyebrow and frowned.

"I really don't think it is, but go on."

"Barrett."

"That's possible," she conceded. "Although if he's doing it for revenge, it's a pretty intricate plan. Even with what he lost, the man did get away with a sizable amount of money."

"You're right," Nathan said. "But revenge is a strong motivation for a lot of people."

"Okay, any other theories?"

"Maybe we should pursue your dad's old cases. Only problem is we don't have his files."

Veronica snapped her fingers. "No, we don't. But I do have a couple of boxes of memorabilia my grandma saved for me. There might be something in there."

"Where are the boxes?"

"At my apartment."

"And you know what's inside?"

Her heart skipped a beat at the thought that she might have hit on something to help. "I've never opened them."

Nathan tossed back his wine and held out his hand. "Feel like taking a look?"

Veronica smiled and summoned her courage. She'd come to Oakland to deal with her past. The odd circumstances surrounding her had frightened her, but she was tired of being scared and alone. It was time for her to take control of her life.

Nathan seemed like a man she could trust, at least with her past. But with her future, she wasn't sure. She'd have to be careful not to fall for him, to guard her heart as she always had. He was a man who lived with danger every day, a man who was too experienced for her, a man who would move on when her case was over. If she got too close to him, he'd break her heart.

Besides, even if there was nothing in the boxes to help find her father's killer or discover who was threatening her, going through the boxes might help her move on with her life. She accepted Nathan's outstretched hand and twined her fingers with his, just as the waiter brought their fortune cookies. "I guess it's about time."

He released her hand and broke open his fortune cookie. Veronica did the same, pausing when Nathan chuckled.

"What does it say?" she asked.

He grinned and kissed her fingertips. "It says romance is at your fingertips. How about yours?"

Veronica tensed as she unfolded the slip of paper. She instantly refolded it and started to stuff it in her pocket. "Hey, let's see," he said, taking it from her. He eased the paper open and read aloud, "Honesty is the key to obtaining trust."

ON THE DRIVE HOME, Nathan tried to divert his eyes from Veronica and how tempting she looked in that sexy bit of a top and the way it clung to her breasts. And he tried to forget how nervous the fortune cookie had made her. Was she nervous because she was keeping something from him? Glancing into the rearview mirror, he noticed a dark sedan behind them. Were they being followed?

He made a quick turn at the red light to see. The sedan turned also. He tried to make out the driver, but the windows were tinted and the sedan stayed just far enough behind them that he couldn't get a make on the car. He eased up to a stop sign and flipped on his left turn indicator. The driver slowed and flipped on his turn signal. Nathan gritted his teeth. He was growing tired of the game. Speeding up, he pulled into the other lane and soared through a red light. The car turned at the stop light and he left it behind.

"Was that car following us?" Veronica asked.

"I'm not sure. I thought so." Nathan ran a hand over his face, deciding he must be paranoid, then mentally ticked off the things he needed to do on the investigation. Follow up with the man in Florida he'd asked to check out Ron Cox. Follow up on Barrett's whereabouts. Find out whose, if any, fingerprints turned up in Veronica's apartment, check with the locksmith Louise Falk had used. He paused as a thought struck him. Perhaps he should also check up on Louise Falk. After

all, she had had access to Veronica's keys. And as her secretary, she could get to her files. Except the ones she kept at
home. Unless those were only backup disks and she had the
information on her hard drive at work. Hmm. Something to
think about.

And find out what connection Gerald Jones had to Barrett.
Come to think of it, he'd seen Gerald talking to Louise at the
party at Eli's that night.

"Thanks for dinner," Veronica said, breaking into his
thoughts.

"It was great," Nathan said as he pulled into her complex.
He stopped and faced her. "You really want to go through
those boxes?"

"Yes." She smiled, and he remembered the picture of her
standing at her parents' graveside. She was a courageous
woman. He couldn't begin to imagine what her life had been
like.

"Do you want me to leave?"

She shook her head. "I know you've heard a lot of things
about me, so if there is something in there about my father's
work, I want you to see it."

Nathan's throat closed. He wanted to believe her so badly
he ached. "Then let's go."

Veronica opened the door and they walked silently to her
apartment. "You know, when I first moved here I couldn't
get used to the cool weather. Most of the leaves had already
fallen to the ground."

Nathan laughed. "I guess it is a switch from Florida."

"But now I like the idea of a change in seasons." She
stopped and stared at the bare trees. "It looks so desolate
without the leaves. But when spring comes and the flowers
bloom, it must be beautiful."

A soft breeze picked up the strands of her hair and tossed
them around her face. Nathan slowly reached out and moved
them back, tucking them behind her ear, certain he'd never
seen a more beautiful sight. "Spring is beautiful," he said
quietly, realizing this year would be the first time she would

experience the magnificent season and remember it. He imagined her standing underneath a blossoming dogwood tree with its dainty white buds showering around her.

Looking through her father's things would be hard for her. He only hoped he could be around when spring finally came for her.

WHILE VERONICA unlocked her apartment door, they heard the phone ringing. By the time they entered, the answering machine had clicked on and he heard a man's agitated voice.

"Veronica, this is Ron. I really wish you were home."

She bit her lip and he stood behind her, watching her reaction.

The man continued in a rush, his voice growing more and more irritated. "I don't know why you haven't returned any of my calls, but I want to talk to you. It's been eight weeks now. For all I know, you could have fallen off the face of the—"

Veronica clicked off the machine, grabbed the phone and turned away from him. "I'm here, Ron." She sighed and ran a hand through her hair. "I'm sorry I haven't called, but my schedule's been crazy and I had to get settled and..."

She rattled on with excuses, and Nathan folded his arms, wondering what Ron was saying on the other end of the line.

"No, don't come here," she said. "Listen, Ron, I really can't talk now."

A long pause followed. Veronica lowered her voice.

"Yes." She glanced at him nervously. "It's business, Ron. Can I call you back?"

Business, huh? He had a feeling they both knew there was more than business going on between the two of them.

"Okay, tell Mr. Raddison I'll give him a call." She hung up and brushed her hands down her skirt.

"Who's Raddison?"

"He's one of the men I represent in the retirement community. He thinks someone's trying to scam them."

"Sounds like a job for the police."

"I'll talk to them tomorrow. I can't let those older people suffer."

Nathan thought of her grandmother and how much Veronica must miss her. "If I can do anything to help, let me know."

"Thanks."

He frowned. "So, is Cox coming here?"

Veronica shook her head. "I don't think so." She turned, obviously avoiding the issue. "I'll find those boxes."

Nathan nodded. He halfway hoped Cox would show up. He'd like to talk to the man himself. And if he had anything to do with the threats on Veronica, he would do a whole lot more than talk.

Chapter Nine

Veronica dragged three boxes into the living room and knelt beside them. The plain brown boxes were sealed with shipping tape, nondescript in every way. But they held precious fragments of a life she remembered nothing about.

"I understand why I blocked out that night," she said, as she cut open the tape. "But I still don't know why I can't recall the earlier years. There must be some happy memories there, too."

"Who knows?" Nathan lowered himself beside her, then squeezed her hand. Veronica gazed into his eyes and accepted the strength he offered. "Maybe you'll find out when you look inside."

She wondered if it were possible. She'd hoped seeing the old house would trigger her memory, but it had only given her the creeps, just as the music box had. What if the same thing happened when she opened the box of keepsakes? What if she found something to confirm the fact that she was responsible for her parents' deaths?

She released Nathan's hand, but hers shook so badly he took the scissors from her and opened the boxes himself. When he finished he placed his hands on his knees and waited. "Take your time, Veronica. It's okay," he said quietly.

Veronica lifted the sheets of tissue paper covering the contents and looked inside. The first box had a family picture on top. She pulled it out and examined the faces. Her mother had been a beautiful woman. She had Veronica's same dark hair and slender build with porcelain skin, a dainty nose and brown eyes. Her father was handsome, with light brown hair, a mustache and hazel eyes that held a commanding look. His nose was prominent and his jaw wide. He'd been a tall man, almost overshadowing her mother's small frame. She favored her mother more than her father.

She was wearing a frilly blue dress and was sitting in her father's lap. Her mother stood behind them with her hand on her dad's shoulder. It amazed her that she could see the three of them together, but she had no recollection of posing for the picture.

"They were handsome people," Nathan said, brushing a strand of hair from her face. "You're beautiful, just like your mother."

Veronica nodded solemnly. She'd almost forgotten he was there.

Next she pulled out a small, worn teddy bear and a raggedy green blanket. "These must have been mine when I was little."

Nathan laughed softly. "Your security blanket. Looks like you wore it out."

Smiling, she stroked the bear and blanket, then laid them down and drew out a long white christening gown. She admired the intricate lace and embroidery design across the front. "It's beautiful. I wonder if my mom embroidered it. Grandma said she liked to sew."

Nathan gave her an encouraging look and she pulled out a rattle, a scrapbook and a journal that had belonged to her grandmother. She opened the scrapbook and saw dozens of pictures of her and her parents. Some were of her as a baby, then a toddler at a birthday party they'd planned for her. A few pages had blank, faded spots as if photos had been removed. Veronica wondered who had taken the pictures out and why.

"You were chubby when you were little," Nathan said in a teasing voice.

"Well, it's no wonder. Look at that cake," she said with a smile. "It's huge."

Nathan took out a small bronzed baby shoe and traced his fingers over it. "You had tiny feet though."

Veronica laughed, her heart squeezing at the sight of the baby shoe. She'd never really thought about having children of her own, but seeing the precious baby mementos brought a vision of a little boy to mind; a little boy with sandy blond hair and eyes a deep amber.

She stared at Nathan, surprised at her thoughts, and their gazes locked. A slow smile spread on his face and she wondered if he had ever thought about having children. He was kind and strong and protective, but gentle; he would make a wonderful father.

But Nathan would leave the minute they solved the case. He was interested in her story, but that didn't mean he would ever fall in love with her.

She flipped through the box and noticed a photograph of her parents on their wedding day.

"She made a beautiful bride," Nathan said, his voice husky.

Veronica pictured herself standing in a long white gown with a lacy veil and a handsome man on her arm. Nathan. His breath feathered against her cheek and she realized he'd dropped a kiss into her hair. She leaned against him and closed her eyes, allowing herself to fantasize about belonging to him. His lips pressed gently along the column of her neck and she shivered. He moved his hands to her waist and paused, leaning with his face buried against her hair. For a brief moment she forgot the horrors of her childhood, the trouble that had happened since she'd moved to Oakland. Then he pulled away, and the sweet moment was broken.

"They had a small wedding," Nathan commented.

She studied the other photographs. "That's odd."

"What?"

"My parents were so close to Eli. I wonder why there aren't any pictures of him in here."

"Hmm. He was senator back then, wasn't he?"

"Yes."

"He probably traveled a lot."

Veronica closed the book. "You're right."

"What's the other book?"

"It's a journal of my grandmother's." Veronica turned several pages, feeling as if she were violating her grandmother's privacy by reading her personal writings.

"How did it get in the box with your parent's things?"

She shrugged. "I don't know. It was dated years ago. It must have gotten mixed in when we moved to Florida. I'll read it later."

"What's in the second box?" Nathan asked.

"Looks like a few of my mom's things." She opened a decorative flower box containing a corsage. "She wore this on her wedding day." Next she dragged out an exquisite wedding gown, trimmed in tiny pearl buttons and lace. Veronica's eyes teared at the sight. Every girl dreamed of marriage and having their mother there. She would never know that as a reality. She touched the slippery satin to her cheek, then quickly wrapped the gown back in its covering before she could become too emotional. When she glanced up, Nathan was watching her with a strange expression in his eyes, a combination of heat and desire and something else: yearning. Veronica smiled and he smiled back, reaching out to wipe a tear from her cheek. Embarrassed, she lowered her head.

The wedding guest book was next. She skimmed over the names, again surprised Eli wasn't there. Perhaps their friendship developed after they were married. Oddly enough though, she noticed Eli's mother's name, Alma Jones. And Arlene Baits, the doctor who had treated Veronica at the hospital.

She thought back to how nervous the woman had seemed when she'd discovered Veronica's identity. Maybe she would go back and talk with her.

"Hey, this looks like a date book," Nathan said, sounding suddenly businesslike as he searched the other box. She glanced over his shoulder.

"It was my father's."

Nathan flipped through the pages. "Do you mind if I take it and look it over?"

Veronica shook her head and he continued to study the small book. She extracted a gold sealed envelope and opened it. It held her parents' marriage certificate and her birth certificate. She'd been born on May 7 at Oakland Community Hospital, weighed seven pounds and eight ounces, and had been nineteen inches long. She traced her finger along her parents' marriage certificate, pausing when she noticed the date of their marriage. Her parents hadn't been married until December 1. That meant her mother was already pregnant when they got married.

Swallowing her surprise, she quickly stuffed the certificate back in the envelope before Nathan could see it. She had enough of her past to be ashamed about. She didn't want him to know that on top of everything else, she'd been conceived out of wedlock.

When he noticed her quickly stuff the papers away, he motioned to the envelope. "What's in there?"

"It's just my birth certificate," she said softly.

He put the date book in his pocket and stood. Other than a pair of bookends and an empty tape recorder, the third box was almost empty.

"Well, I guess that's it," Veronica said, pushing up from the floor. "It doesn't look like we found anything to help."

"I want to get a closer look at the appointments your father had before he died. It might give us a clue." He patted his pocket where he stuck the book and Veronica followed him to the door. "I suppose I should be going," he said, pausing.

She started to speak, but clutched the doorknob, her gaze straying to her bedroom.

"I'll clean the lipstick off your mirror before I go," he said, as if he'd just remembered it.

Veronica shook her head firmly. "No, I need to do that."

His hand covered hers. "Will you be all right?"

"I may sleep on the couch, but I'll be fine."

He lifted his hand and rubbed her chin with the pad of his

thumb. "I've got a car watching your apartment again. I'll make sure he's in place before I go." She smiled shyly and nodded, her heart thudding painfully at the concern shadowing his husky voice. "You need to get the locks changed again. And this time, you stay here while they change them."

"I will."

"And don't let anyone have an extra key."

"I won't."

He gazed into her eyes, then back at the couch, and she desperately wanted to ask him to stay. Instead she clamped her hand over his and squeezed it tenderly. He lowered his mouth and gently brushed his lips across hers. When he raised his face, she saw again the raw yearning in his eyes as they darkened.

Then remorse or some emotion that looked like uncertainty filled his eyes, and he left, closing the door behind him.

Veronica leaned against the door, wondering if Nathan realized how close she'd come to begging him to stay. Only he would have been playing bodyguard, and she didn't want him to sleep on the couch to protect her. She'd never wanted anything as much as she wanted to feel his arms around her. She wanted him to lie in her bed and bring her to ecstasy with his hands and mouth.

How could she be falling in love with the man, when he was doing nothing more than offering his comfort and expertise as a detective? She was going to make a fool of herself and drive away the only man who'd ever heard her story and not gone running.

She glanced outside, saw the blue-and-white car, then locked the door, pushing aside thoughts of Nathan. She stared at the boxes, still shaken by the fact that her mother had been pregnant when she'd married her father. Her grandmother had told her she was premature, but that obviously had been a lie. What else could her grandmother have lied about?

She walked over and picked up the journal. Still feeling as if she were intruding on her grandmother's thoughts, she laid it on the end table. After changing into her gown and robe, she settled on the couch with some tea and the book. She took a deep breath and opened it to the first page.

Skimming the few pages in front, she learned her grandmother had started the journal when her grandfather had taken ill with cancer. Her grandmother had described her feelings while she'd cared for him.

She found a section describing her grandmother's reaction to her mother's pregnancy. She could hear her grandmother's voice in her writing; it was almost as if she were in the room.

I pray she will marry the man and not make my grandchild grow up a bastard. Amelia is already growing heavy with the child, and unless they marry soon, the whole town will know. I've considered moving away to hide our shame, but Amelia seems to be coming around, and I've talked with Amelia's doctor about keeping her pregnancy a secret. She's agreed to tell people that the baby was premature.

Veronica closed her eyes and squeezed back tears. Her grandmother had considered her birth the family's shame. She remembered the way her grandmother had cried and taken care of her. Had her grandmother loved her? Or had she only taken her in out of pity?

Curious, she turned a few pages.

Amelia is to be wed today. I thank God for answering my prayers. I have made her wedding gown to disguise the soft mound of her belly in hopes that no one will notice. Her morning sickness has finally gone and she is starting to talk about the child as if it is already alive. I regret the way my daughter has behaved, but I think she will make a wonderful mother. She is kind and loving and I see the way Robert looks at her, and I know he is a good man who will provide a living for her and the baby.

Veronica wiped a tear from her eye and read on. Her grand-mother had always told her that her mother loved her, but somehow reading it in print made it so much more real. She could imagine her mother pregnant, smiling at the thought of her birth.

As the day draws near for the baby, I am nervous. Amelia's doctor has taken ill and I hope the new doctor Baits will keep our secret.

Veronica paused—Arlene Baits, the woman she'd met in the emergency room. Had she delivered Veronica? Excitement made her turn the pages faster and skim for details.

May 7—Dr. Baits helped Amelia bring a baby girl into the world today. It will be hard for people to believe she is premature since she is such a nice healthy size, but Dr. Baits has told people Amelia would have had a ten-pounder if she'd carried to term. And Robert is such a tall man that I think folks may accept the story.
   The baby is beautiful, with soft dark hair and big brown eyes. She reminds me of Amelia, but I think Robert is a little disappointed that she doesn't favor him. She may change as she gets older. Babies do, I told him.

Veronica continued to read, tears slipping down her face as her grandmother described her visits to see her, how much her mother loved her and how proud she was her father's law practice was doing so well. She skimmed over her early child-hood, forcing herself to try and remember the incidents her grandmother described. But nothing seemed familiar.
   Later, the handwriting grew disjointed, as if her grand-mother had been upset. She read on and realized her grand-mother had written the entries after her parents' deaths.

My heart aches with the loss of Amelia and Robert, and to think that they destroyed themselves is more than I can bear. But I must protect my little Veronica, who the doctors say is severely traumatized from witnessing their deaths.

She lies so still with her eyes so wide, and her skin feels cold and clammy, like she has taken ill. In a way I suppose she has. She has taken an illness in her mind and she may never be right again.

The doctors talk to her, but she doesn't respond, and the reporters hover outside the door and window, trying to get in. I want one day to see her run and play and be normal again.

Veronica's chest squeezed as she sensed the pain and frustration her grandmother must have felt. She had never felt normal.

Weeks have passed and my little Veronica has finally come out of the shell she was locked inside. But her memory has gone with her parents' deaths. Some say it is a terrible thing. I think it is a blessing in disguise.

Veronica wiped her eyes and lay down on the couch, hugging her grandmother's journal to her chest. "How could it be a blessing in disguise, Grandmother?" she whispered. Not only could she not remember their deaths, but neither could she remember them when they were alive.

NATHAN FELT LIKE growling the next morning as he lumbered into the police station. A long night with only his electric blanket, his dog and the hum of his ancient refrigerator to keep him company had destroyed his sleep.

Hell, who was he kidding? Veronica had destroyed his sleep.

Or rather, the fact that she wasn't with him.

He'd studied her father's date book and made a note of all

the appointments Mr. Miller had the weeks prior to his death. Interestingly enough, Alma Jones, Eli's mother, had scheduled a meeting with him only two days before he'd died. Had the woman been soliciting campaign contributions for her son or had she some other business in mind?

He had to remember that Miller was the only attorney in town back then, so most of the people had used him. It was likely half the town had made appointments with him that month. Including Scroggins, the former police chief who had been less than eager to talk about Veronica.

He slurped his morning coffee and made a list of the phone calls he needed to make. Last night after he'd finished with the book, he couldn't sleep and he couldn't get Veronica out of his mind. He wanted her. Emotionally stable or not, he wanted her.

"Got that report on the fingerprints," Ford said, slapping a file down in front of him. "Only fingerprints in the apartment were hers and yours," Ford said.

"Even on the mirror?"

"Yep."

"How about the computer disks?"

Ford lit up a cigarette. Nathan really felt like growling. He'd come close to driving to the store the night before and buying a pack. He didn't need this temptation now.

"We got part of one, but couldn't match it. Whoever touched them isn't in the system."

"Meaning there could have been someone there, but they didn't have an arrest record. Or they used gloves."

"It's a long shot," Ford said, raising his eyebrows in skepticism.

"Did you find anything on Barrett?"

"He's got several offshore accounts. Could be anywhere."

"Keep checking. And run a background check on Louise Falk."

"Who the hell is she?" Ford snarled.

"Veronica's secretary. She's one of the few people who had access to Veronica's keys."

"And while I'm doing all the legwork, what are you doing?"

Nathan gritted his teeth. "I'm checking up on her former boyfriend. And digging up the past."

"Found the shrink who treated the Miller broad after her parents' deaths," Ford said, waving a slip of paper in front of Nathan. Nathan snatched it and read the name. Dr. Sandler.

"I'll head over there after I make this phone call."

Ford shook his head as if he already knew what the psychiatrist would tell Nathan and ambled over to his own desk. Nathan punched in the number of his friend in Florida.

"Bill, this is Dawson. What do you have for me?"

The man on the other end laughed. "Always straight to the point, aren't you?"

"It's important," Nathan said. *Too important. Veronica's starting to mean too much to me.*

"Well, I found out something interesting on the Miller woman."

His stomach knotted at Bill's tone. Guilt warred within him at checking up on her. He wasn't sure he really wanted to know.

"She was seeing a psychiatrist in Florida, but he wouldn't give me any information. Said her file was confidential."

Nathan sighed audibly and clenched the slip of paper in his fist. He shouldn't have been surprised, but if Ford got wind of it, he'd be certain Veronica was mentally incompetent. "How about Cox?"

"Cox is pretty boring. I could fall asleep just looking at him."

Nathan laughed.

"Goes to work at six, out to lunch with several suits every day, night he works late, goes to a local gym once or twice a week, eats takeout dinner."

"Any women in his life?"

Bill chuckled. "A couple of uppity attorneys. Certainly not your type."

"I didn't mean that," Nathan said, realizing his type had

never been dark-haired, dark-eyed mysterious women—
until now.

"Naw. Man's a workaholic. Nothing interesting, including
the car he drives."

"What kind?"

"A dark sedan. Tinted windows. Real conservative."

Nathan remembered the dark sedan he thought had been
following him and Veronica on their way from the restaurant.

"And he's been in Florida all week?"

"Until yesterday. Left on business."

"Do you know where he went?"

"Drove to Savannah."

Hmm. Savannah was near enough to Atlanta for Cox to
drive over in an evening. Veronica had talked to him the night
before, too. What if he hadn't been calling from Florida? What
if he'd been right here in Oakland?

VERONICA TUGGED her jacket around her shoulders to ward
off the chill of the January wind and glanced over her shoulder
to see if someone was following her. She thought she'd seen
a black car behind her on the highway, but it hadn't turned in
to the hospital. Maybe it was only her imagination.

She intended to see Arlene Baits and question her about her
birth. Somehow talking to the people who'd known her parents
made her feel closer to them.

All night she'd tossed and turned on the sofa, thinking about
her grandmother's journal and her reaction to the death of her
parents. Which doctor had treated her after they'd died? If
Arlene Baits had helped deliver her, maybe she had been
around when she was taken in for trauma and could give her
some answers.

If she had to, she was prepared to visit the former police
chief and ask to see the records on the investigation of her
parents' deaths. After finding out how much her parents loved
her and each other, she couldn't make herself believe the murder-suicide theory. Or that she had hurt them.

And if she'd seen the real killer, whoever it was had gone free, because she'd been afraid.

She might have been a traumatized little girl twenty years before, but now she was a grown woman and an attorney. Justice hadn't been served, and if getting her memory back was the key to finding the person who'd ripped her childhood to shreds, she was determined to face it, no matter how painful.

The small county hospital was a buzz of activity when she entered. She had a little over half an hour before she'd have to be at the office, and she'd promised to meet Tessa Jones, Eli's daughter, for lunch.

She still hadn't understood the woman's phone call this morning and her insistence on the meeting. She seriously doubted Tessa wanted to talk about her taxes. Certainly Eli had all his children's financial matters well in hand. Distracted with her thoughts, she almost ran into an orderly pushing a wheelchair with an older woman sitting in it. It reminded her of her grandmother. And her reason for being there.

She scanned the nurses' station and spotted a friendly looking young woman. "Hi, I'm Veronica Miller. I'd like to see Dr. Arlene Baits."

The girl held out a clipboard. "Fill this out, please."

Veronica smiled. "No, I'm not here as a patient. I need to speak with her."

The young woman pointed to the waiting area. "I'll see if I can find her." She checked the clock. "It's just about time for her shift to end. She'll probably be out in a minute."

Veronica stared at the faded yellow paint on the walls and thought about Nathan. Had he found out who'd broken into her apartment and written the threatening message?

"Ma'am, Dr. Baits can see you now."

Veronica followed the young woman to a small lounge where the doctor waited.

"Dr. Baits, I'm glad you could talk with me."

The older doctor turned around, sloshing hot coffee over the rim of her cup. "Oh, my."

"Are you okay?" Veronica asked, approaching cautiously.

The woman recovered, her hand trembling as she placed the coffee on the table and settled into a chair. Veronica sat down beside her. "Seeing me upsets you, doesn't it, Dr. Baits?"

"Please call me Arlene," the woman said, patting her gray hair in place. "That's what your mother called me."

"Really?" The thought of this woman and her mother being friends warmed her and slightly settled her jangled nerves.

"Yes, you look so much like her, dear. It's uncanny." Dr. Baits took a sip of coffee. "You have the same dark hair and those eyes. I always thought your mom was a beautiful lady."

"She was," Veronica said, her throat closing. She took a moment to get her emotions under control. "And you delivered me?"

The older woman nodded. "Sure did. Course I delivered half the babies in the town back then. Wasn't as many specialty doctors around, you know?"

"I suppose not," Veronica said, studying the woman's neatly trimmed nails.

"So what can I do for you, dear?"

Veronica's voice came out barely above a whisper. "You can tell me about my mother."

The woman smiled gently. "She was a sweet young thing. Delivery went fine, although a little long. Thought Robert was going to wear the floor out with his pacing."

Veronica laughed. "Did you treat me as a child?"

"Oh, yes. But you were a healthy little thing. Never had much more than a cold or an occasional bout with the flu."

"And my parents—they loved me?"

A look of surprise crossed Dr. Baits's face. "Of course they did, child."

The lump in Veronica's throat grew. "Dr. Baits, were they happy together?"

Dr. Baits paused, her forehead furrowing. "They had a good marriage, a spat here and there, but nothing big, you know."

"They wouldn't have killed each other, would they?"

The sudden silence was deafening. Dr. Baits fidgeted in her seat, folding the cuffs of her lab coat.

"I have to know the truth, Dr. Baits. I know I was with them when they died, but I don't remember it." Veronica paused, then went on in a more heated voice. "Maybe I'm grasping at straws, but from everything I heard about my parents, they weren't the volatile type. I read my grandmother's journal. I know my parents loved each other, even though they got married because my mom was already pregnant."

Dr. Baits shifted, her hands toying with the cuffs of her coat again. "I didn't know you knew about that. What else did you read in the journal?"

"Not enough," Veronica said. "That's why I'm here." She sensed the doctor didn't want to discuss the forced marriage. Perhaps she thought she'd get in trouble for lying about Veronica's premature birth. "I can't believe their death was a murder-suicide," Veronica continued.

The warm hand that covered Veronica's was both gentle and strong. "I never believed that, either," Dr. Baits finally said.

"I have these nightmares. And I see this shadow. I think it's a vision of somebody else who was there."

"You know that for sure?"

Veronica shook her head in frustration. "I can't see the face. But I was hoping you might have known if either one of my parents had any enemies. Who could have killed them?"

Dr. Baits sighed. "I don't know, child. I really don't. It was a sad, sad time."

Veronica stood and wrapped her arms around herself. "Were you the one who treated me after they died?"

Dr. Baits cleared her throat. "Yes, I was here. But you were in shock. Severely traumatized. We called in a specialist."

"Was it someone here on the staff? Are they still here?"

Dr. Baits nodded. "A man named Dr. Sandler. You probably don't remember much about him. He evaluated you, but you moved away before he finished treatment."

"No, I don't remember him. But I have to talk to him,"

Veronica said. She glanced at her watch, remembering her luncheon appointment.

"He's on the fifth floor," Dr. Baits said.

Veronica thanked her and rushed out the door. A long elevator ride later, her stomach was roiling. As she sidled off the elevator, she checked the nurses' station.

"Dr. Sandler's with someone right now," the nurse said, checking her calendar. "Then he has patients scheduled the rest of the day. I can give you an appointment tomorrow."

"That would be fine," Veronica said. "Ten o'clock."

"Ten's good," the nurse said, scribbling the time in the appointment book.

Veronica exhaled, feeling as if she'd finally made a start. Then a familiar face caught her eye. "Nathan?"

He was sitting in the waiting area, his fingers steepled, his brows drawn in concentration. When he spotted her, his face registered surprise. "What are you doing here?" he asked.

Veronica stopped in front of him. "I was going to ask you the same question."

"I—"

The nurse cleared her throat. "Detective Dawson. Dr. Sandler will see you now."

Chapter Ten

When Veronica's eyes narrowed, he wondered if she'd some-how guessed his agenda. Guilt nagged at him, but he wasn't prepared to tell her the truth. "I came by to check the profile of a perp in a case I'm working on."

"Oh, well…of course." She looked embarrassed, and sud-denly he felt like a big heel for lying to her. But what was he supposed to say? *I came by to find out about you, to talk to the psychiatrist who treated you when you were a child.*

"Your turn?" he said, quickly recovering.

She chewed her bottom lip, and he could tell he'd caught her off guard. "I had a checkup downstairs, that's all. Thought I'd say hello to Dr. Sandler, see if he remembered me."

She was lying. He had no idea why, but the fact that her voice squeaked slightly and her pulse was jumping in her throat gave her away. Relief momentarily filled him. If lying about this was so difficult for her, perhaps she'd been telling the truth about everything else that had happened to her.

But the realization she would lie to him also infuriated him. Couldn't she see he was trying his damnedest to help her? Why didn't she trust him?

"I see," he said, not bothering to hide his skepticism. "And did everything check out okay?"

"Yes, well…" She checked her watch in a nervous gesture. "I've got to get to work. I'll see you later."

Definitely. Nathan watched her tug her jacket around her

and rush away, the wind whisking her hair around her face in long wild streaks of ebony, her long legs gliding like a dancer's. He wanted to have her wrap them around him.

Hell, he wanted to bury his hands in her wild tresses and sink himself inside her—in spite of the fact that she didn't trust him or that he didn't know whether she was lying about the attack. He'd never felt this way before, beguiled to the point of not caring if he lived on the edge, so turned on by one woman that his judgment was starting to feel impaired.

And that was dangerous.

He rubbed the base of his spine and hip. He knew the possible consequences of losing his objectivity. He had the scars to prove what happened when a cop let his personal feelings get in the way of his professional code. A siren wailed in the distance, reminding him he'd actually come here on business, to find out more about Veronica, not just to lust after her.

Dr. Sandler met him at the door. "Hi, I'm Detective Dawson. I called earlier."

"Yes, come on in." The tall, lanky doctor ushered him into a small office and motioned toward a chair. Nathan eyed the leather chaise lounge and wondered if he should lie down and ask for therapy—he had to do something about this emotional stuff going on inside him. If the investigation were over, it would be different, but he still—

"Detective, you wanted to talk?"

Nathan glanced up to see the doctor watching him with avid curiosity. He realized his silence had been more revealing than he'd intended.

"I need some information about a case I'm working on."

The doctor removed his glasses and twirled them around with his fingers. "If this is about a patient, you know files are confidential."

Nathan nodded. "I understand that. But she's not a patient now. It's someone you treated years ago."

"Still—"

Nathan held up a hand to stop the protests. "We can speak in hypothetical terms if you want, but I have reason to believe this woman is in danger. And I think it may be related to her past.''

The gray-haired doctor crossed his long legs and linked his hands around one knee. ''I see.''

Encouraged, Nathan went on. ''Her name is Veronica Miller.''

A twitch in the doctor's left eye was his only reaction. ''I heard she moved back to town.''

''Yes, and ever since she has, she's had some strange things happening to her. Someone broke in and attacked her, left several threatening messages.''

''Oh, my,'' Dr. Sandler said, shaking his head. ''It was bad enough what the poor child went through years ago, but now someone is trying to hurt her.''

''I'm afraid so,'' Nathan said, realizing the man truly seemed concerned. ''And I need to know as much as you can tell me about her condition after her parents were killed.''

''Haven't you read her files? I gave an in-depth statement to the police years ago.''

''I did. But I wondered if she gave you any clue, no matter how small, about who might have killed her parents.''

''No.'' Sandler's word was emphatic.

''Are you sure?''

''I'm certain.'' Dr. Sandler's gray eyes narrowed. ''I hated all the gossip about the child and would have done anything to have saved her from the ordeal she went through.''

''Do you remember anything strange, anybody who showed up to visit her at the hospital that seemed odd?''

The doctor scratched his chin in thought. ''Not that I recollect. Her grandmother came immediately, Dr. Baits, Daryl Scroggins, the police chief back then, and the Jones family. Eli came every day, practically kept a vigil till she came out of shock. Even missed a debate, everyone thought that was real decent of him. And his mother was here almost as much.''

''How did you diagnose Veronica's condition?''

''It was a classic case of childhood trauma. I told her grandmother I wasn't sure she'd ever remember what happened. Her grandmother seemed to think it was a blessing.''

''And you?''

''I've always been of the theory that the mind remembers things when the person is ready to accept it. However, I do think a loss such as this can have devastating effects on a person.''

''How so?'' Nathan started to scribble in his notepad.

''There are all kinds of latent effects. Schizophrenia, multiple personality disorder, paranoia, to name a few. In some cases if the person isn't treated, they may become delusional. There're a variety of psychotic behaviors a traumatized child may show later in life.''

''Is it possible the person might actually do things to harm themselves?''

''It's possible.'' Dr. Sandler unfolded his long legs. ''The conscious mind has its own way of taking care of repressed issues. It's unpredictable. Varies with each case.''

Nathan didn't like what he was hearing.

''Do you really think someone's trying to hurt Ms. Miller now, after all these years?'' Dr. Sandler asked.

''As a child, Veronica witnessed the murder. If the murderer is still in town, he may be afraid her memory will return.''

''I see. Well, I hope you find the person, then, before he hurts Ms. Miller any more than she's already been hurt.''

Nathan shook Dr. Sandler's hand and left. The doctor had confirmed two of his theories. One, it was possible Veronica could be doing these things herself. And two, if her parents' case wasn't a murder-suicide, but a double homicide, the threats to Veronica could be very real. He wasn't sure which one frightened him more. He was still concerned about her former boyfriend, too, who was supposed to be in Savannah.

Things seemed to be growing more complicated. And he was determined to find the answers—before Veronica was hurt again.

AFTER WADING through her morning paperwork and talking with the retirement community about the problems the elderly people had complained about, Veronica had a major headache nagging at her temple. She was ready for a nap, not lunch with Tessa Jones. She hadn't talked with Eli since his last visit, since he'd subtly suggested she not date his son, the future senator. Her feelings were still hurt, and all morning she'd wondered what Tessa had in store for her. Did she want to warn her to get out of Dodge, too?

"I'm taking the afternoon off," Louise said, poking her head in Veronica's office. "I made some fresh tea if you want some."

"Thanks." She shuffled a few papers and remembered about having the locks changed. "Did you get that new locksmith on the phone?"

"Yep. He said he'd meet you at your place at five."

"Great, thanks."

"And Ms. Jones called and said she'll see you at that little French café around the corner."

Veronica had a cup of tea to calm herself, then checked to make certain her hair was in place as she headed to meet Tessa. After she'd left the hospital, she'd tucked the wind-blown mass into a topknot and added a jacket to look more professional for her meeting. Visiting with Tessa was intimidating and she wanted to look her best. A few minutes later she found Tessa waiting at a corner table.

Tessa beamed as Veronica walked over to greet her. She was wearing a stunning green silk dress and green suede heels. Her gold bracelets jangled as she shook Veronica's hand.

"Hi. Great café." Veronica indicated the simple French decor of the restaurant.

"I love this place," Tessa said, settling down in her seat again. "The wines are fabulous. And they have a divine French onion soup." She nodded toward an already-filled glass. "I took the liberty to order us a glass of wine."

She normally skipped the wine for lunch, but Veronica didn't want to offend Tessa, so she simply smiled and sipped the Chablis. "The food smells heavenly," Veronica said.

"It is." After they ordered quiche and salad, Tessa unfolded her napkin and toyed with the long gold loop dangling from her ear. "I thought we should get to know each other."

"Really?" Veronica couldn't hide her surprise.

"Yes, Daddy's talked about you for years. And Gerald mentioned he took you to lunch the other day."

Oh, boy—here it comes.

Instead Tessa gave her a sugary smile. "Since you're Father's goddaughter, I figured that makes us kind of like sisters."

"I hadn't thought of it that way." *Although once upon a time, I wanted it to be that way.* Veronica stiffened, wondering where that thought had come from.

"Dad said when you were small, your parents brought you to one of his fund-raisers and you followed me around all day."

"I did?"

"Yes, isn't that cute?"

"I...I suppose so." Veronica took a mental count. When she was seven, Tessa would have been nineteen. She could see how she must have been drawn to her.

"Anyway, I'd forgotten all about that," Tessa said in a chatty voice. "Dad said you wanted me to tie bows in your hair."

Veronica laughed softly. "I must have been a pest."

"Not really. So, after the party the other night, Dad told me what a tough time you had after your parents died, when you went to live with your grandmother." Tessa's eyes teared, and Veronica couldn't help but feel she was being sincere. "I can't imagine losing my father."

Veronica swallowed several sips of water, hoping to dislodge the lump forming in her throat.

Tessa gave her a sympathetic look. "What made you decide to move back here after all those years?"

Veronica had expected subtlety. Instead this woman had no qualms about asking what she wanted to know. "I wanted to work for myself instead of a large firm," Veronica said, sipping her wine.

"Yes, but you could have done that anywhere. Why come back to this town? You must have bad memories." She brought her hand to her cheek in a dramatic gesture. "I just can't imagine."

"That's just it," Veronica said, meeting Tessa's curious gaze head-on. "I don't have any memories of this town at all."

"None?" Tessa asked sympathetically.

"None," Veronica said matter-of-factly.

"So when those doctors said you have amnesia, it was true. I thought they were just making it up."

"It's true," Veronica said, suddenly losing her appetite. "I've tried everything to remember. Even hypnosis. But nothing worked."

"That must be horrible."

"Yes." Tessa's smile radiated warmth and sincerity, but Veronica's head was starting to throb even more, and she felt nauseated.

"But I see you've already found a man. You're seeing that handsome detective?"

Veronica took a sip of water. "He's a—Tessa, I'm not feeling well," Veronica said, massaging her temple as a wave of pain rocked through her. "It seems I'm getting a migraine."

"Oh, dear, do you want to take something?"

"No, I have something at home. I think I need to lie down."

"I'm so sorry." Tessa seemed concerned, and Veronica felt even worse for skipping out on their lunch. Perhaps she and Tessa could be friends, after all. "I hope I didn't upset you by bringing up your parents," Tessa finished.

"No, no, lunch was a lovely idea. Actually I woke up this morning not feeling well." Veronica rubbed the base of her neck. "Must be a bug or something."

Tessa patted her hand. "I hope you feel better. Let's do it again sometime soon."

"Sure." Veronica clutched her purse and avoided looking

at the quiche as she hurried out. She certainly couldn't stomach any food.

Once outside, she blinked to ward off the dizziness. Hoping the fresh air would do her good, she walked back to her office, breathing deeply and trying to suppress the throbbing at her temple. She clutched the stair rail and slowly climbed the steps, then shuffled into her office by sheer willpower. Two painkillers later, she stretched out on the sofa in her office and fell sound asleep.

WHY WASN'T VERONICA answering the phone?

The hairs at the back of Nathan's neck stood on end. He was too damn worried about her to even think. First, the threatening message last night. Now, she wasn't answering her phone. What if something had happened to her?

"They found Barrett," Ford said, leaning against his desk. "In some little hotel downtown. All holed up with a new mistress."

"Right under our noses. How the hell did they trace him there?"

"His wife. She had a PI on him the whole time."

"So, he's been there since the day Barrett Pharmaceuticals called?"

Ford nodded. "Looks that way. Means he's probably not responsible for that little Miller gal and her wolf cries."

Nathan let out several curse words and grabbed his jacket. "Maybe, maybe not. He could have orchestrated the whole thing from the hotel. Besides, I don't think she is crying wolf, Ford."

"You're a sucker," Ford said.

Nathan ignored him and rushed to his car. He might be a sucker, but his gut said something was wrong. He had to listen to his instincts. Veronica was in danger. He knew it; he just didn't know who was after her.

VERONICA WOKE with a start, her vision cloudy, the sound of a tree limb scraping against the windowpane drawing her gaze to the darkening sky. Her heart was pounding, her breathing erratic. She covered her face with her hands and took several deep breaths to remind herself that the dream was over. And it was just a dream—just like she'd had thousands of times before.

The shadow had been pursuing her again, chasing her through the forest, and as she ran through the safety of the woods, the branches had snatched at her hands and legs and tried to grab her. She'd seen a bright light up ahead and heard music playing, the soft lyrics of "Somewhere over the Rainbow" fading in and out. She tried to run faster, but suddenly teetered on the edge of a deep hole. She dove for a tree branch to swing across it, but her hands slipped and her fingers scraped the bark, the prickly wood splinters digging into her palms. She felt herself falling, falling, swirling through the air, sinking into nothingness, then slowly waking up.

She shook off the exhaustion and fear that came with the dream and stared at the clock, groaning as she noticed the time. Ten minutes before five. She had to meet the new locksmith in a few minutes.

She padded into the bathroom and washed her face, then retrieved her keys and purse and a few files to work on at home. Switching off the lights, she made her way down the stairs. The remnants of fatigue and her earlier headache weighed on her body, and her muscles felt heavy and achy.

Stepping outside, she wrapped her coat around her and scanned the grassy area. Empty. The gray sky was cold and dark, signifying possible snow, and a chill crept up her spine as the wind howled and whistled through the bare trees. She shivered and glanced around for other people, but the parking lot was amazingly vacant for so early on Friday, and the sunset had diminished with the impending bad weather. She should have listened to the weather forecast. It hardly ever snowed in Georgia, but occasionally an ice storm or light snow would blow through, immobilizing the city. No one was prepared for icy roads, and snowplows were reserved for the major expressways.

Hurrying home would be best, so she opened the car door and climbed in, fighting with the wind as it caught a few strands of her hair and swiped them from her topknot. Something white caught her eye. A towel lay in the passenger seat, all wrapped up. Odd. She hadn't put it there.

Reaching across the seat, she slowly unfolded the edges of the towel, her heart thumping as a red stain came into view. The ends of the towel flopped open and she saw the shiny glint of metal. Blood trickled onto the soft leather of her car seat, and a scream locked in her throat. It was one of her own kitchen knives, covered in blood.

Someone grabbed her arm and a male voice penetrated the eerie silence, calling her name.

"Veronica, what the hell is wrong?"

She turned, wide-eyed, to see Nathan standing beside her car.

"Veronica, what is it?"

A muffled cry escaped her and she pointed with unsteady hands to the seat. Nathan's jaw tightened as he spotted the bloody knife. He helped her from the car.

"Come on, sit in here." Without preamble, he gently shoved her into the front of his own car and radioed for a crime unit. "I want this car searched with a fine-tooth comb."

"I...I got in and it was there," Veronica mumbled, still shivering uncontrollably.

"This game is getting tiresome," Nathan said, gritting his teeth. He pulled Veronica into his embrace, and she relaxed against him, grateful for the warmth of his strong arms.

"It's okay." He rubbed his hand along the base of her spine, and Veronica felt his calm soothing voice wrap around her like a tender caress. "When the crew gets here, I'm taking you home."

"I was supposed to meet the locksmith," Veronica whispered.

"We'll meet him," Nathan said. "And I'll make sure your apartment's secure this time."

"Stay with me," she pleaded, burying her face in his chest.

"Don't worry." He threaded his fingers in her hair. "I'm not going to leave you, Veronica."

Not ever.

Nathan knew the silent vow was a mistake, but he could no more stop himself than he could push Veronica away and let someone else take her case. That would be the smart thing to do. He was definitely too involved. But he would not leave her until he figured out who was trying to hurt her.

And then—he would leave her only if she asked him to.

Her soft body sagged against him, and within minutes he felt the tension drain from her as she relaxed in his arms. She was safe. He knew it now, but he couldn't erase the heart-pounding fear he'd experienced when she hadn't answered the phone. Her firm breasts were pressed against his chest, and the whisper of her breath on his neck had him clinging to her. He'd been scared out of his mind on the way over, imagining all sorts of things that could have happened to her. He buried his face in her hair and inhaled her sweet scent, oblivious to his vow to remain professional.

He needed the reassurance. He needed to know she was safe. And dammit, he needed to hold her as much as she needed to be held.

The blue-and-white rolled up, and he pulled away from Veronica only long enough to give them orders. "I'm taking her home. Be sure to fingerprint the car and the knife. Check the bloodstains for type and bag it all for evidence." He lowered his voice. "I'm going to catch this bastard."

The officers nodded and set to work while he climbed in the car. Veronica looked pale, but she'd composed herself and he glimpsed the courage she'd drawn from all her life. The ride back to her house was silent and filled with tension. He didn't force her to talk, and he realized he needed the time to gather his own thoughts. He'd been frightened. When he'd seen she was safe, he'd wanted to lavish her with kisses and hugs and tear off her clothes, sate his need for her right there in the parking lot. Damn. He'd never felt this way before.

Gathering his calm, he parked, hopped out and went around to the passenger side. She was already climbing out. The locksmith was waiting. Nathan watched the man work while Veronica excused herself. He heard the shower running and imagined her standing naked under the spray of water. He desperately wished he could join her. But he had to make certain the apartment was secure.

And he needed to give Veronica time. He wanted her to be sure she wanted him, not just a warm, comforting body. Because once he took her, she was going to be his.

Forever.

It couldn't be any other way. Not with Veronica.

"Finished," the man said.

Nathan paid him and checked the dead bolts, then called for a pizza and found a bottle of wine in Veronica's cabinet. Making himself at home, he pulled two glasses from the cabinet and poured them nearly full. When the pizza arrived, he paid for it and put it in the oven to stay warm.

Then he settled on the couch with the wine and sipped, thinking of how he'd have to be patient with Veronica. She was a classy woman, an attorney, not a rough-and-tumble sort of woman. If he took her like some macho, needy jerk, he'd scare her to death. He'd have to go slow, to be tender, to make sure his rough callused hands did nothing but pleasure her. Yes, he would take it slow. He would pleasure her before he found his release. Even if it killed him.

Then he would do it over and over and over again until she begged for him to take her one more time.

The fire in his body intensified when she came out wearing a short silky robe. Water droplets lingered in the curve of her breasts and were much too tempting for him to resist. And the bravado she showed made his chest tighten with a feeling he was too afraid to label. He stood, closing the distance between them, until he held her with his legs spread wide, and her delicate body was wedged so close to him he could feel her breath on his neck.

"Veronica, I—"

"Shh," she whispered as she pressed two fingers to his lips. She took the wineglass from him and ran her tongue gingerly around the edge, then brought the clear liquid to her mouth. He watched her inhale the sweet scent of the wine, saw the pleasure it gave her the moment it touched her tongue, and saw the urgent need reflected in her eyes when she licked her lips and swallowed. The curve of her throat was so pale, so enticing, and his body ached with a need only Veronica could satisfy.

He opened his mouth to speak, but she shook her head slowly and the soft sway of her long tresses tumbling around her shoulders sent waves of desire thrumming through him. He looked toward the window where the gray sky had begun showering the earth with light snowflakes.

"It's snowing," he said in an effort to divert his mind.

"It's beautiful," Veronica whispered, not once tearing her gaze from his.

"No, you are."

A slow smile spread on her mouth. The hunger in his body grew at the sight. Veronica finger combed a lock of his hair off his forehead, and the shy gesture seemed so intimate he knew he could never let her go. Even if she wanted him to.

"I was so worried about you," he finally said.

She closed her eyes and leaned against him, and he wrapped his arms around her. "I'm okay now. As long as you're here."

He wound a strand of her beautiful hair around his finger, resisting the temptation to dig his fingers in the long locks. His chest ached with the fear he'd felt earlier. He needed to forget his own needs, though, and take care of her. "Are you hungry?"

He felt her soft laughter against his chest.

"I meant for food. There's a pizza in the oven."

She looked into his eyes, her face serious. "Do you always take care of your...cases so well?"

He swallowed against the sudden rise of emotion in his throat. "You're more than a case and you know it."

Her gaze locked with his. Then she smiled, slow and sweet, and spoke so softly he could barely hear her. "I think we'd better have the pizza."

He laughed and hand in hand they walked to the kitchen. He carried their wine and she took their plates to the den where they sat down on the floor in front of the coffee table. As Veronica sank her teeth into the gooey cheese, he ate his own slice, barely tasting the rich sauce. She smiled and licked her fingertips, and he sipped his wine, his heart hammering in his chest.

"This is nice," Veronica said quietly.

"What? The pizza?"

"No, being here...with you. Just relaxing." She ran her finger along the rim of her glass, and he downed his wine. "It feels so normal, so peaceful."

He tipped her chin up with his thumb and wiped a crumb from the corner of her mouth. "It's okay to feel that way. Things have been difficult for you."

She shook her head. "It seems my whole life has been hard."

He forced her to look into his eyes. "It won't be forever, Veronica. I promise you." He wanted to reassure her, to let her know she had solace from her troubles for a while. But when he lowered his mouth and tasted the tangy wine mixed with Veronica's sweetness, with her strength and determination, he knew he was taking more than he was giving. He needed her courage, her strength, her soft womanly way of facing things and still managing to have a sweet vulnerability about her. Something he'd lost on the force. Something no one could give him but her.

"Veronica, I need you," he said softly.

She cupped his face with her hands and he felt her nod against his chest. Her arms slipped around his waist and she hugged him, ever so gently, then ran her hands up his back and held on to him. She felt so right, so perfect in his arms.

His resolve broke. He captured her mouth in a kiss, his lips devouring everything she offered, his mind a million miles from work. His soul floated in a space it had never been before, mingling and joining with her every breath.

Then she inhaled and the soft curve of her breasts swelled, her nipples pushing taut against the silky fabric, and he grabbed her to him with a need that he could longer hide or deny. "Veronica, if you want me to stop—"

"I don't."

Relieved, he frantically lowered his head and ravished her sweetness, inhaled the soft scent of her soap and tasted the wine and the need in her own urgent mouth as she opened for him. She grasped at his arms and he felt his muscles clench at her seeking hands. Her mouth felt warm and inviting and he plundered the inside with his tongue until her own tongue met his in slow uninhibited thrusts. He nibbled at her lower lip and drove his lower body against hers, crushing her breasts against the fabric of his blue denim shirt and rubbing his hands up and down her back and down to the soft curve of her hips.

"Veronica, I—"

"Don't talk," she whispered. "It feels too good."

It felt like heaven and hell all mixed together as he tortured himself by trying to hold back. Then she dug her fingernails into his back, and he lost control. Sweeping her up in his arms, he carried her to the bedroom, kicking off his shoes as he went, nibbling at her neck and the soft shell of her ear until she writhed in his arms and tugged at his shirt. She pulled it loose and covered his chest with the palms of her hands, raking her fingernails across his hard nipples until he thought he was going to burst from the pleasure.

Still, he forced himself to pause, to drink in the moment when he would see her naked before him. She kicked off her shoes, and he grinned. Easing her to the floor, he met her gaze and read the urgent hunger, and his vow to go slow evaporated like ice on a hot August day. He shoved her robe aside, revealing the creamy mounds of her full breasts, and she moaned and pushed his own shirt over his shoulders, smiling wickedly when it dropped to the floor.

She kissed the base of his throat while he covered her breasts with his hands. Then he squeezed and rolled her nipples with his thumbs until he felt her pushing herself against him and knew she was hot and aching for more. Gently he eased her robe to the floor. Pausing in awe, he drew in a harsh breath as his eyes took in her small waist, her bare torso, her glorious bosom, then drifted lower.

She smiled that shy kind of smile that melted his insides, and his body instinctively pulsed and thrust against her. "Sweetheart, you are so beautiful."

She found the snap of his jeans, and the sound of the snap popping open and the slow rasp of his zipper being lowered made his muscles quake with desire. She pushed his jeans over his hips, and her blatant perusal of his body only heightened the urgency.

"I can't believe you're here like this," Veronica whispered.

He held her hands with his own and studied her face. "You want to stop?"

She shook her head. "No. Will you stay all night?" Veronica asked softly.

"You'll have to kick me out," he said, taking her mouth again and lowering her to the bed. He lay beside her, propped himself on his elbow and gave himself time to enjoy the beauty of her lying naked in the moonlight. Streaks of yellow and bronze streamed through the window, highlighting the tips of her hair and illuminating her face with a golden glow. The soft scent of her shampoo and the fresh bed linens were enticing, the air filled with her womanly fragrance like the aroma of honeysuckle on a warm, spring day. She ran her hands through his hair, down his arms and body. He kissed her again, warming her with the touch of his hands and mouth, tasting the saltiness, the sweetness of her smooth skin.

Then he was on top of her, stroking and petting her, reveling in her soft cries and her pleas for more, loving her body in ways he'd never loved a woman before. Rising above her, he cupped her breasts and licked the tip of her nipple, suckling it and circling it with his tongue, then laving the other nipple as he probed her soft womanhood with his need. He quickly found a condom and slipped it on, then thrust gently until he felt the tip of his body enter hers and saw her tense and close her eyes.

"Veronica, look at me, baby," he ground out. She opened her eyes, and the smile of pleasure and the blatant need he saw made him pause. "You are so wonderful."

She caressed his face with her fingers, and he kissed them, one by one. He traced a path down her arms to her waist, then lower, teasing her body with playful fingers. Veronica groaned and cupped his buttocks with her hands. He lowered his mouth again and consumed her with a kiss that deepened as he pushed inside her, and she moaned with pleasure. She was tight, and her body hugged his as he filled her and pumped himself in and out, her dark eyes wild with emotions. Her chest heaved as he drove her crazy with his hands, taunting her nipples over and over again with his tongue until she begged for more, and when he felt her body convulse around his, he fisted his hand in her hair and dragged her mouth to his, never once letting his gaze leave her face. He wanted to see every moment of her pleasure. Then she gripped his hips and wrapped her legs around him and he groaned in total ecstasy.

Chapter Eleven

Veronica snuggled into Nathan's arms, taking solace in his protective embrace and reveling in the euphoric aftermath of their lovemaking.

She wanted him again. And again. And again.

The soft sandy hairs on his chest tickled her chin as she buried her face against him, and the fact that he kept stroking her back and holding her told her he, too, wanted more. The danger and fear she'd felt earlier evaporated in the face of his strength, and a sense of peace filled her. With Nathan's arms around her she felt safer than she had in a very long time. But what would happen in the morning?

"That was incredible," Nathan whispered in her hair.

Veronica nodded against his chest, then moaned a reply. A deep chuckle resonated from him. He rolled her over and pinned her beneath him, rubbing himself up and down over her body in an intimate gesture that made her gasp. "I want you again."

Veronica smiled. "Well, what's stopping you, Detective?"

He threw his head back and laughed again, so hard that Veronica laughed with him.

"You know that's the first time I've really heard you laugh," Nathan said, his face serious. "It sounds great."

She traced her finger along his stubbled jaw. "It's all because of you."

Their gazes locked and a moment of silent understanding

passed, then Nathan lowered his head and took her mouth in a kiss just as hungry as the first one, and Veronica knew the night was going to be filled with loving and laughter. She prayed it would never end.

Hours later as a sliver of early-morning sunshine peeked its way through the venetian blinds, Nathan awoke with a start. He'd heard a sound.

Someone was outside Veronica's apartment.

Easing his arm from underneath her head, he paused for only a second to take in her quiet beauty as she lay sleeping, her long hair fanned across the pale yellow sheets, her porcelain skin rosy from his lovemaking. He yanked on his jeans, pulled on his shirt without buttoning it and reached for his gun.

Then he heard it again. Footsteps—quiet and slow as if someone were easing their way around the side of the apartment toward her front door.

"Veronica," he whispered, shaking her gently.

Sleepy-eyed, she rolled over and stretched, her breasts rising above the edge of the sheet. Jesus. He wanted her again.

Instead he grabbed her robe. "Here, put this on."

She gave him a puzzled look, but he pressed his finger to her lips to keep her quiet. "I think I hear something outside. I'll be right back."

She sat up, immediately tense. "Don't go."

He smiled slowly, then cupped her face with both his hands. "I'll be okay. It's probably just someone walking their dog."

She nodded, obviously not buying his explanation, but slipped on her robe. "Be careful."

He gave her a quick kiss, then handed her the phone. "Call 911 if you need to." Moving slowly, he made his way through the living room and paused at the door.

He could hear the faint rustle of footsteps in leaves through the hollow wood. He gripped his gun in one hand and eased the door open. A tall man with light brown hair wearing a designer jogging suit was standing in the doorway.

"Freeze. Police."

The thin man's eyes bulged, and he jammed his hands up in the air. "I'm not armed. Don't…don't shoot."

Nathan kept the gun aimed at the man's chest. "Who the hell are you and why are you creeping around outside?"

"I'm—"

"Ron?" The sound of Veronica's voice broke off the man's stuttered words. It took Nathan a moment to realize he was standing face-to-face with Ron Cox, Veronica's old boyfriend. The man who was supposed to be in Savannah.

He felt Veronica move up behind him. "What are you doing here?" he demanded.

"I should be asking you that," Ron said snidely. He started to lower his hands, but Nathan shoved them up and glared at him.

"Let me pat you down first, buddy."

"What?" Ron asked indignantly.

"Nathan, I don't think—"

He ignored them both and did a quick brisk search. When he found Ron clean, he lowered his gun, but not his distrust of the man. He didn't like Cox on sight. He was too clean, too polished, too whiny looking. And he was snooping around Veronica's when he was supposed to be miles away.

"Veronica, what's going on here?" Ron asked, recovering enough from Nathan's intimidation tactics to push his way inside.

She glanced nervously at Nathan and back at Ron. Nathan folded his arms and made no attempt to move.

"I…this is Detective Dawson. He…"

"I'm here to protect Veronica," Nathan supplied.

"Protect her? Is this standard police procedure?" Incredibility hardened Ron's voice as he did an obvious perusal of Nathan's and Veronica's appearances. "It looks like you're doing a whole lot more than that, *buddy*."

Nathan almost laughed at the man for throwing his own word back at him. His anger only made him look more wimpy. Nathan could take him with one simple blow to the solar plexus and the man would never know what hit him.

He also realized Veronica's hair was mussed and she was wearing nothing but her skimpy robe. Her cheeks and face were slightly red from whisker marks. His shirt was unbuttoned and he'd skipped the socks and just slipped on shoes. It looked as if they'd been in bed—doing exactly what they had been doing.

And he wasn't going to apologize or make excuses to this weasel. Veronica, on the other hand, appeared mortified.

"I asked you a question," Ron said to Veronica.

She wrapped her arms around her middle. "It's a long story, Ron. Why don't you come in and I'll make some coffee."

Coffee—Nathan wanted to bark. Were they going to entertain this little bozo? He felt like arresting him, for… for…what, he didn't know yet. Just for being alive and being on Veronica's doorstep.

"Okay," Ron said. "You know I like mine with cream and sugar."

"And you know how I like mine," Nathan added.

Veronica rolled her eyes and hurried to the kitchen. He and Ron simply stood and stared down each other.

"You'd better have a good explanation," Ron said.

"So had you," Nathan replied.

Veronica brought in a tray and pointed to the couch. "Sit."

Nathan smothered a grin at the commanding tone of her voice. She was a little thing but strong and stubborn. Maybe that was the reason he'd fallen in love with her.

In love? He froze, automatically feeling his heart pound at an odd rhythm. He was in love with Veronica. What a fine time to realize it—right in the middle of a confrontation with her former boyfriend.

And lover? Had she slept with this turkey?

"You go first," Veronica said to Ron. "I want to know why you're here."

Ron sighed angrily and pushed his wire-rimmed glasses up on his thin pointed nose. "I was worried about you. I couldn't figure out why you wouldn't return any of my calls."

Nathan saw Veronica's gaze shift to him and back. What

was she thinking? Did he have something to do with the reason she hadn't phoned Ron?

"I told you when I left that it was over, Ron. That I wanted to move on."

"I know," Ron said, avoiding looking at Nathan. "But I thought once you got here, you'd miss me and change your mind." Then he did look at Nathan, a glare that only a man could understand. "But I see you haven't been lonely."

"It's…it's not what you think."

Nathan arched an eyebrow at Veronica. It damn well was what the man thought, and she'd better not deny it.

Ron clicked his teeth. "Come on, Veronica. I'm not stupid."

She ran her hands up and down her thighs in a nervous gesture. "Well, maybe partly. But there's more." She went on to explain about the attack and the threats she'd been getting. Ron's already-white skin turned ghostly pale. His eyes bulged beneath his glasses.

"Oh, my God. You think someone's trying to kill you?"

Veronica shrugged. "Or drive me crazy. I really don't know what to think, except somehow I think everything may be related to my past—the parts I can't remember." She started to explain, but Ron stopped her.

"I know about your parents, Veronica."

She stared at him with her mouth open. "How…when?"

Ron leaned his elbows on his knees. "I've known from the beginning. Old man Owen checks out all the potential employees before he hires them."

"So everyone knows?" Nathan's chest ached at the horrified expression on Veronica's face.

Ron nodded. Nathan watched the exchange with interest. If Ron had known, he could have used her past to torment her. But even though he disliked the man immensely, he sensed Ron genuinely cared for Veronica. Another thought to ponder.

"I'm sorry, Veronica," Ron said, reaching for her hand.

She pulled back. "But why didn't you say something?"

Ron frowned at her withdrawal. "I figured if you wanted to talk about it, you would."

"So I hid it from everyone there for no reason."

"I...I didn't understand why you wouldn't talk about it," Ron said.

The true concern in Ron's voice struck a nerve in Nathan. At least the man had one good point—he hadn't cared about Veronica's past. And his gut instinct told him Cox wouldn't hurt her.

So, did Veronica still care for him?

"How long have you been in town?" Nathan asked, remembering the dark sedan that had followed them.

"A couple of days," Ron said, looking sheepish.

"So you were here in Oakland when you called me?" Veronica asked.

Ron nodded. "Yeah, I wanted to ask you if I could come over, but you sounded too distracted. I couldn't figure out what was going on. Then I saw you with him." Ron glared at Nathan.

"And you followed us?" Nathan asked.

"Yes."

Veronica's eyes widened. "You did what?"

"I only wanted to find out who he was. And how involved the two of you were." Ron gave Veronica a hurt look. "I guess I got my answer."

"I'm sorry, Ron," Veronica said quietly. "I really am. You're a good friend, but like I told you in Florida, that's all it can ever be. When I met Detective—"

"You don't have to explain about us," Nathan cut in.

"Yeah, I think I'd rather not hear the details," Ron said sarcastically.

Veronica wrung her hands together as the tension crackled through the room.

Ron finally stood, jammed his hands in his pockets in a gesture of defeat and faced Nathan. "You'd better not take advantage of her."

"I can take care of myself," Veronica snapped.

Nathan pushed himself up and shook his head. "I'm going to catch the creep who's doing this."

"Can I see you alone for a moment?" Ron asked Veronica.

Nathan waited, hoping she'd say no. Instead she looked to him and arched her beautiful eyebrows. "Do you mind?"

Nathan's hands fisted by his sides, but he gave her a brief nod and stepped into the bedroom. He paced back and forth across the room, his mind reeling. What did the two of them have to talk about that he couldn't hear? What was Veronica saying to him? When this mess was over, would she go back to that wimp?

No. He damn well wouldn't let her. She was his now. And if he had to make love to her over and over all day, he'd prove it to her.

A few minutes later he couldn't stand it any longer. He opened the door and saw Ron lean over and kiss Veronica on the cheek. "I hope you find what you came here for," he told her softly. Then he turned and walked out the door.

Veronica had wondered if the "morning after" would be uncomfortable, but *awkward* didn't begin to describe the incident with Ron. She stole a glance at Nathan over the fresh blueberry muffins she'd made after Ron left, and saw him watching her, something he'd been doing intently since Ron had walked out the door.

"These are delicious," he said.

Forcing a smile, she broke her muffin in two and watched Nathan lick his lips. A crumb clung to the corner of his mouth and she was tempted to lick it off. Last night she would have.

This morning she didn't feel quite so bold.

"So what did Ron want during your little private talk?"

His tone sounded mild, but Veronica could read his eyes now, and they held more than simple curiosity. And more than just interest in her case. They held heat and the remnants of their night of passion—the same wonderful memories hovering in the front of her own mind. And she also thought she detected a hint of jealousy. Could the handsome detective have feelings for her?

"He wanted me to be careful, that's all."

"And?"

"And that's all. It's over between us," Veronica said quietly. She didn't know if that was the answer he wanted to hear, but she wasn't into playing games, not with either man.

"Good." Nathan slurped his coffee and grinned. "I don't share my women, Veronica."

Veronica almost choked on her food. "Your what?"

Nathan wiped his mouth. "Excuse me—my woman."

Veronica stared at him, remembering the mindless pleasure he'd given her. What a totally barbaric thing to say. Then suddenly she laughed and so did Nathan.

"It's Saturday. Do you have to work?" he asked.

She cleared the table. "I need to do some errands."

"Want a bodyguard?" Nathan asked coming up behind her and circling her waist with his arms. "'Cause I like guarding your body."

Veronica moaned as he nibbled at the sensitive skin at the base of her neck. "Don't you have work to do?"

"Protecting you is my work," he whispered against her hair.

"Is that all I am? A job?" Veronica bit her tongue as the words came out, mortified she'd revealed so much of her feelings.

Nathan spun her around. The anger in his eyes made her stiffen in his arms. "You know you're not."

"I…I'm sorry."

He cupped her face and lowered his head, devouring her mouth with his. When he finally broke the kiss, she could hardly breathe.

"I need to take a shower," she said softly.

Nathan grinned. "So do I."

An hour later, after they'd made wonderful love in the shower, Nathan drove Veronica to her office to retrieve her car.

"I'm going to the precinct to check on the labwork. Will you be all right?"

"Yes," she said. "I have a little paperwork to catch up on."

"I'll bring steaks tonight," Nathan offered.

"I'll pick up some wine."

After he walked her to her office and checked the inside, he kissed her and waved goodbye. She waved back, and a strange feeling overcame him. He zeroed in on her hand. Veronica was right-handed.

Aha. That was it. He'd known from the beginning she hadn't tried to commit suicide. And he couldn't wait to explain his theory to Ford and watch the detective's face.

A few minutes later he stood in front of Ford's desk. "I figured something out today."

"What?" Ford asked as he wolfed down his second bear claw.

"Veronica is right-handed."

"So?"

"When her wrist was cut during that first attack, it was her right wrist. If a right-handed person tried to commit suicide, she'd cut her left wrist, not her right."

Nathan saw the moment Ford conceded. His furrowed eyebrows formed a straight bushy line. "You might be right."

"I am right," Nathan said. "Tell me what you found on the prints off her car."

"Nothing," Ford said. "Oh, except her secretary's. You asked me to check into her, too."

"Her prints were on Veronica's car?"

"Yeah, but she works with her, doesn't she? Maybe she took something to her car for her."

Nathan nodded. "It's possible. Does she have a record?"

Ford licked the powdery sugar from his lips. "For prostitution in '88."

"Ahh, interesting." Nathan let the idea churn around in his mind. Louise Falk worked for Veronica, had access to her keys, her car and perhaps her house. But why would she hurt Veronica? Even if Veronica had known about her past, which he didn't think she did, Veronica had given her a job.

"Final report on the bloody knife in the car," Ford said. "Blood was from a butcher shop, not a human's."

"So, someone is trying to drive Veronica crazy."

"But why?"

"It has to be her past. But Louise Falk doesn't fit. If she did know Veronica as a child, she was just a kid herself."

"I'll check into Falk's family," Ford said.

"Good work," Nathan said, realizing the two of them were actually working together. "I'm going to check out some of the people in Mr. Miller's date book. Maybe the key in discovering who's threatening Veronica is to find the person responsible for murdering the Millers."

"So you don't think it was a murder-suicide?"

"Veronica doesn't," Nathan said. "And I believe her."

Ford shook his head. "I hope you're right."

He remembered a similar conversation with his former partner, only his partner had been wrong. But this was different. And sometimes a cop's instincts led him to the truth.

Only problem was, Nathan wasn't sure he hoped he was right—if he was and the murderer was in town and afraid of being discovered, Veronica was in terrible danger.

VERONICA WAS LEAVING her office when the phone rang. Thinking it was business, she hurried back to answer it. "Veronica Miller speaking."

"Ms. Miller, this is Alma Jones. We met at my grandson's campaign kickoff party."

"Yes, you're Eli's mother. I remember." How could she forget the withered old woman who'd been so unfriendly to her?

"My granddaughter, Tessa, said she had lunch with you yesterday."

"Well, it wasn't exactly lunch. I'm afraid I wasn't feeling well and had to leave before our food arrived." Had Eli's family decided to welcome her into their tight-knit group?

"Listen, I'd appreciate it if you would stay away from my family. What with Gerald running for the senate, our family can't use any negative publicity right now. You understand, don't you?''

"What?" First Eli didn't want her to see Gerald, now his mother wanted her to stay away from the whole family.

"Murdering your own parents was bad enough, but I won't let you harm any of my children."

Veronica gasped. She'd heard rumors that some people thought she was a child murderer, but no one had ever said it to her face. Anger hurriedly replaced her hurt. "Look, Mrs. Jones, I don't have any intention of interfering with your family. In fact, I don't even want to be a part of it." Veronica slammed down the phone and dropped her face into her hands, her pulse racing. How dare the woman.

Still reeling fifteen minutes later when she parked at the hospital for her appointment with Dr. Sandler, she did the relaxation exercises the psychiatrist in Florida had taught her. Taking deep breaths and imagining herself on a quiet, deserted island helped. Only the island wasn't deserted—Nathan was there. And it was perfect, a romantic haven where problems didn't exist, where their love could blossom and they could make love beneath the stars every night with only the moon watching them and the sound of waves lapping at the shore.

Feeling better, she made her way through the quiet hospital corridors and up to Dr. Sandler's office. She offered him a calm smile when he greeted her.

"Well, Ms. Miller, it's a pleasure. You've turned into a beautiful young woman."

Veronica blushed as he gave her a firm handshake. You could tell a lot about a person from a handshake. "Thanks. I'm afraid I don't remember much about you."

"Of course not. The last time I saw you, well, it wasn't under the best of circumstances." He offered her a sympathetic look, which she tried to ignore.

"I know." Veronica settled into one of the leather chairs flanking his massive oak desk. "I wanted to talk to you about what happened."

Dr. Sandler folded his hands, and Veronica had an eerie

feeling that the next few minutes were crucial. "I want to know what I said when I was a child. You know, after my parents' death."

"Why now?" Dr. Sandler asked.

Veronica told him about the threats.

"I know. I talked with that young detective yesterday who's working on your case."

"You what?" Veronica felt as if the wind had been knocked out of her.

"Dawson, I believe he said. I thought you probably gave him my name."

She shook her head, stunned. He'd lied to her. Why hadn't Nathan told her? Was he checking up on her? Hurt spiraled through her, and it took her several seconds to regain her composure.

"Relax, Ms. Miller. I didn't disclose anything confidential. I pride myself on my ethical practice."

"Of course." Veronica breathed a sigh of relief, her anger growing. He had spent the night with her, made love with her until dawn, but he hadn't told her he'd asked a psychiatrist about her. Did he think she was crazy? Or did he believe she could have killed her own parents?

"Um, Ms. Miller?" The doctor checked his watch. "I have to see patients soon."

"Oh, yes." Veronica collected herself. "I've had these recurring nightmares all my life. A big ominous shadow is chasing me, trying to catch me. One doctor told me it was a child's way of compensating for the fear I felt, that the shadow represents death. But I think the shadow is a person's face. I think I'm seeing a vision of the person who killed my parents."

Dr. Sandler's eyes narrowed in concentration. "Either one is possible. Have you tried hypnosis?"

"Yes. But nothing happened. I wondered, did I say anything to give you a clue as to who killed my parents?"

The doctor shifted, obviously uncomfortable.

"Please tell me the truth."

"Ms. Miller, you were very small and fragile, in shock."

"What did I say?"

"You mentioned a big, dark shadow."

"But the police didn't think anyone else was there?"

Dr. Sandler shook his head. "No." He paused, then continued. "The only other thing you said was that it was your fault. You kept saying it over and over—'It was my fault. My parents died because of me.'"

Veronica's throat closed. It couldn't be true. She couldn't have killed her father and mother. But if she hadn't, then who had? And why did she feel so guilty?

AFTER CHECKING Veronica's father's date book and the list of people presently living in the town against those who were around at the time of his death, Nathan found only four names that ranked as possibilities. Alma and Gerald Jones were two of them. Scroggins was another. The last was a girl named Susan Pritchard. At the time she'd been seventeen, and would now have been thirty-seven. Only, she had died in a car accident within a few days of Veronica's parents' deaths. Her parents still lived in town. Nathan made a quick phone call, but the Pritchards weren't home, so he decided to swing by and visit Gerald and his grandmother.

The Jones family had been a founder of the town, and Alma knew everyone who lived in Oakland. He'd heard the woman was a society matriarch and would do anything to ensure her son's future in politics. Now Gerald had been added to the repertoire of her protective arms.

He drove to the mansion and pulled up in the big circular drive, amazed to see gardeners tending the lawn in the heart of winter. A distinguished, stiff-looking butler greeted him and showed him to the formal sitting room where Alma Jones sat. Wearing a long golden robe and feathered slippers, she looked as regal as a queen on a throne. Her gnarled fingers took away slightly from the powerful image, but her cool assessing eyes and pointed chin made up the difference.

"What can I do for you, Detective?"

The obvious distaste she had for his position in life came

through loud and clear. "I want to discuss something that happened a few years ago."

"Is this about that Miller woman?"

Nathan hesitated, wondering how she knew. Then he quickly realized Alma knew everything. She probably paid spies to collect gossip for her.

"Yes, in a way. Why do you ask?"

"I saw the two of you cavorting at Gerald's party."

Perceptive woman. "Actually, I'm looking into an old murder case—the Millers."

"You mean that murder-suicide?" The woman's lower lip curled into a look of disdain that only a true snob could pull off. "It was a horrid thing for the community. And I did feel sorry for that poor child."

"I heard that you and your son visited her in the hospital."

Shock widened the woman's eyes momentarily, but she quickly masked it and fanned her face, her diamonds glittering as she waved her hand back and forth. "Yes, Eli was… worried. And in his position, we thought it was a good move to show concern for the child."

"So, you did it to impress the cameras?" A bitter taste filled Nathan's mouth.

"That was part of it. And as senator, Eli felt a certain responsibility. The town supported him, he felt he owed it to help console that little girl in her tragedy."

"You scratch my back, I'll scratch yours."

The old woman smiled as if she was glad he understood. His stomach clenched.

"Mrs. Jones, Mr. Miller's date book indicates you and your grandson visited him the week before he died."

Yellow tinged the old woman's white pallor as she dug her bony fingers into the kerchief in her lap. "Yes. He was the only lawyer in town. He handled some financial affairs for us."

"And Gerald? He was only—what, around twenty back then?"

"Eighteen, but he had a trust fund. Miller was overseeing its executions."

She had an answer for everything. The quickness of her reply struck him as odd, almost as if she'd practiced her response. "Actually, Detective Dawson, I hated to mention this after the poor family's death, but I was withdrawing my accounts from Mr. Miller."

"Oh?"

"Yes." The old woman tethered. "There was some gossip that he wasn't quite on the up-and-up. And my family certainly couldn't have had our name associated with someone of that caliber."

"I see." Nathan studied the old woman. She was cunning and definitely out to protect her family. But at what cost? "And you think that might have had something to do with the deaths?"

"Who knows?" The woman toyed with the emerald on her left hand. "Perhaps someone found out and Mr. Miller was so distraught he killed himself."

Or he was in with the wrong people and they murdered him. The implication came through loud and clear. Nathan's gut pinched. He didn't want to tell Veronica this latest insight. If it were true, she would be crushed.

"Was Eli here the night the Millers died?"

"Oh, no. He was away on the campaign." She smiled, fluttering her long gray eyelashes. "But he came back right away to check on the child."

Nathan stood. He'd had enough of Alma Jones and her condescending snobbery. "Is Eli here?"

"No, he and Barbara are hosting a charity event tonight."

"How about Gerald?"

As cool as Mrs. Jones appeared, anxiety streaked her face. "He's in his office. But I believe he's busy. You could make an appointment with his secretary."

"That's okay. I think I'll just knock." Nathan remembered seeing an office on the main floor the night of the party. He had a feeling it was Gerald's. "Thanks for your time, Mrs. Jones."

"Certainly." The woman nodded stiffly, dismissing him.

He found Gerald's office and tapped on the door.

"Come in."

Nathan opened the door and tried not to gawk at the elaborate furnishings. Gerald's office contained more furniture than his entire apartment, and the price of his sleek cherry desk probably tripled the cost of Nathan's entire living room set.

"To what do I owe this visit?" Gerald asked with his usual smooth politician's smile.

Nathan made himself comfortable in one of the leather wing chairs. He gave a short rendition of his search into the Miller case. "I wondered what business you had with Mr. Miller years ago."

Gerald's false smile slipped slightly. "I didn't have business with him," Gerald said. "I was only a young boy."

Nathan hesitated, remembering Alma Jones's story. "You didn't go to see him about a trust?"

Gerald looked puzzled for a moment. "Oh, yes, I did have a trust. I don't remember what day it was that I was scheduled to see Mr. Miller, though. In fact, I never made the meeting."

"You didn't meet with him at all that week?"

Gerald shook his head. "Not at all. Now, if there isn't anything else, I have an important call to make."

Feeling dismissed, Nathan stood and left, an uneasy premonition settling inside him. For some reason he couldn't pinpoint, he sensed Gerald was lying.

VERONICA GATHERED the mail, and after flipping through the assortment of junk pieces and bills, stared at an unmarked envelope. Ripping it open, her chest squeezed at the sight of the newspaper articles enclosed. They were all about her parents' deaths. She immediately glanced around her to see if anyone was watching. Who had sent the unmarked envelope? And why?

Tired of being afraid, she summoned her courage and opened the door to her apartment. The minute she stepped inside, she knew someone had been there. Were they still there?

The apartment smelled like a man's cologne, but not like Nathan's. It was some sickly sweet smell that lingered in the air like rotten fruit. And the furniture had all been rearranged in her living room. Her hands trembled and fear mushroomed in her stomach. Her sofa was against the far wall, the chairs sectioned off to form their own conversation group and the coffee table had been pushed to the side. Magazines lay scattered on the floor, and the cushions from the couch were stacked in a tall pile. Who would do such a strange thing? Was someone playing with her mind?

Her temper flared. An intruder had once again violated her personal domain. Some sicko who wanted to drive her crazy.

Pausing at the door, she listened for the intruder and prepared to bolt. How had they managed to get in with the new locks she'd had installed? Anger overrode her fear. She wasn't crazy. Someone was out to get her. Maybe the same person who had killed her parents.

A deep voice sounded behind her, and she screamed. Firm hands grabbed her.

"Veronica, stop, it's me, Nathan."

It took a second for his voice to register and when it did, embarrassment flooded her face. "I'm sorry."

"Shh. No, I am." He gently wrapped his arms around her, and she sagged against him. "I'm so sorry, sweetheart. I didn't mean to startle you. What's going on?"

"I just got home," she said in a dull voice. "It looks like the new locks didn't work."

Nathan cursed and released her. He drew his gun and pushed her behind him. She remembered her talk with the psychiatrist, and followed Nathan into the apartment, a mixture of anger and hurt spiraling inside her. He hastily searched her apartment, but Veronica knew it would be empty. Whoever was doing this was too clever to be caught. And right now, her heart was breaking from wondering why Nathan had seen Dr. Sandler behind her back. She'd told herself that having his comfort and body was enough, that if he walked away from her, once the case was solved, she would be fine. But she realized she wanted much more. She wanted his love. And she didn't want him to leave. For the first time in her life, she'd started to envision a future with a man instead of being alone.

She stood silently in the living room, one hand clinging to the sofa arm for support. When Nathan sauntered back into the room, he threw the dead bolt, then stuffed his gun inside his jacket and stared at her, fury in his eyes. "Are you all right?"

Veronica nodded as her mind filled with memories of his hands pleasuring her and his arms closing around her. He was beside her in a flash, curling his hands around her arms. "What's wrong?"

"I went to see Dr. Sandler today," she said quietly. "Only he told me he'd already talked to you about me."

The look of guilt that washed over his face only made her feel worse.

"Why did you do it?" Veronica asked. Then she finally voiced the question that had been eating at her all afternoon. "Do you think I killed my parents?"

Chapter Twelve

Sensing the importance of his answer to her question, Nathan considered lying. But he wanted a relationship with Veronica based on trust, and that came from being honest. So he forced a calm into his voice he didn't feel after seeing her apartment disturbed, and stroked her arms up and down with his hands.

"Do you?" Veronica asked. Hurt kindled in her eyes.

"No," he said. "I don't."

He saw relief flicker briefly across her face, then the anger returned. "Then why did you talk to him about me?"

"Let's sit down and I'll explain," Nathan said, leading her to the sofa. She sank down beside him, her posture stiff.

"I went because I'm trying to find out what's going on here." He motioned around the apartment. "And if your old boyfriend or one of your clients isn't responsible, then it must have to do with your past."

"I think so, too," Veronica said in a quiet voice.

He took her hand in his, but she remained tense. "I thought it might be helpful if the doctor could give me some information about your condition when they brought you in as a child."

"You want to know if I'm a basket case," she accused.

"No, that's not it," Nathan said. "I want to understand you, Veronica." He ran his finger in a circle around her palm, speaking softly. "I want to help you."

His comment silenced her. She simply stared at him in disbelief.

"That's the truth." He squeezed her hand between both of his. "I don't know much about amnesia, especially when it results from childhood trauma. I hoped the doctor could help me understand it." He paused, watching her face as her anger faded. "I also thought he might have remembered something you said that could help us."

"That's the reason I went," Veronica admitted. "What did he tell you?"

"Nothing confidential," Nathan said.

She smiled. "He didn't tell me much, either, except that I blamed myself."

"That's probably normal for a child," he said. "I know kids from divorced families who think it's their fault."

"I guess you're right." Veronica shivered, and Nathan warmed her hands between his. "I can't help but think there's more to it, though."

"What makes you say that?"

"I don't know. Just a feeling." She leaned back against the sofa, her face weary.

Nathan drew her into his arms. "Don't be angry with me, Veronica. I really want to understand you." He caressed her back with his hands, easing the tension from her shoulders with his tender ministrations.

She gazed into his eyes. "I'm not angry. But it's important to me that you believe me."

Nathan cupped her face in the palms of his hands, his mouth a whisper away. "I do believe you. And we're going to solve this together." Lowering his head slowly, he inhaled her intoxicating scent and pressed his lips onto the soft edges of her mouth. "You're not alone, Veronica. Not anymore."

Seducing her with words felt so heavenly and so right, and as Veronica relaxed in his arms, he absorbed the excited shivers of her body into his soul. He loved her, with every breath and inch of his body and heart, and he intended to show her.

Her hands eagerly clutched him, and when she pulled at his

clothes, he grinned and bit the sensitive area of her throat, pleasuring her with his tongue as he plunged inside her welcoming mouth and thrust his body against hers. She gripped his muscles and dug her fingernails into his skin, tugging him closer, and he slid her silken blouse down until he saw the soft crevice between her breasts, the glorious peaks already rising for his attention. Pushing her lace-covered bra down to expose her flesh, he laved her nipples until she cried out and begged for more.

"Nathan, please. I want you."

"I want you, too, sweetheart." With one quick movement he shoved her slacks down her thighs, his tongue tracing a pattern from her pelvis to her delicious toes. Then he feathered kisses along the insides of her thighs. She moaned and tried to pull him up. "No, let me love you," he whispered against her soft delicate skin. She dug her hands in his hair, and he pushed her legs open to reveal the heart of her womanhood, then lowered his mouth and loved her until she writhed beneath him. Then he drank of her heat and reveled in the pleasure of her sweet taste.

"Please, oh, please, Nathan, I want to feel you." Jerking off his clothes, he rolled to his back and pulled her on top of him. She straddled his thighs and the look of pure joy in her expression made him crazy. She tortured him with kisses.

Her tongue caressed him and her fingers gripped his buttocks until he jerked her hands away and pulled her over him. She straightened slowly, her breasts a beautiful vision as her long hair swept against her creamy skin. And when she sank onto his manhood he moaned and clung to her, kneading her breasts, rising up to suckle the rosy tips, then pulling her down harder and faster until they were both crying out in release.

Nathan tightened his arms possessively around her and closed his eyes. The moment was perfect. Feeling sated and still hot at the same time, he knew it would be another long night of lovemaking. He wished he'd never doubted her, wished he'd been able to say he believed her from the start, but he was too much of a detective not to question every aspect of a case. This time his investigation had led him to love.

Should he tell Veronica his feelings, or was she too confused to know what her feelings were? He was experienced enough to know danger heightened adrenaline and sexual interest, and it was easy for a cop and the person he was protecting to get involved. But usually it didn't last. If she had feelings for him, would she still have them when things calmed down?

She turned to him with her dark eyes sparkling and threaded her hands in his hair. "You make me feel whole."

Nathan hugged her to him, touched by her admission, then carried her to bed. He had never been happier, and he wanted to tell her, but not until the case was solved and there was nothing between them. Then she smothered his mouth with a mind-boggling kiss and he forgot to talk. And when dawn broke the next morning, and she was still sleeping in his arms, he lay there watching her, savoring every moment.

VERONICA AWOKE the next morning, patted the bed beside her and felt a moment's disappointment when it was empty. Had Nathan left? Her heart stopped momentarily, and she realized the feeling was nothing compared to what she would feel if he left for good.

"Hi, sleepyhead." Nathan grinned as he carried a tray into her room.

She tried to hide her surprise. "I thought you'd gone."

"I'd never leave without saying goodbye."

Veronica's smile slipped and Nathan arched an eyebrow. "I told you I'm not going anywhere, darling. Trust me." He leaned over and planted a quick kiss on her lips. "Now let's eat."

"Eat?" Veronica stared at the tray in surprise. "You made French toast?"

"Sure," Nathan said, wiggling his eyebrows. "I'm a man of many talents."

Veronica laughed, wrapped the sheet around her and shoved her hair from her eyes. "Okay, sit."

Nathan stretched out beside her. "Actually I'm so tired from slaving over the stove, I was hoping you'd feed me."

His puppy-dog expression and sudden look of fatigue was so comical Veronica burst into laughter. "Okay, baby, open wide."

Nathan did. And seconds later he had his mouth full, but the French toast sat untouched.

Several long minutes later, Veronica lay back, thoroughly sated and Nathan once again handed her the breakfast tray.

"It's cold," he said, feigning disappointment.

"I thought it was pretty hot myself," Veronica said.

He laughed. "The food, silly."

She nuzzled his neck. "It was worth it."

Nathan kissed her soundly, then they both sipped juice and devoured the food. "Did you find out anything else yesterday?" Veronica asked.

"I checked your father's date book."

"And?"

"And Gerald Jones and his grandmother both had appointments with him the week he died."

"Gerald? He must have been a teenager then."

"Eighteen. Sonny was a kid, closer to your age," he said, dabbing his mouth with a napkin. "His grandmother said he talked with your father about a trust. But something about the way Gerald acted made me think I didn't get the whole story."

"Hmm." Veronica tucked the sheet around her. "That gets us nowhere. We know my parents and Eli were friends."

Nathan scratched his chin. "Yeah, but Eli's mother acted suspicious to me, like she might be covering up something."

"Really?" She furrowed her brow. "I had an interesting chat with her yesterday myself."

He tucked a strand of her hair behind her ear. "What happened?"

Veronica told him about Alma's less-than-friendly phone call.

"What a witch," Nathan said, chopping his toast into pieces.

"Snobbery's everywhere," she said. "Believe me, I know."

"And politicians are the worst. Always worried about their image."

"That's what Gerald said. It must be awful at times."

"It's the life they choose." Nathan squeezed her hand. "There's one other family I need to talk to. And I'd like to talk to Daryl Scroggins again. He seemed reluctant for me to dig up the past."

"I'd like to go with you," Veronica said.

"Okay. You want the shower first?"

"Who says we have to take turns?"

Nathan laughed and motioned for her to lead the way, but as he crept off the bed, he heard a thump. Something slipped from between the mattress and boxspring and fell to the floor. A hypodermic syringe. He stared at it, his thoughts racing back to the first time he'd been called to Veronica's apartment when she'd been attacked and they'd found a sleep-inducing drug in her system. She had insisted she hadn't taken anything.

"Nathan?" When he looked up, Veronica stood beside him. He pointed to the syringe.

She gasped. "Where did that come from?"

"It must have been caught in the mattress. It fell out when we got up."

"Well, what's it doing here?" She leaned over and started to pick it up, but he ordered her not to touch it.

"Do you keep hypodermics here for any reason?"

"Of course not." Her mouth dropped open as she realized the implications. "It's not mine. I've never seen it before. I don't even like needles."

Nathan hurried to the kitchen, retrieved a plastic bag and sealed up the needle. When he went back to the bedroom, Veronica had her robe on and her arms folded. She glared at him. "You still suspect me?"

He shook his head. "I'm going to have it dusted for prints. Maybe it's the missing clue we've been looking for."

"What do you mean?"

"Remember that night you were attacked?"

"I'll never forget it." Veronica shivered, and he hated that he'd reminded her of that horrible night.

"The report confirmed a sleep-inducing drug in your system. But you insisted you didn't take any sleeping pills."

"I didn't."

"Well, maybe someone helped you along."

AFTER DROPPING OFF the needle at the lab, Nathan drove to Daryl Scroggins's house. For a retired cop, he certainly seemed to have done well for himself. The thought hadn't occurred to him the first time he'd visited Scroggins, but this time a seed of awareness niggled at his consciousness. How had Scroggins been able to retire and pay for this place on a cop's salary?

"Are you sure you want to do this?" Nathan asked as he parked and faced Veronica.

"Yes." She gave him a brave smile.

"It can't be easy for you to hear about your parents."

"It isn't," Veronica said. "But it's important I do. I've been running from it long enough."

Nathan kissed her hand. "Remember, I'm here with you."

When Scroggins saw Veronica and Nathan at his door, he tried to shut it.

"No, you don't." Nathan wedged the door open with his foot. "We have some unfinished business, Scroggins."

"I told you to leave the past alone," Scroggins said, glaring at him and then Veronica.

"I don't give a damn what you said," Nathan barked. "I want some answers." He nudged Veronica into the doorway. "And I think you owe Ms. Miller the truth."

Beads of perspiration exploded on Scroggins's forehead, and Nathan thought for a moment the man was going to have a heart attack. Scroggins pressed his hand over his chest and heaved for air.

"I'm not going anywhere," Nathan said more calmly. "So why don't we have a little chat, Scroggins."

Scroggins dragged a handkerchief from his pocket and wiped his forehead. Finally he waved them into his den. Nathan was struck again by the plush surroundings. "You sure did well for yourself when you retired," Nathan said casually. He met Scroggins's gaze. "Must have had some investments on the side."

Scroggins glared at him and settled his round body into a chair, then picked up a glass of whiskey and downed it.

Veronica seated herself in a chair. She knotted her hands in her lap as her gaze swept the surroundings. Several photos of the Jones family caught Nathan's eye. He focused on an eight-by-ten of Scroggins accepting some kind of award. The senator was congratulating him. So…they were close.

Scroggins was probably in the senator's pocket.

"I want to know everything you know about the Millers' deaths," Nathan said.

Scroggins gestured toward Veronica. "Is that what you want, little Missy?"

"My name is Veronica, Mr. Scroggins. And yes, I want to know. Everything."

Scroggins winced at her irritated tone, then rubbed his balding spot. "Well, there ain't much to tell that ain't already been said. I got a call, disturbing the peace. Raced over to your place."

"How long did it take you to get there?" Nathan asked.

Scroggins thought for a minute. "I'd say about fifteen minutes."

"Fifteen minutes?" Nathan asked incredulously. "Then someone else could have been there and left?"

"I know that," Scroggins said. "But there wasn't any evidence to prove it. Believe me, I looked."

"So, you deemed it a murder-suicide?" Veronica asked.

"Wasn't nothing else I could do."

Nathan kept one eye on Scroggins while glancing around the room. "You wouldn't be covering up for someone, would you?"

Scroggins bolted up from the chair. "What the hell are you implying?"

"That someone paid you to keep quiet," Nathan growled.

"I would never cover up murder," Scroggins snarled back.

Nathan raised his brows in question. He saw Veronica shift uncomfortably. "What *would* you cover up?" she asked.

Scroggins's long pause only confirmed his guilt.

"Answer her," Nathan said. "If you don't, I'll make sure the lieutenant brings you in for questioning. And you know how reporters in a small town can make that look."

Scroggins dropped into his chair, looking defeated. He wiped his forehead with his handkerchief. "The report on your parents was accurate," Scroggins said. He looked at Veronica with such remorse that Nathan found it hard to believe he wasn't telling the truth. "I really did try to find out who killed them. But there wasn't any evidence. And once reporters got wind of the fact that you were holding the bloody knife... well..."

"You let them believe it was a murder-suicide to protect me?"

Veronica's face paled. He hadn't considered the fact that Scroggins had protected Veronica.

"I knew you were too little to do such a thing. But the media thought it was a great story, and I've seen the way they do things before. They can't convict you through the paper, but they can ruin your life." Scroggins exhaled loudly. "I figured you'd been through enough already. If I couldn't find the killer, least I could do was let you off the hook from those leeches. And if the killer was still around, I was afraid he'd come after you."

Veronica dabbed at her eyes, and Nathan fought the temptation to comfort her. She straightened her shoulders, and once again he admired her fortitude. "Thank you, Mr. Scroggins," she said. "I appreciate what you did."

"You realize Veronica's life may be in danger now," Nathan said. "She may have seen the real murderer. If there's anything you can tell us that will help, we need to know."

Scroggins folded his fingers in his lap. "I did cover up something, but I didn't think it was connected to the murder. I ain't proud of it, but I didn't see any harm at the time."

"What?"

"I think I know the person who might have burned Miller's files."

Veronica's eyes widened. "Who? Why would someone do that?"

"That's just it. It didn't have anything to do with your parents' death."

"Explain, Scroggins," Nathan said.

"I had a theory but I never could prove it. This little teenager in the town got pregnant. She'd been to see your daddy, Ms. Miller."

"For what?"

"A paternity suit?" Nathan guessed.

Scroggins nodded.

Nathan snapped his fingers. "Let me guess—Susan Pritchard?"

Scroggins poured himself another drink. "She was just a young little thing. Turned out files didn't even need to be burned."

"Why is that?" Nathan asked.

"Little gal died in a car wreck a few days later. No one would ever have known about the baby."

"And who do you think burned the files, the baby's father?" Veronica asked.

Scroggins leaned on his knees. "Seems logical."

"Who was the father?" Nathan asked, losing his patience.

"You'd have to ask the girl's parents."

"Come on, you have an idea," Nathan said.

Scroggins looked down at the floor. "My best guess—it was our next senator—Gerald Jones."

"I WONDER if Eli knew," Veronica said, once they'd settled back in the car.

"Probably," Nathan said in disgust. "If not, I'd say the

odds were his mother did. Alma Jones struck me as the type who'd take care of her family at all costs.''

Veronica shivered. "Do you think she'd murder for them?''

"Who knows? I'd like to talk with the Pritchards next though.''

Ten minutes later they arrived at a wooden clapboard house situated on an old country road. The house needed a paint job, and various car parts as well as an old Mustang jacked up for repairs littered the front yard.

"Far cry from the Jones's,'' Nathan said under his breath.

"You think that's why Gerald wouldn't marry her?'' Veronica asked.

"Eighteen-year-old boy, son of a politician in the middle of a campaign, with his own goals set for office—yeah, I think that's why.''

"That's awful,'' Veronica said. "How could Eli raise a son so shallow?''

Nathan clutched her hand in his as they made their way up the overgrown drive. "That's the life of a politician, remember?''

"But Eli wasn't that way,'' she said.

Nathan studied her. "You really care about him, don't you?''

"Well, he is my godfather. He wrote me all those years and helped finance my college.''

"Like I said, I have a feeling Alma Jones took care of Gerald, and Eli.''

Nathan knocked on the door. They heard a dog barking, then the door screeched open. A small, frail-looking woman wearing a black knit shawl peered at them though the mesh of the screened door. "Who is it?''

"Mrs. Pritchard, my name is Detective Dawson, and this is Veronica Miller. We'd like to talk to you.''

"'Bout what?'' The woman wrapped the shawl tightly around her. "Has my husband been selling moonshine again?''

Nathan smothered a laugh. "No, ma'am. I'll explain if you'll just let us come in."

The older woman took a minute to decide. "You got five minutes, buddy boy," she said, pointing to a raggedy blue couch. Nathan and Veronica sat down, and Nathan explained briefly who he and Veronica were, skipping the details about the threats on Veronica, but focusing on the fact that she couldn't remember her parents and was trying to piece together the past.

"We thought you might help us." Nathan lowered his voice in sympathy. "I understand you lost your daughter twenty years ago, and that she was pregnant."

The old woman's gray eyes grew angry. "Who told you that?"

"It doesn't matter," Nathan said. "But it is important to us to find out the truth. Ms. Miller may be in danger." The lady's eyes softened as she looked at Veronica. She started to cry. "We still miss our Susan. Joe didn't even know about the baby."

Veronica patted her hand. "I'm sorry you lost her, especially at such a young age."

"That's right. You understand about loss, don't you, hon?" The old woman smiled at Veronica, and Nathan decided to let her continue.

"We think my father's files might have had something to do with my parents' murder. But the files were burned."

"What's that got to do with my Susan?" she asked.

Veronica's voice softened with concern. "We suspect whoever burned the files did so because Susan went to see my father."

"Yes, she did," the old woman said, folding her hands together. "Susan wanted to keep the baby, but the father wanted to pay her to have an abortion."

"So Susan went to see Mr. Miller?" Nathan asked.

"Yes, she planned to bring a paternity suit against the father."

"Mrs. Pritchard, I know this is hard for you, but it's important.'' Veronica continued to pat the old woman's hand. ''Would you tell me who the baby's father was?''

A worried look knitted her brows. ''I reckon so. That woman can't hurt us anymore. We've done lost everything.'' She dabbed at her moist eyes.

''Who are you talking about?'' Veronica asked.

''Alma Jones. Why, that was the meanest woman to ever walk the face of this earth. She killed my Susan and my grandbaby.''

''I don't understand,'' Veronica said.

''See, her grandson was the baby's father.''

Nathan glanced at Veronica and saw her face tighten. ''But Gerald, he was one of them ladies' men. Thought he was God's gift to every woman in a skirt, strung our little girl along.''

''Then she got pregnant, and he abandoned her?'' Nathan asked.

''Shore did,'' the old woman said. ''And if that weren't bad enough, his grandmama come over here offering to bribe Susan. Wanted to pay her to have an abortion and leave town.''

''But you said she killed Susan?'' Veronica asked.

Mrs. Pritchard's face crumpled. ''Susan was so upset and depressed about the way Gerald done her. Told her she was a tramp and he'd never had any intentions of marrying a poor little country girl like her. Said she was dumb as dirt for even thinkin' such a thing. Broke her heart.

''Then that woman came over here one night and kept badgering her. Susan got so upset, she got in the car and took off, driving like a maniac.''

''That's the night she had the accident?'' Nathan asked.

''Yes. 'Cause she was so upset,'' the old woman said bitterly. ''See, Alma Jones killed her. And I won't never forget it.''

A few minutes later, Nathan and Veronica climbed in the car to go to her apartment. ''That was a terrible thing for Mrs. Jones and Gerald to do to that girl,'' Veronica said. ''And I can't help but wonder…''

"Eli might not have known," Nathan said, reading her thoughts. "Alma Jones could have hidden the whole thing from him."

Veronica sighed, and Nathan ran his hand along the seat and threaded it through the back of her hair. "You okay?"

"Yes." She leaned against him. "I'm glad you're here." But Veronica couldn't stop thinking about the young pregnant girl and how Alma and Gerald had been so callous toward her. She wondered if Eli had known. After all, when he'd warned her not to date Gerald, she'd sensed he didn't want anyone to destroy his son's reputation and career. To what lengths would Eli go?

Chapter Thirteen

As Veronica entered her apartment, thoughts of Gerald, Eli and Alma tormented her. She'd forgotten she'd left the newspaper clippings she'd received in the mail scattered across the coffee table. Nathan immediately zeroed in on them and sat down to study them. Veronica retreated to the kitchen to put the takeout Mexican food they'd bought on a tray. Part of her felt shameful; another part wondered what he thought as he looked at the pictures. He'd said he didn't think she killed her parents, but did he think she was unstable or strange? And what would happen once he solved the case?

Since she'd met Nathan, she'd started dreaming of a future and a family—like the one she'd lost as a child. But each time she thought of having a baby of her own, fears bombarded her. Since she couldn't remember her own mother, how would she know how to be a good one herself?

Poor Susan Pritchard hadn't gotten the chance to find out. How many other women had found themselves in the same position with Gerald and been paid off to keep quiet or have an abortion? And if Eli had known, what kind of a man did that make him? When she'd first moved to Oakland, she'd dreamed of becoming a part of Eli's family, but now she wasn't sure it was the kind of family she wanted to belong to.

"Both Eli and his mother were at your parents' funeral," Nathan said, holding up one of the articles.

"They were friends."

"You know, I got a different feeling from Alma Jones." Nathan grabbed a nacho and dipped it in salsa. "I'm not sure she considered your father a friend."

"Why not?" Veronica cut the quesadillas in half and bit into one.

"Eli's mother said she visited your father to tell him she was taking her business to another attorney."

"But why? I thought Dad was the only lawyer in Oakland."

Nathan ate his quesadilla, suddenly quiet. Veronica sensed he was hiding something. "What is it, Nathan? What aren't you telling me?"

Nathan's gaze met hers. "I don't know if there's any truth to it."

"To what?"

When he looked away, Veronica braced herself for bad news.

"Mrs. Jones suggested your father might have been…um, less than honest."

"My father?" She bolted off the sofa so quickly she almost knocked over the coffee table. Nathan's glass skidded sideways and he caught it, his fingers folding tightly around the rim.

"I don't believe it," Veronica said angrily. "I've heard a lot of accusations and gossip over the past few years, but I don't believe for a minute my dad was a crook."

"I didn't say it was true," he clarified. "I only said that was what Mrs. Jones implied."

"And I suppose she implied someone killed him because of his dishonesty."

Nathan nodded.

"Well, she's wrong." Veronica crossed her arms and paced across the room. "If anybody was shady, it would have been her. After all, look how she treated that Pritchard girl."

"I agree," he said calmly. "Although I found a couple of excerpts in the papers that suggest the same theory."

"Nosy reporters," Veronica said. "They'd do anything for a story. I wonder why they didn't catch wind of that Pritchard girl's accident and splatter the fact that she was pregnant all over the papers.''

"You're right," Nathan said. "I imagine somebody got paid off along the way.''

She stared out the window at the fading sunlight as it formed shadows on the lawn and sidewalk. Just like in her nightmares, she thought she saw the dark shadow of a man lurking behind every tree. She was more certain every day that the visions in her dreams were visions of the man who'd killed her parents. And if she could just remember that night and see his face, she could make him pay for destroying her life and murdering her family. Did Eli's family have something to do with it?

"Veronica?" Nathan's calm voice broke into her thoughts. She pivoted and saw him watching her, concern darkening his eyes. "I have a theory. You want to hear?"

She nodded.

"Suppose Susan goes to your father for help. She wants to file a paternity suit. Mrs. Jones and Gerald wanted to hide the fact that Susan Pritchard was pregnant.''

"And?''

"Then Gerald or Alma go to your dad to try and talk him out of it.''

"Or to buy him off," Veronica said, her heart pounding at the scenario. It made perfect sense.

"Right. And suppose your father wouldn't go along. They were worried about Gerald's reputation and about Eli's campaign.''

Veronica sank into the chair, her heart racing. "Then Gerald or Alma killed my father to keep him quiet." Veronica hesitated. "But why kill my mom?''

"She must have come in and seen the whole thing. So they killed your mom and made it look like a murder-suicide.''

"Oh, no," Veronica muttered under her breath. "Do you think Eli knew?''

Nathan shook his head. "I doubt it. His mother said he was out of town the day your parents were killed. When he got word, he rushed back.'' He hesitated. ''Of course, they could have lied about him being out of town. It's been so long ago I'm not sure if we can find out for sure.''

''He came to see me at the hospital.'' Veronica felt a chill creep up her spine. ''He couldn't have known, Nathan. He just couldn't have. He's been so kind to me.''

Nathan started to go to her, but the phone rang and Veronica picked it up. ''Hello.''

''Veronica, darling, it's Eli.''

''Eli.'' Veronica's legs folded beneath her. Nathan helped her sit down.

''Yes. Tessa said she enjoyed having lunch with you.''

''Yes,'' Veronica croaked.

''That's great. I'm calling to invite you and a date, of course, to my house for a private dinner party tomorrow night. Can you make it?''

Veronica searched Nathan's face for support. ''I thought you didn't want me becoming close to your family.''

''Veronica, honey, listen. That was a misunderstanding.'' Eli's breathing became labored.

''Are you all right, Eli?''

''Yes, but I don't want you to be upset. Please, I really want you to come.''

Veronica hesitated. ''Just a minute, Eli.'' She whispered an explanation to Nathan and he nodded.

''Fine, Eli. I'll be there.''

''Good. It means a lot to me. Cocktails are at seven.''

''See you then.'' When she hung up the phone, her hands were trembling.

''A family get-together?''

''I suppose.''

''That should be interesting.'' Nathan took her hand in his and stroked it. ''Maybe we can find out more about Gerald and Mrs. Jones.''

''Yeah.'' Veronica squeezed his fingers. ''But first I have to do something.''

''What?''

"I have to go back to the old house." Once again, she looked to Nathan for support. His amber eyes glowed with understanding, and what looked like admiration. "Last time it didn't jog my memory, but maybe if I go inside it will, and I'll finally remember what happened." Then she looked at Nathan and voiced another worry. "But if it is Eli's mother or his son, how will I ever tell him?"

Nathan put his hand on her back. "I don't know sweetheart, but I'll go with you."

A FEW MINUTES LATER, Nathan had his hands clenched around the steering wheel as he drove Veronica to her childhood home. He wanted to find out who was threatening her and see them rot in jail, and the detective in him wanted to find it out at any cost.

But the man in him, the person who cared about Veronica, didn't want her to suffer in order to find the answers. He wanted to protect her. If she relived the horrid memory she'd blocked out twenty years ago, what kind of an effect would it have on her mentally? Would she be able to handle the truth?

Should he call a doctor to go with them?

He reached over and covered her hand with his. "You don't have to do this now."

"Yes, I do." She raised her delicate chin and he recognized strength and courage in her profile. Yet fear shaped her dark brown eyes into pools of liquid chocolate. "I never came back here after they died. My grandmother took me away as soon as I left the hospital."

"I can understand that. I'd probably have done the same thing." When he parked the car in front of the overgrown yard and saw Veronica bite down on her lip, he stroked the column of her neck and kissed her gently on the cheek. "You may not remember anything, even when you go inside."

"I know. But I have to try." She opened the car door and climbed out. Nathan followed her, letting her set the pace as he mentally prepared himself for whatever might happen. He needed to step back and to become invisible inside the house in order to let her concentrate. But if she struggled with her memory or became too frightened, he'd have to step in. He'd never be able to stand by and watch her in distress.

She looked cautious and thoughtful as she made her way past the weed-filled patch that had once been a flower garden. She paused and glanced at a magnolia tree in the yard, and he wondered if she had any recollection of it. Of course it had to have been tiny when she lived in the house.

Gingerly, she reached out and wiped spiderwebs from the boarded doorframe. Nathan pulled the rotting boards loose, then tore the boards from the windows. Sighing deeply, she gave him a slow smile before she opened the door.

AS SOON AS THE DOOR squeaked open, Veronica thought she heard music playing. The familiar tune "Somewhere over the Rainbow" drifted into her mind, but instead of the comforting, beautiful melody, the screeching gyrations grated on her nerves, consuming the space in the room and sucking the air from her lungs with the haunting clarity of impending doom. Her heart pounded, blood running hot through her veins and roaring in her ears.

The musty odor was a swift reminder that the house was devoid of life, empty of love and laughter. A cloud of dust and cobwebs streaked the outdated Early American style furniture. The avocado and gold colors made Veronica painfully aware she'd truly stepped back in time. Thick rust-colored shag carpet covered the floors, and a magazine rack filled with old *Life* and *Time* magazines overflowed the wooden holder. These were her parents' old things. The faded gold couch with the flowers, the ruffled pea green chair, the worn vinyl recliner.

Immediately her eyes were drawn to the ugly words vandals had painted on the yellowed walls. A mouse skittered out from the sofa and darted into the corner. A brown clay ashtray in the center of the table surprised Veronica because as far as she'd known, neither of her parents smoked, then she noticed the ashtray had been made of clay. It was a child's art project. She must have made it for her parents. Why hadn't her grand-

mother taken it from the house and put it with the other memorabilia?

She bypassed the table and paused to wipe the thick dust
from a book on the pine end table. An old copy of Dickens.
Was it her mother's or father's? Or maybe they'd read it together. A musty smell filled her nostrils as she opened it and
read the inscription. ''For my darling wife. With all my love
on our wedding day.'' Veronica's vision blurred as she read
her father's name.

She clutched the book in her hands and walked slowly toward the kitchen. The strong scent of mildew lingered in the
air and she stopped to stare at the rusty porcelain sink. Mouse
droppings littered the floor. Something seemed familiar about
the room—the yellow gingham curtains, the dingy white ap-
pliances. The kitchen was supposed to be the heart of the
home. Had her family cooked and had nice, cozy family din-
ners in here? Had she thrown baby food on the floor or helped
her mother make cookies for preschool?

Closing her eyes, she hugged the book to her chest and
conjured up a vision of her parents. She could imagine them
standing in the kitchen, her mother baking biscuits, her father
sipping juice and reading the morning paper. Or maybe her
father had cooked and her mother had read the morning paper?

No, it was all wrong.

She tried to picture a Christmas tree in the den and the smell
of cinnamon or gingerbread, but her vision became foggy with
images of blood and the sounds of her parents' screaming.
Then she heard her own voice as a child's. She was crying
and begging her parents not to die, not to leave her. The memory shook her to the core, and she began to shiver.

Darn it, why couldn't she at least remember some happy
memories. Surely their family had had some.

Opening her eyes, she gripped the counter and saw Nathan
watching her. ''Are you all right?''

She simply nodded, too stunned by the vivid memory to
speak. She stared through the broken glass of the back window
and spotted a swing. It seemed vaguely familiar, but once

again no details registered. Gathering her courage, she walked down the hall. A room to the left—a room to the right. Which one had been hers?

She caught a glimpse of blue and rose wallpaper. It seemed familiar. Then she remembered the wrapping paper on the gift that had been sent to her office and how she'd reacted to it. This room must have been hers. And the person who'd sent her the music box had known.

She heard Nathan's shallow breathing behind her and felt grateful he was there, grateful also that he wasn't pushing her to talk. She sidestepped a section of the wall where vandals had painted obscenities. Her finger traced the small rosebuds, and she smiled as she noticed a child's drawing on a small pink bulletin board. It was obviously supposed to be the sun, but if she'd drawn it, she must have gotten carried away with the orange marker, for it looked more like a giant pumpkin. Then she realized that she didn't know if she'd drawn it or if another child had given it to her.

Anger filled her. By forgetting that night and blocking out her childhood, she'd lost some treasured memories as well as the bad. She had to get them back. Spurred on by determination, she studied the white French Provincial furniture and tried to imagine herself as a child curled up in the bed asleep. She picked up a worn brown teddy bear and pressed it to her chest. Had this been her favorite bear? If so, why hadn't her grandmother taken it with them? She studied the bear's floppy ears and the place where a button was missing, hoping it would conjure up a familiar image. But her mind refused to focus, and her head started to pound. She rubbed her temple and felt Nathan's gentle hands massage her shoulders.

"Don't push it. You'll remember when you're ready."

"No." Veronica let anger drive her. "It's time. I just need to concentrate."

She pushed past him and examined the small box of toys: a broken doll, chalkboard, cards, blocks, puzzles and a sketch pad. She opened the pad and gasped in surprise. The first few pictures vaguely resembled the good witch in *The Wizard of*

Oz and oddly, she'd scrawled her mother's name above them. She'd named her father the Wizard. A childhood drawing of a nasty-looking witch filled several pages.

She'd labeled a stick picture of a man "Eli." To her surprise, the picture had been colored over with black crayon.

Why would she have done that?

"I wonder if you drew those before or after the murder," Nathan said. "And I wonder why the police didn't take them."

"It must have been before," Veronica said. "Grandma said she never brought me back here afterward. I don't understand why I would color over Eli."

"Hmm, interesting. Maybe you didn't. Another child could have done it. You know how kids are."

"I suppose you're right," Veronica said, although a strange feeling came over her. It was as if she knew she *had* drawn the pictures. The dark, dank air in the room closed in around her, and she noticed a shadow rise above her from the window frame as the last remnants of the sun slipped away.

She turned the page of the sketch pad, and fear completely clogged her throat. Someone had drawn a picture of a little girl kneeling over a woman's and a man's bodies, and the little girl had a bloody knife raised above her.

When Nathan saw Veronica's face pale at the sight of the picture, he decided he had to get her out of there. Slowly, he tried to ease her fingertips from the sketch pad. "Come on, darling, let's go."

Veronica shook her head, her eyes glazed.

"You've seen enough today. We can always come back."

She shook her head vehemently and her lower lip trembled, but her voice sounded amazingly strong when she spoke. "No, I have to see something."

"What?" Was she remembering?

Her eyes still dark, her face as pale as the faded walls, she pulled away from him and turned to cross the hall. Immediately Nathan realized she was going to her parents' bedroom. The room where they had died.

Sweat beaded on his forehead as he watched her enter the room. She stared at the simple maple double bed. The mattress and boxspring were missing, but the chalk lines the police had used to mark where her parents had died still remained on the floor. Although the lines were faint and marred with dust, the outline was clear.

She inched toward the bed, touched the worn lime green chenille bedspread piled on the end of the frame, then blew the dust from one of her parents' pictures. A small smile spread on her face at the sight of her dad and mother holding her. The idyllic expressions on their faces made it clear they loved her.

"Dr. Baits said my father was disappointed I didn't look like him," Veronica whispered. "I think I might have his chin."

Nathan took the photograph. He couldn't see the resemblance, but then he never had been one to notice things like that with families. He sensed it was important he confirm her thoughts so he smiled. "Yeah. Maybe you do."

She pivoted, her gaze moving to the faded shag carpet where the chalk marks served as an aching reminder of the tragedy that had taken place in the house. "Look at those pictures of them together. You can't make me believe they killed themselves," Veronica said quietly.

He had to agree. Domestic violence was common, but Veronica's father had been an educated man, a pillar of the society. And the glow on his wife's face was evidently one of admiration and love for her husband.

A lace doily covered the dressertop, its yellowed edges frayed. Veronica wiped a thin layer of dust from an antique music box that sat on top of it. He was amazed there was anything left in the room. In some cities, vandals would have robbed the place or the homeless would have moved right in. The neighbor who'd kept an eye on the place must have done a good job.

Veronica opened the box and paused, the look on her face strange when it started playing "Love Is a Many-splendored Thing." Then she pulled out a small pin, and Nathan moved closer. It was a pin like the one the lady in the flower shop had mentioned, exactly like the one Veronica owned. Where had it come from? Veronica said there were only a few like it in the world.

"Can I take this and have it fingerprinted?" he asked.

Veronica nodded, still dazed. Then she surprised him by moving over to the chalk marks and kneeling beside them. "This is where they found me," she said in a voice barely above a whisper. "I was right beside them."

A sudden chill swept through the air and the lacy curtains ruffled. The sky had darkened and Nathan wondered if a thunderstorm was on its way. He pulled the curtain back and peered outside. One of the window panes had been broken, and the wind whistled eerily through the jagged glass. In the distance he thought he saw a dark car skid around the curve. Had someone been following them?

When he glanced back, Veronica was staring at her hands, her face ashen. Then she brought her hands to her head and pressed them against her temples. He raced to her and encircled her with his arms. "Veronica, come on, let's go."

"My head hurts," she whispered. "I want to remember, but I can't."

"Shh, it's okay."

"No, it's not," she said. She raised her face to look at him, and the pain and agony in her eyes made his chest ache. "I have to remember. I have to."

"You will, sweetheart." He started to pull her into a standing position, but she groaned and pressed her hands tighter over her head.

"Make it stop. Please make it stop." She closed her eyes and rocked herself back and forth in his arms. Nathan gritted his teeth. He didn't care if she remembered or not. He couldn't stand to watch her suffer. Sweeping her up into his arms, he carried her to the car.

Once they arrived at her apartment, Nathan helped Veronica change into a nightshirt, gave her two painkillers and tucked her into bed.

"Stay with me," she said softly. Her eyes were closed, her face etched with fatigue, and although Nathan knew he should be working on her case, he couldn't resist her simple plea. He lay down beside her and pulled her into his arms. "Go to sleep, sweetheart. It's been a long day."

Veronica nodded. "I wish I'd remembered more."

"It's a start," he said, stroking her back to calm her. "Just relax." He talked softly and continued to stroke her until she fell asleep. For a long moment, he watched her sleep, reveling in her beauty and quiet strength. She was dealing with past demons he could hardly imagine. Her eyelashes fluttered and she jerked in her sleep. He stroked her again and curled his fingers in her hair, once again soothing her until she stilled. Finally, when he was sure she was sound asleep, he eased off the bed and went into her den to use the phone.

After dialing his partner, he relaxed on the sofa with a beer and contemplated the things he'd learned from the Pritchards and the former police chief while he waited for Ford to get to the phone. Could Eli's mother or Gerald possibly be responsible for everything that happened to Veronica—her parents' deaths, the threats, the attack, the music box, the crushed flowers? But if they had killed her parents and didn't want her to remember, why send her things that might trigger that memory?

Unless…unless they thought she was unstable and might become so distraught she'd take her own life.

He certainly didn't like that line of thinking.

"Dawson, Ford here."

"Yeah. What did you find out on the Falk woman?"

"No relation to anyone who lived in Oakland in the seventies. Can't find any connection or motive as to why she'd want to hurt the Miller woman."

Nathan had to agree, but still she'd had access to Veronica's keys. "Maybe someone paid for her help."

"That's a possibility," Ford said. "She sure took a cut in pay when she quit prostituting."

"Yeah," Nathan said, wondering if Gerald or Alma Jones could have paid her to help.

"I'm meeting her at Richard's. Maybe she'll open up over a few drinks."

"Sounds like a plan," Nathan said. "How about the hypodermic I dropped off? Any prints?"

Ford paused. "Only one."

Nathan swallowed hard. "Veronica's?"

"Nope."

"So she didn't lie. She hadn't given herself the shot."

"She could have wiped them off."

Nathan sighed in disgust. "You're still determined to make her out as a crazy woman, aren't you?"

Ford laughed. "I'm looking at all angles. Remember, I'm not the one thinking with my hormones."

"Shut up," Nathan growled. "Now, tell me whose prints you did find."

"They weren't registered."

"Damn." Nathan rubbed his face in frustration. Every time he thought he had evidence, it turned out to be incomplete. Then he remembered Eli's party the next night. He would escort Veronica and find some way to get Gerald and Alma Jones's fingerprints. "Well, keep it on file. Maybe we'll find a match."

"All right." Ford hesitated. "And what have you learned— other than Ms. Miller's bra size?"

Nathan cursed vehemently.

Ford laughed. "Settle down, man."

Nathan reined in his temper and gave Ford the details about his visit with Scroggins and what he'd learned from the Pritchard family about Gerald. Then he briefly described Veronica's visit to her homestead.

"I think you're barking up the wrong tree if you're looking at Gerald Jones. He's done nothing but good for this town,"

Ford said. "Everybody's got a few ghosts in their closet. It doesn't make them killers."

Nathan bit his lip. "You may be right. But if he isn't involved, we have to find out who is. And I damn well intend to do it, with or without your help." He hung up the phone and cursed Ford. After talking with him, Nathan felt as if he'd made no progress at all.

A low moan came from the bedroom and he realized Veronica must be having a nightmare. Slowly, he opened the door and saw her tossing from side to side, her eyelashes fluttering as she clutched the covers with her fingernails. He took off his shirt and jeans and beeper and stretched out beside her, then pulled her into his arms. He wanted this whole ordeal to be over for her, yet he still didn't know what would happen between the two of them once it ended.

Would she go back to Florida or to Ron Cox? Would she realize she'd only been drawn to him because of the danger? He was, after all, a cop. And cops made lousy husbands. He had a dangerous job, a profession many women weren't able to accept. Would Veronica be able to tolerate his crazy hours and the fact that when he left every day, they would both have to face the fact that he might not come home at night?

He knew he could. He would live each moment with her as if it might be their last. With that thought on his mind, he drew her next to him, and closed his eyes.

Sometime during the wee hours of the morning, the telephone jangled, waking him from a deep, warm sleep. Nathan jumped and reached for it, his mind instantly alert in case it was another threat to Veronica. She bolted upright and hugged the covers to her chest, her eyes wide in the moonlight.

He waited for the caller to speak. "Hello. Hello, this is Lieutenant Stevens. Is someone there?"

Lieutenant Stevens—how had he known where to find him?

His already-agitated voice grew louder. "Hello, I'm looking for Detective Dawson. Ms. Miller—"

"Lieutenant, I'm here."

"I'm not going to ask what in the hell you're doing," Stevens said. "But you need to get down here."

"Why?" Nathan asked, reaching for his jeans.

"Your partner, Ford." When Stevens paused, Nathan lost his breath. *Your partner*—the words reverberated over and over in his head. Nathan felt dizzy as déjà vu struck him. No. It couldn't be happening again.

"What happened?" he finally choked out.

Stevens sighed. "I hate to tell you this, Dawson. But Ford's dead."

Chapter Fourteen

Nathan felt his windpipe close. "What? How?"

"Ran his car off a cliff," Stevens said. "Happened a couple of hours ago."

"Damn." Nathan scrubbed his hand over his face and glanced at Veronica.

She looked frightened to death. "What's wrong?" she whispered.

Nathan shook his head, self-recriminations exploding in his mind. It was his fault. He shouldn't have been here in bed with Veronica. He should have been working with Ford.

"Any sign of foul play?" Nathan asked.

"Not yet, but we've got a team going over the car right now. Thought you might want to be in on it."

"Hell, yeah."

"Do you know what Ford was up to tonight? Were you two working on something?"

Nathan stared at Veronica, his chest clenching painfully. "He was supposed to meet a woman named Falk tonight," he said. "Around ten at Richard's Bar and Grill."

Stevens mumbled something under his breath. "I'll check it out, but it looks like he was on his way when he had the wreck. I don't think he ever made it to the bar."

Veronica clasped his hand. He squeezed her fingers, guilt fogging his mind.

"Who is this Falk woman, anyway?" Stevens asked.

Nathan paused, reluctant to say anything in front of Veronica. She had enough to deal with. But then again, she was involved. She had to know. "She's Veronica Miller's secretary. I asked Ford to check her out because she had access to Ms. Miller's keys."

Veronica's eyes clouded with confusion.

"I see. And you think Ford's accident might be related?"

"It's possible," Nathan said.

"I'll see if we can locate Ms. Falk."

"I'll be there as soon as I can."

Nathan lowered the phone and turned to Veronica. The shock in her eyes made his stomach churn.

"What happened? What about Louise?"

Nathan took her hands in his, trying to ignore his own turbulent emotions. "My partner had an appointment with her tonight."

The expression on her face turned to horror. "Did something happen to Louise?"

Nathan shook his head slowly. "No. Ford never made it to see her. He had an accident."

"Is…he all right?"

He shook his head again, unable to speak. Veronica wrapped her arms around him, but he couldn't accept her comfort. He didn't deserve it. His first partner, Rick, had died because he believed in a woman. Ford had died doing legwork for him because he believed in Veronica—because he was in bed with her.

"Nathan?"

Her soft voice barely penetrated the coldness around him. He had to find the truth now. Not just for Veronica. But for Ford, the partner he hadn't liked, the partner who hadn't believed him, the partner who'd died because of him. Hadn't he learned that police work and personal relationships didn't go together?

It certainly cast suspicion on Louise Falk, but like Ford said, what possible motive could she have to hurt Veronica?

"I have to go." Nathan pulled away and stood, then reached for his shirt.

Veronica's eyes shimmered with hurt. She'd had a terrible night, and he felt like a heel for leaving her, but he couldn't stay here—not when Ford lay dead, and the person who'd been tormenting Veronica was still on the loose.

"Are you all right? I can drive you," Veronica offered.

Nathan quickly buttoned and tucked in his shirt. "I'm fine. I'll call you later." Then he grabbed his gun and headed for the door. Before he closed it, he turned to Veronica. "Lock the doors. And don't let anyone in. Not anyone." He pointed to his beeper. "And if you need me, call."

FIFTEEN MINUTES LATER, he was standing at the scene of the accident watching a wrecker tow Ford's truck up the hill. It would be taken in for a complete workover. By tomorrow they would know if the car had any mechanical problems and if it had truly been an accident.

"No witnesses?" Nathan asked Stevens.

"None." The lieutenant leaned over and stared at a dark smudge on the back of the bumper, then pointed to the street. "Possibility the car might have been helped off that cliff, though. See the extra set of tire marks?"

"Yep. And by someone who drives a black car." Nathan examined the paint spot. He remembered Cox's black sedan. Was he still in town? He recalled seeing another black car at Veronica's house the day before.

"Did you have someone question the people at the bar and grill?" Nathan asked.

"Done," Stevens said. "No one saw Ford. And the waitress didn't remember a woman coming in alone."

Nathan scratched his chin. "Any news on the Falk woman?"

"She's not at her place. And her apartment's been cleaned out."

Nathan's thoughts swirled. What in the hell did Louise Falk have to do with all this? Had Eli helped Veronica hire Louise?

Was she just a paid assistant in someone's demented game or was she some psycho who had planned the whole scheme to torment Veronica on her own? And why? Even psychos usually had some twisted logic.

"I'll run a complete background check on her," Nathan said. "I'm going to find out everything there is to know about Louise Falk."

"Get on it," Stevens said. "I hate to lose one of my men."

Nathan swallowed. And as much as he disliked Ford, he hated to lose another partner.

VERONICA PACED the apartment, her nerves on edge. She'd showered and tried to finish some paperwork, but her mind raced with worry. Nathan had been upset when he left.

And rightfully so. His partner had been killed because of her—because he was investigating her case. Death followed her everywhere she went. Maybe she should just leave town and forget about her past. If Nathan's partner had been killed because of her, then Nathan was in danger. And she loved him too much to let him die.

She collapsed onto the couch, brushing away the tears as nausea overwhelmed her. Why did everyone she cared about have to die? Was loving her some kind of awful curse? Had she caused Nathan's partner's death as she had her parents'?

The shadows closed around her, clawing at her skin and screaming her name over and over until she buried her face into a pillow and sobbed. She wanted her parents back. She wanted her grandmother back.

And she would not lose Nathan. At least not to death. She wasn't worth dying over.

Making a hasty decision, she scrambled into her bedroom and started to pack.

ON THE WAY to the precinct Nathan swung by his apartment and picked up clothes for the evening at Eli's. If he ran short on time, he could change at Veronica's. Then he went to the station and found everything he could on Louise Falk. She'd been born an illegitimate child, lived with a drug-addict mother and carted from one homeless shelter to another until she was fifteen. Louise had run away and lived the life of a prostitute until she was twenty. After that, she'd gone from one live-in relationship to another.

She'd come to Oakland, volunteered on Gerald Jones's campaign, and learned general office skills at a local business school. From there she'd taken the job with Veronica. So her connection to the Jones family was Gerald, not Eli. Checking further, he discovered she'd invested in Barrett Pharmaceuticals at the advisement of Gerald. Had she lost a bundle as well?

Why hadn't he guessed Gerald was the key? They could be lovers. When Veronica returned, Louise had helped him torment Veronica because she was in love with him. A logical reason for a poor, former prostitute to help Gerald.

He stuffed the information into a folder and headed to the car. He wanted to see Veronica, but he'd had a disturbing thought while driving to the station. He knew the sketches she had found at her old house had bothered her, and they had concerned him, but he hadn't been able to put his finger on it. What if she had drawn the pictures after her parents were killed? Perhaps there was a clue to the murderer in her childish sketches.

He hurriedly drove to her old home. Once there, he stared at the decaying house. It symbolized a host of horrible memories for Veronica, memories that had almost destroyed her life as the termites and weather had destroyed the paint and wood. But she had inner strength. Enough, he hoped, to face the truth, if he found it. And strong enough to go on when they had to part. He couldn't endanger anyone else because of his own sloppy work or his personal ties.

He went inside the house to find the sketch pad. It was missing. Why would someone take it?

Unless…unless Veronica had drawn the sketches after the murder. When he got back to her house, he would call the psychiatrist and ask. He searched the house but discovered the teddy bear and Veronica's mother's music box were also gone. She would be upset. But not as much as seeing the brutal way her bedroom had been vandalized. Someone had completely slashed the comforter, then shredded the curtains into a million pieces.

Hurrying to the car, he fought the panic building inside. What if they had gotten to Veronica? He'd left her alone— totally alone. What if Ford's accident had been a decoy and she'd been hurt?

He pressed the gas pedal and floored it, zooming through traffic and honking his horn for people to let him by. Ten minutes later he raced into Veronica's apartment complex. Damn. There wasn't a parking spot in sight. He didn't see her car and his pulse accelerated. He skidded to a stop, jumped from his car and left the engine running. His heart pounded as he ran toward her building.

They were supposed to go to Eli's tonight. She should be home getting ready. Earlier, he'd hoped to solve the case. Now he just wanted to know she was safe.

He ran to the door and knocked, but no one answered. He picked the lock and rushed inside. "Veronica, where are you? Veronica, answer me!"

He quickly searched her apartment, his pulse racing when he noticed her dresser drawers opened, clothes hanging haphazardly from the edges. Either she'd left in a hurry or someone had ransacked her place.

His heart constricted as the silence in the apartment enveloped him. She was gone.

VERONICA THOUGHT she was being followed. She glanced in the rearview mirror and tried not to panic as she turned onto Fourth Street and drove toward her office. The black car was still behind her. Not close enough for her to see the driver, but not far enough away for comfort. Somebody wanted to antagonize her. To scare her. But who?

If Nathan's partner had been killed because he was meeting

Louise, his death implied Louise's involvement. But how? And why? She'd never met Louise before she'd come to Oakland. What could her secretary have against her?

Then she remembered seeing Louise talking to Gerald at the campaign party. Were they romantically involved? If Gerald wanted to hurt her, that might make sense. She glanced up and saw the black car still two cars back. A shudder rippled through her. Dammit, she was tired of all these cloak-and-dagger games. She would go to Eli's dinner party and find the truth herself.

She slammed on her brakes to pull into the parking lot adjacent to her office and stifled a scream. A stream of smoke billowed from her office. Was the whole building on fire? Panicking, she drove onto the lawn, shoved the door open, and ran toward the building. If the fire was small, maybe she could save something. She raced up the steps and reached for the door, but someone grabbed her from behind and she screamed. Something sharp and hard slammed against her head and knocked her off balance, and a blinding pain exploded behind her eyes. She reached for something to hold on to, but just like in her dreams, darkness surrounded her and she went spinning and falling, then dropped into a bottomless hole where there was nothing.

A DULL ACHE spread through Nathan. Where was Veronica? Was she still alive?

He rounded the corner near her office going eighty-five and nearly choked when he saw the smoke billowing from the building. Tall orange flames licked the roof and spiraled toward the sky. He jumped from his car and ran toward the building. *Please don't let Veronica be inside.*

A small crowd had gathered on the lawn, and he ran up the steps, ignoring their warnings not to go inside.

"We've called the fire department!" someone shouted.

But Nathan shoved his weight against the door and burst inside. Heat enveloped him and the smell of burning wood seeped into his nostrils, but his eyes scanned through the haze of thick smoke for any sign of life.

"Veronica!" He screamed her name over and over, then fell to his hands and knees and crawled, coughing at the fog of smoke. Someone at the door yelled for him to come back, but he crawled past the burning desk and gasped when he saw a foot.

"Veronica." She groaned and he slid on his stomach, dodging splinters of broken wood and burning papers. When he reached her, he dragged her out of her office. Most of it was already in flames and he could barely see through the thick haze of smoke. He coughed and jerked a handkerchief from his pocket and covered her mouth. Quickly he pulled her toward the front door, then swept her up and ran outside. The fire truck rolled up, sirens wailing. People raced toward him but he ran for the grassy area, for clean, fresh air, coughing and choking as he carried her to safety.

"Dear God, Veronica, come on. You have to be all right. You just have to be," he said in a strangled voice.

"Here, let me examine her." A paramedic eased down beside him, and Nathan relinquished control so the emergency worker could give her oxygen. Veronica tried to open her eyes, then brought her hand up to the back of her head and moaned.

"She has a gash on her head," the paramedic said. "Some wood probably fell and hit her."

"No," Veronica said, reaching for him. "Hit me before... before I went in."

Nathan clenched his jaw in fury. Someone had tried to kill her. "Did you see who it was? A car, anything?"

Veronica closed her eyes, her voice barely discernible. "Thought a car was following me...black." The emergency worker pressed the oxygen mask over her face.

Damn, Nathan muttered silently. "Is she going to be all right?" he asked, gripping her hands in his.

"Yeah. Her lungs sound good. She must not have been in there long."

Nathan's heart pounded with relief. He leaned down and hugged her. "I was so scared," he whispered.

Veronica pushed the mask away and gently touched his cheek. "I'm okay."

"What about her head?" Nathan asked.

"A bad lump. She'll probably have a major headache for a couple of days. But she'll be all right. We should take her to the hospital overnight."

"No, please, not the hospital," Veronica protested.

Nathan read the fear in her eyes and wondered if it related to her childhood. "It'll just be overnight," he said. "You need to have medical supervision."

"They already examined me," she argued. "I'm fine. I'm not going to the hospital."

Nathan and the paramedic exchanged worried looks. "She seems fine. But someone should watch her overnight. You can call the hospital if she has trouble breathing."

"I'll take care of her," Nathan said.

Veronica stroked his face. "Thank you."

"I'm so glad you're okay." He kissed her again and she kissed him back fervently. "I'll be right back," he finally said, glancing at the policemen. He rushed over and ordered them to call the arson unit. "I want the place detailed," he said. His gut clenched as he heard the burning embers crash to the ground and saw the smoke billowing into the dark sky. Veronica could have died in that fire. Once again he'd failed to protect someone—and this time it was the woman he loved. He never should have left her alone.

Guilt-laden, he hurried back to Veronica and knelt beside her. In spite of the smoke and her head injury, she smiled. Nathan blinked moisture from his eyes. He loved her more than his own life. How would he ever say goodbye?

VERONICA CLUNG to Nathan's hand, wondering if she would be strong enough to let him go when it was time. She'd planned to go to the party at Eli's without him, but now…now, she didn't know. She was too weak to even stand alone.

He helped her to a sitting position, and she fought back tears as she watched the firemen hose down her office. All her files were destroyed. She had backups at home, but this was the place her father had worked. The business she'd wanted to operate for the rest of her life. And it had gone up in flames. Why?

"Do you want to go home now?" Nathan asked.

She looked into his eyes and saw a wealth of understanding, a feeling she'd never expected from a tough cop like him. Tenderness for him swelled inside, and tears blurred her vision. He pulled her into his arms and carried her to his car.

"Do you want her bag?" One of the firemen stopped Nathan. He was holding her suitcase. "I found it when I had to move her car."

He glanced at the brown suitcase, then back at Veronica. She nodded toward the fireman. "Thanks."

Nathan helped her in the car and scooted into the driver's seat, his jaw clenched hard, his amber eyes flickering with anger. "Where were you going, Veronica?"

She twisted her fingers in her lap. "I don't know."

He leaned back in the seat and faced her. "Were you running away from all this or from me?"

How could she tell him she was running away to protect him? "I thought it might be best if I left town," she said softly.

Nathan nodded. "I see." Then he cranked the engine and drove toward her apartment. He remained silent until they were inside.

He picked up the phone and called Eli's. A few minutes later, he hung up. "Eli is postponing the party until tomorrow night. He really wants you there."

Veronica nodded, too weary to do anything else.

His face softened slightly. "Why don't you rest for a while, then shower. I have some phone calls to make."

"Okay." She reached for her bag, but he refused to relinquish control.

"I'll put it in your bedroom."

Veronica felt like weeping. He looked so angry, so rigid and untouchable. She had to say something, to try and explain.

"Nathan, I don't want anyone else to get hurt because of me."

"What are you talking about?" he asked.

"Your partner." Veronica's voice shook.

"Is that what this is about?" He grabbed her arms. "Listen to me, Ford didn't die because of you. Cops face danger every day. It's part of the job. You…you can't blame yourself."

She tried to accept what he said. She knew he was trying to absolve her of guilt. But she heard the anger in his voice and wondered if he really believed his own words or if he blamed her as well. And if anything happened to Nathan…

She pushed the thoughts aside. She would go to Eli's tomorrow and see if she could figure out this whole mess. And if that didn't work, she'd go back to her parents' house—alone. She would remember who killed her parents, and then she could get on with her life. And he would be free to do the same.

NATHAN WATCHED Veronica retreat to her bathroom and silently fumed. He wanted to hold her and make love to her so badly he ached. But he'd let her down. He hadn't protected her, and he couldn't forget it. And he couldn't let his defenses down again. If he did, this time the person who was out to get Veronica might succeed. And if that happened, there would be no reason for him to go on with his own life.

He called the station. "Any news on Ford's car?"

"Looks like he was run off the road. Rear-ended by a late-model black car, paint job was high-class, custom job. Most likely someone with money."

Alma Jones or Gerald fit that picture. But was Alma strong enough to hit Veronica over the head and drag her inside a building? Maybe Alma and Gerald had conspired to kill her.

"Any further information on the bloody knife or the syringe in the Miller case?"

"Definite DNA of another person on the bloody knife. The syringe has been traced to a pharmaceutical company."

"Let me guess, Barrett Pharmaceutical."

"You got it. There's more. The towel the second knife was wrapped in."

"Yeah?"

"Came from Italy."

"Well, well, well," Nathan said. That might prove helpful. "Think it was imported?"

"We'll find out."

Now who might have recently taken a trip? Maybe he'd find out at Eli's.

"Thanks, Lieutenant. I suppose there's no news on the fire at Ms. Miller's office."

"Not yet, but it looks like arson. I'll let you know."

Nathan hung up and heard the shower dwindle to a stop. Veronica would be stepping out of the shower, her beautiful naked body glistening with water droplets. He wanted to make love to her with a fierceness that almost overwhelmed him. Instead he slumped on the couch and dropped his face into his hands.

A few minutes later he tiptoed to the bedroom to check on her. She lay on the bed, sound asleep. He felt her forehead, listened to her breathing, then covered her and lay down beside her. For a long time he simply watched her sleep, thanking God she'd survived. He'd definitely let her down.

Then he set the alarm so he'd wake every two hours and check on her. Reaching inside his pocket, he absentmindedly dug for a cigarette, then remembered again he'd given them up. He craved one so badly he thought he would die. Hell, that was nothing compared to how it would feel to give up Veronica.

THE NEXT NIGHT, Veronica dressed in a long black skirt and a white silk blouse, added a simple gold bracelet, necklace and earrings and wound her hair in a chignon. She thought she'd never cleanse the smell of smoke from her hair and body, but finally she felt clean. She wanted to look her most poised to meet with Eli's family. Her stomach rumbled and she swallowed to calm her nerves, pressing her fingers to her temple to massage her headache. Hopefully the painkillers would kick in soon. Tonight might be the night she unlocked the key to her past.

And if it was, it would be her last night with Nathan. The case would be over, she would deal with the past, and he would move on. She blinked back tears and powdered her face, then opened the door. Nathan stared at her intently.

"You look beautiful."

"Thanks." She rushed out of the room.

"It won't take me long to shower," he called.

"The towels—"

"I know where the towels are," Nathan said in a deep voice.

Veronica turned and met his gaze. She knew they were both remembering the last time he'd showered here. Tonight though, the tension crackled between them. Nathan reached for the buttons of his shirt and Veronica clenched her hands into fists so she wouldn't be tempted to help him. "Like I said, I won't be long." His gaze lingered a moment longer.

She hurried into the kitchen and made tea, hoping to calm herself. She tried not to fantasize about Nathan's hard, muscular body standing underneath the same shower head she'd stood under only moments before. She'd been alone most of her life; she would survive without Nathan. Then he would be safe.

She thumbed through the pages of her photo album, smiling at the picture of her parents, once again curious at the missing photographs. Then she spotted Eli and stared at his face. He had been so good to her over the years. Even if his son Gerald had been involved in some way in the deaths of her parents, Eli couldn't have known. He was too kind and loving.

"How's the suit?" Just as Nathan said, it had taken him only minutes in the shower.

She looked up and saw him standing in her den, freshly

showered and dressed in a dark suit and navy tie. He looked so handsome she wanted to wrap her arms around him. "Great." Veronica could barely speak past the lump in her throat. His hair looked darker with water still clinging to the ends and she detected the fresh scent of her own soap on his body.

"Are you ready?" he asked.

She nodded and grabbed her coat. On the drive Veronica mentally prepared herself for confronting Eli's family members. When they walked to the entrance of the mansion, she felt as if she were walking to her own tombstone.

A maid greeted them at the door and ushered them into the formal sitting area. Eli came toward Veronica, his face aglow.

"It's so nice to see you, darling." He wrapped her in a warm embrace, and all the doubts Veronica had had about him vanished. Eli loved her. He could never do anything to hurt her. Nathan stood in the background, then shook hands with Eli when he finally let her go. "It's nice to see you, Detective Dawson."

"And you, Eli."

"Would you like a drink?" Eli offered.

Veronica shook her head. "Club soda will be fine." After taking the painkillers for her head, she was afraid the alcohol would knock her out. And she wanted her wits about her for the duration of the evening.

Nathan smiled. "The same for me."

Eli clinked ice into three drink glasses and filled them, then turned with a smile. "My favorite also." He raised his glass. "Here's to my goddaughter."

"Yes, she's lucky to be here," Nathan said. "Especially after that fire yesterday."

Veronica almost choked on her drink. She hadn't expected Nathan to bring up the topic.

Eli's face turned ashen. "My dear, are you okay?"

She felt a moment of guilt. "I'm fine, Eli. Really."

Eli clutched the chair edge. "What happened?"

Nathan spoke up. "It looks like arson. I have a team investigating it."

A butler rang the dinner bell.

It took Eli a moment to recover. "Were you there, Veronica?"

"When I arrived the fire had already started. I tried to save some files. Then Detective Dawson showed up." She purposefully left out the part about the attack. She saw Nathan scrutinizing Eli.

"You shouldn't have gone inside," Eli said, dabbing at his pale face with a napkin. "You could have been killed, Veronica."

"Look, I'm fine. Let's talk about something else," she said.

The butler cleared his throat. "Sir? Dinner is served."

"Yes, let's go to dinner," Veronica said, taking Eli's arm.

When they entered the large, formal dining room, Veronica tensed at the formidable-looking Alma Jones, who stood at the head of the table.

"Mother, you remember Veronica?" Eli said.

"Certainly. How are you, Ms. Miller?"

Veronica forced a smile and ignored the sharp look the old woman gave her. "I'm fine."

A surge of quiet voices echoed from the hallway, and suddenly Eli's family filled the room. Tessa gave her a hug. "Hi, Veronica. I'm so glad you could make it. I was sorry you had to leave our luncheon. Are you feeling better?"

"Yes, thanks." Veronica smiled, grateful to have an ally in the family.

Nathan arched an eyebrow. "Veronica wasn't feeling well and had to leave early," Tessa explained.

"Yes, I'm sorry," Veronica said. "But I'm glad you're here tonight, Tessa."

Gerald looked polished and neat in his three-piece suit. He gave her a peck on the cheek. Veronica noticed Nathan's jaw tighten, but she returned the kiss. Her stomach knotted as she considered the possibility she was kissing her parents' murderer. And quite possibly, the man who'd attacked her this afternoon and burned down her office. Or was it Alma? Or Louise?

Eli's wife, Barbara, greeted her with a tight smile. "Nice of you to join us, Ms. Miller."

"Thank you for having me."

The room grew suddenly silent. Eli cleared his throat. Tessa started to babble about the elaborate menu to fill the awkward silence. Sonny, Eli's youngest son, stumbled in.

"Hi, Pops." Sonny slapped his dad on the back, then hugged his grandmother.

Alma winced. "Remember my sore arm, dear."

Veronica paused, her attention drawn to Alma. The older woman's wound was the same place she thought she'd stabbed her attacker.

Eli gave Sonny a harsh look. "It looks like you've been at it again, son." He wrinkled his nose. "Smells like it, too."

"Eli," Alma admonished. "Sonny, we have guests."

Always the formal hostess, Veronica thought, as Eli's wife pointed to their assigned seats and everyone took their places. Veronica had been seated between Sonny and Gerald while Tessa and Alma Jones surrounded Nathan.

"Bring Sonny some coffee," Eli told the maid. "And make it strong."

"No way. Get me a scotch," Sonny said, slurring his words.

The evening couldn't have been more uncomfortable. Veronica picked at the fancy seafood dish and listened to Alma Jones chatter about the latest society news. She made a futile attempt to ignore the foul smell of Sonny's whiskey breath and his constant rude interruptions.

Nathan asked about the antiques.

"I love Europe," Mrs. Jones said. "Many of my antiques are imported from France and Italy. I brought in only the best Persian rugs for the house."

Tessa smiled at Veronica across the table and helped ease some of the tension while Gerald tried to change the topic of conversation to politics; primarily his own campaign.

"How's it going?" Nathan asked.

"Very well," Gerald said, wiping his mouth with his napkin. "I think I have support over most of the state."

"Dessert everyone. Look, it's chocolate mousse," Eli's wife announced. She turned to Nathan. "Our cook makes the best mousse in Atlanta." The maid served each of their desserts, bypassing the elder Mrs. Jones.

"Aren't you having some?" Nathan asked.

"No, I'm afraid not," Mrs. Jones said.

"Grandma's diabetic," Tessa interjected.

"Yes," Mrs. Jones said. "I must watch my sugar."

"And take her insulin regularly," Tessa said with a shiver. "I don't see how Grandma gives herself shots."

Veronica met Nathan's gaze over the table. Was he thinking about the hypodermic he'd found in her bedroom?

Suddenly Sonny, who'd been thankfully silent for a few minutes, leaned forward, his elbows on the table.

"Well, Dad, are you going to tell everyone what this little dinner party is all about?"

Eli broke into a cough and Gerald slapped him on the back. "Are you okay, Father?"

After downing a glass of water, Eli wiped his mouth and stared at Sonny. "I don't know what you mean, Sonny. We're simply having a friend over for dinner."

Sonny chugged another scotch. His words were slurred when he spoke. "Oh, come on, Pops. I know why you invited Veronica. You want us to get to know her."

"Well…that's right," Eli stuttered, his face turning red. "She was the daughter of a close friend of mine."

Barbara glared at Eli.

"A friend?" Sonny sputtered.

Alma Jones's spoon hit her plate with a thud. Gerald frowned at Sonny. "Must you be so rude? We have guests." Gerald turned to Eli. "Father, you really should ship him off. He's an embarrassment to this family."

Veronica's fingers tightened around her spoon. She looked at Nathan and saw him studying the scene with a detective's eye. All she could see was humiliation on Eli's face. His youngest son obviously had a drinking problem. What a hardship for Eli.

Sonny stood up, knocking the table. Silverware clinked and Tessa caught her water glass just before it overturned. Sonny slapped the table edge. "You guys are such bozos. You're so caught up in your stupid politics and society pages, you don't even see it. Dad's trying to pull one over on all of you."

"What are you talking about?" Gerald asked angrily.

Tessa looked shocked at her brother's outburst.

Eli gulped and reached for Sonny's hand. "Sonny, let's talk in private."

"Shut up, Dad." Sonny shoved Eli's hand away and waved his arm in the air. Alma Jones gasped.

Eli's wife, Barbara, stood up. "Now, Sonny—"

"Mom, you aren't going to let Dad get away with this, are you?" Staggering, Sonny tried to walk around the table but stumbled against his mother's chair.

"With what?" Gerald asked.

Sonny steadied himself and pointed his finger at Veronica as if she had committed a crime. "I just found out Dad's going to put *her* in his will."

Chapter Fifteen

"No!"

"What? That's not possible!"

"Dad?"

The room erupted into chaos. Veronica froze, too stunned to move as Eli's wife, mother, Gerald and Sonny all verbally attacked Eli.

"You can't do this," Alma Jones shouted. "You'll disgrace us all."

Barbara's face turned murderous. "Eli, how dare you!"

In a more calm but equally puzzled voice, Gerald jumped up. "Father, what is the meaning of this?"

"She's not a part of the family," Sonny yelled.

Tessa's expression was unreadable as she observed her family fighting. "I think you're overreacting," she said calmly. "Father's probably just giving her a small token since her family is all gone."

"Stay out of this, Tessa," Gerald snapped.

"You little gold digger," Eli's mother said, pointing an accusing finger at Veronica. "You came back to Oakland to try and get money—"

"Mother, that's enough!" Eli yelled.

"Don't you talk to me that way, Eli Jones," Alma snapped. "I'm your mother!"

The air in the room grew hot and heavy. Veronica tugged at the neckline of her blouse, unable to breathe. Darkness descended around her, and a haze covered the room, blocking out all the faces. She closed her eyes so she wouldn't have to see the anger and fury as the people in the room fought and cursed.

But she still heard their voices. The ugly names. The people talking about her as if she wasn't there, blaming her, telling her she wasn't a part of the family, arguing about her. Then, in her mind she saw the distant image of a man's face, etched with grief and anger. The man stretched his arms toward her, but his face was distorted, his hair hardly visible in the dim light. Then music began to play "Somewhere over the Rainbow," and the face moved closer, his eyes a gray mist in the glow of the bedroom lamp.

It was Eli.

Her mother screamed, her father cried out in agony, Eli called her name. Blood dripped down her mother's face and arms and collected in a pool on the floor.

"No!" Veronica screamed. She wrenched herself free from the memory and stared at the people around her. Apparently her outburst had silenced them all, because they hushed and stared at her, shocked at her emotional display.

"Veronica?" Nathan reached for her, but she pulled away and ran toward the door.

"Veronica, wait!" Nathan called.

Her feet pounded the concrete steps, and she flew across the grass, panting and heaving for air. She had to escape. She had to get away from Eli.

Suddenly someone's arms caught her, jerking her to a stop. Thinking it was Eli, she struggled against him.

"Stop running."

She struggled, but the person's arms tightened.

"Veronica, it's me, Nathan. Stop fighting me."

His calm, soothing voice penetrated her panic, and she fell limp in his arms. "Let's get in the car. Then we'll talk."

Veronica sensed the others watching. She heard Eli's concerned voice as he asked Nathan about her. Nathan promised he'd call him later, then he climbed in and started the car. His breathing sounded erratic and she noticed a scratch on his face. Had she done that?

"Are you okay?" he asked, once he'd pulled away from the house.

Veronica nodded.

"You want to tell me what happened in there?"

Her jaw clenched, she twisted her fingers in her lap. She was shaking all over.

"Sweetheart, come on, I'm trying to help you. Trust me."

Veronica took a deep breath. She'd come there to find out who her parents' killer was, and now she thought she knew. Only it was too hard to believe. She didn't want to believe it.

"You remembered something, didn't you?" Nathan's warm hand covered hers, and he massaged her fingers. "Take your time and tell me about it."

Veronica waited until the house disappeared from sight. Finally she closed her eyes, hoping the image would disappear, too. She had to be wrong. But the vivid image of Eli remained.

"Tell me what you saw," Nathan prodded.

"Eli." Veronica almost choked on the word.

"What do you mean, Eli?"

"He was there. At my parents' house the night they died." She stifled a sob. "I heard them arguing. My mother screaming. My dad. The blood." Veronica covered her face with her hands, and Nathan pulled her to him. She was trembling so hard she felt like she was going to come apart in a million ragged pieces.

"Veronica, Eli was at your house a lot since he was friends with your parents. Could you possibly have things mixed up? Could he have been there another night and you're confusing the nights?"

Veronica shook her head. "I know what I saw. It was the vision in my dreams. Only this time I saw his face."

Nathan stroked her back. "Honey, I have a hard time believing Eli would have killed your parents. He has an impeccable reputation, was a great senator. Besides, he wasn't in town that night."

Veronica tried to listen to logic. "But I know what I saw," she said quietly. "The image was fuzzy, but I'm certain Eli was there. Maybe you should bring him in for questioning."

Nathan's hands tightened around the steering wheel. "I can't bring Eli in without some proof. He's a powerful and important man. And don't forget, he helped take care of you. I'd have to have some strong evidence for anyone to believe him guilty of wrongdoing."

Nathan didn't believe her. Veronica's heart squeezed.

"Maybe he showed up after the murder. I still think it's Gerald or Alma Jones," Nathan continued. "Did you notice the animosity radiating from that woman?"

Veronica nodded. "From his wife, too."

"And I managed to get Gerald and Alma Jones's fingerprints," Nathan said with a smile. "I'm going to drop them off at the lab. Alma is a diabetic and Gerald owns part of a pharmaceutical company. Either one had access to a syringe."

"Yes, but Mrs. Jones isn't that strong. I don't think she could have attacked me."

"Maybe not," Nathan said. "But Gerald could have." Nathan rounded the curve and glanced in the rearview mirror for the first time. He'd been so worried about Veronica, then so caught up in the case he hadn't realized the dark car was on his tail.

"Hold on. I think we're being followed."

She glanced back. "The black car again. Who is it?"

"I don't know, but I intend to find out." Veronica cringed. Nathan swerved and sped up, turned onto a side road and screeched the car to a stop, then spun it around in the other direction. He was headed back down the small road when the dark car came barreling around the curve. Nathan raced toward it, but the car swerved to the right. Then it passed them at riproaring speed and a gunshot exploded through the windshield. Veronica screamed. Nathan winced and grabbed his shoulder as a bullet pierced the area right above his heart.

HELL. HE'D BEEN HIT. Nathan moaned and tried to steer the car, but the blood seeped from his chest, and his vision blurred. The gun fired again, and he floored the car and sped down the road and onto the main highway. Feeling dizzy, he blinked and reached for Veronica. She had her hand pressed to his chest, trying to stop the bleeding, but her hand was soaked. She ripped off the end of her skirt and pressed it to his chest. He felt weak and light-headed.

"Pull over. I'll drive," Veronica said, taking control. Her face looked white as milk.

"Is the car still behind us?"

"No, it went the other way," Veronica said.

He stopped the car and crawled to the passenger side. The last thing he remembered before he passed out was Veronica planting a heavenly kiss on his mouth.

SHE PEELED into the hospital parking lot and jumped out at the emergency room exit. "He's been shot, someone help me!" Nurses and doctors rushed to her aid. They eased Nathan onto a stretcher and wheeled him into the examination room, firmly pushing Veronica aside.

Please let him live. Veronica prayed the same prayer over and over while she paced the faded floor of the waiting room. The odor of antiseptic and alcohol permeated her nostrils, and she willed herself not to be sick. At least until she found out if Nathan would be all right. And if he wasn't…she closed her eyes, driving away the awful images of his blood-soaked clothes. He had to be okay…he had to.

"Excuse me, miss? Did you bring Detective Dawson in?"

Veronica swirled around to see a dark-haired young doctor who looked as if he'd just finished med school. She forced her voice to work. "Yes, how is he?"

"I'm Dr. Byrne. We're taking the detective to surgery to remove the bullet."

"Is he going to be all right?" Veronica asked. Her heart was pounding so hard the blood roared in her ears. She leaned against the dingy wall for support.

"He should be. The bullet missed his heart, but we need to remove it. I'll let you know when the procedure's over."

A nurse approached her. "We're required to report all gun-shot wounds. Is there someone you want me to call?"

Veronica thought about the car that had been following them and wanted to kick herself for not getting the license plate number. She'd been too frightened to even think about it.

"Yes, Lieutenant Stevens."

The nurse smiled sympathetically. "I'll phone him right away." She handed Veronica a foam cup. "Go in the lounge and pour yourself a cup of coffee. It's not much better than the machine's but it'll take the edge off."

Veronica tried to sip the dark, rich coffee, but it tasted bitter to her mouth. The cup warmed her hands, though, and gave her something to hold on to while she sat and stared at the lines on the floor. Lieutenant Stevens rushed in several long minutes later and went straight to the nurses' station. "Where is Dawson? How bad is he hurt?"

The nurse explained his condition. Veronica glared at the man. When she'd first gone to him complaining of the threats to her life, he'd laughed her right out of his office. She'd wanted him to believe her, but not at Nathan's expense.

Now she wanted him to find the person who had hurt Nathan. "Lieutenant Stevens, I can explain." To her surprise, he listened patiently while she rambled through her story.

"And you weren't hit?" he asked, glancing down at her blood-covered shirt and torn skirt.

"No. I think the bullet was meant for me, but it missed." Veronica bit her lip to hold back the tears burning her eyes. The lieutenant shook his head. "Don't do that to yourself, Ms. Miller," he said. "Dawson's a cop. A cop puts his life on the line every day. It's his job." Exactly what Nathan had told her before.

His words gave no comfort. Neither did they assuage her conscience. Nathan was more than a cop. He was the man she loved. Stevens ordered a team to check her car for the other bullet, then paced the waiting room. Two hours and three cups of cold stale coffee later, the young doctor finally returned. Veronica's fingers felt raw from wringing them together.

''He's lost some blood and he's weak, but he's going to make it,'' the doctor said.

Veronica said a silent prayer of thanks, then begged the nurse to let her in the recovery room to see Nathan.

He was pale and so still that tears filled her eyes. Nathan had been hurt because of her—the very thing she'd wanted to avoid. She truly was a curse to the people she loved. Moving slowly, she tiptoed to his bedside and held his limp hand in hers, stroking the lines of his fingers. She pressed his hand to her cheek and kissed his palm, her heart breaking at the sight of the bandage across his bare chest and shoulder. The nurses had shaved off part of his sandy blond chest hair, and a dark bruise showed beneath the edges of the bandage.

She glanced down at her own blood-soaked clothes, then closed her eyes and whispered another prayer. But as she prayed, Nathan's image became blurred, and instead of his handsome face, she saw her parents lying on the floor of her old house, their blood covering her as she prayed for them not to die. The image was so strong she gasped for air and clutched Nathan's hand more tightly. The shadow hovered above her—Eli's face. He was upset, calling her name, and her parents were yelling at him. They were all screaming and fighting. Then he was gone.

Pieces of the night jumbled in her mind. Her parents lay on the floor, covered in blood, the knife sticking out of her father's chest. She heard her own scream, saw herself pull out the knife, saw another shadow hovering in the corner. Sirens wailed, and then she was crying and rocking herself back and forth over and over, begging her parents not to leave her.

''Ms. Miller?''

Veronica started when a hand touched her shoulder. She glanced up, breaking herself out of her memories. ''I need to check his vitals now,'' an elderly nurse said gently.

Veronica nodded and kissed Nathan's hand, then slowly laid

it down beside him. She'd remembered more of that night. She needed to remember the rest. Eli had been there, but was the other shadow Eli returning or someone else? She had to know.

"He's going to be fine," the nurse whispered, giving her a pat on the back.

"Thank you," Veronica said. She leaned over and kissed Nathan on the cheek. "I love you." Then she slipped out the door. He had almost died because of her. He'd jeopardized his career and his life for her. She'd blamed herself for her parents' deaths all her life. Anger and rage stormed inside her. She wouldn't let him take a bullet for her for nothing.

She was going back to her old house and see if she could remember the rest of the story. His love and support had gotten her this far. She could do the rest on her own. Then she could say goodbye to her past and Nathan. And he would be safe.

NATHAN STRUGGLED to open his eyes, but they felt as if they'd been pressed down by boulders. And the rest of his body felt worse. What the hell had happened?

Then he remembered. The fight at Eli's. Veronica's memory. The car following them. The bullet. He groaned and tried to raise his arm, but one side was taped with a bandage, the other secured with an IV. Damn. He couldn't move. Then the white walls started closing in on him.

He couldn't just lie here. Not when Veronica was in danger. Where was she, anyway?

He made a feeble attempt to call for help, but his words came out garbled, and his eyes were so heavy he couldn't keep them open. Medication. He must still be on the anesthetic. God, he needed to wake up and find Veronica. He flailed his arms and legs, but nothing happened and he realized the drugs were so strong he couldn't fight their effects. A heaviness weighted him down as his eyes drifted shut. His mind screamed for him to get help, to tell someone to watch out for Veronica, but the rest of his body wouldn't cooperate. He fell into a fitful sleep and dreamed that she was running from someone and calling his name. But he couldn't find her. And he knew if he didn't hurry, it would be too late.

THE POLICE WERE FINISHED with her car, so Veronica slid inside, painfully aware of the bullet hole in the windshield. She drove slowly, checking behind her to make sure she wasn't being followed. So far, so good.

As she drove down the long country road, dread mushroomed inside her. She wanted this to be over, but she realized the answers she found would not be pleasant. Before she went into the house, she paused and grabbed a flashlight and Nathan's gun from the glove compartment. She stashed them in her purse and walked up the steps. The minute she opened the door, she knew tonight was going to be different.

It was already after midnight, and darkness enveloped the house, so she switched on the flashlight. She almost stumbled over a loose board on the porch as she entered the den. She shone the light around the room and saw the same sparse, dusty furnishings, then proceeded to the bedroom, where it had all happened.

Snatches of memories flashed through her mind—the music, ''Somewhere over the Rainbow,'' a woman's soft soprano singing a lullaby, her father's deep rich voice calling her name. The floor creaked behind her and she turned to look out the window. An opossum skittered across the porch. She passed her room and stopped, appalled as she noticed the bedcovers and curtains had been demolished. Who hated her enough to do such a thing?

She forged ahead, intent on remembering the past no matter what the costs, and knelt beside the place on the floor where her parents had died. Then she heard the creaking of boards again and she smelled a strange smell, something like gardenias. She closed her eyes and remembered it was her mother's favorite perfume. The curtains fluttered and a cool breeze filtered in through the broken window. The music in her mind suddenly stopped, and a chill swept through the air, the moonlight outside fading as a shadow formed behind Veronica in the doorway. Was it real or a shadow from her memory?

She slowly turned and squinted in the heavy darkness. An outline was framed in the doorway, silhouetted by faint ripples of moonlight so the features looked stark. An image of Eli came to her mind and the argument at his house, then another fight he'd had with her parents the night they'd died. Horrible angry voices, shouting, screaming, her mother crying. Her head pounded with the sounds. Then she saw Eli's back as he ran out the door.

"It was *you*," Veronica said as she looked into the doorway and recognized the shadow, the one from her nightmare. Except this time it was real.

NATHAN PUSHED the nurse away and bellowed for her to remove his IV. Eli rushed in. "Where's Veronica? Was she hurt? I came as soon as I heard."

Nathan saw the worry lines on Eli's face. Veronica had suspected Eli, but he still couldn't believe her godfather would hurt her. "I don't know where Veronica is," Nathan snapped. "But if these nurses would let me out of here, I'd find her."

"You've just had surgery, young man. You're not going anywhere." A heavyset nurse folded her arms and glared at him.

Nathan snarled. "I'm a detective, and the woman I love is in danger."

"You're in love with Veronica?" Eli asked.

"Of course I am," he yelled. "Now tell these people to let me out of here. I have to save Veronica."

"What do you mean?" Eli asked, his eyebrows drawn upward.

"I mean someone tried to kill us after we left your house. And they're after Veronica."

Eli dropped his face in his hands. "Why?"

"I have an idea," Nathan said, trying to control his impatience. "But I need to find her. And we need to do it fast."

Eli motioned to the nurse. "Why don't you have one of the doctors give his officer in command a call?"

The nurse nodded and left. "If you help me, I'll fill you in on the way." Nathan yanked out the IV, wincing in pain as Eli helped him up. "Get me some damn clothes."

"This may be a mistake," Eli said.

"No way," Nathan said. "You don't want Veronica to be hurt, do you?"

"No." Eli's voice broke. He hurried out and returned seconds later with a surgical scrub suit.

Nathan dressed, then Eli slid his arm under Nathan to give support and opened the door. When they were in the car, Eli paused. "Dawson, you said you love Veronica."

"Yes, sir, I do."

"Then that gives us something in common."

"You really do care about her, don't you?" Nathan asked, wincing again as he tried to buckle his seatbelt.

"Yes, I do," Eli said quietly. "I love her very much. And I have to tell you the truth, Dawson. Veronica is my daughter."

VERONICA CLENCHED the purse to her side as her memories crashed back in a torrent of scattered, painful moments.

"Tessa, it was you. You were here that night. But why?"

The woman Veronica had thought was her friend moved inside the room, her body as sleek and cunning as a bobcat in the woods, but her voice sounded wild and razor sharp. "You knew it all the time. You never lost your memory. You played this stupid game so you could come back and get Father's money."

"What are you talking about?"

Tessa waved a knife in front of her. Her eyes blazed with hatred, and she wore an all-black warm-up suit, a drastic change from the silk suit she'd worn at the dinner party.

Then a cold, eerie feeling crept over Veronica. Yes, she had seen it before. Those eyes. She'd seen that crazy look on Tessa's face the night her parents had died.

"You wanted Daddy's money," Tessa ranted. "You came back to destroy our family. You wanted to take him away from me, just like you would have years ago." She stalked around the room waving the knife in wide circles.

"That's not true," Veronica said, pressing her hand to her temple as a dull ache throbbed behind her eyes. Then she saw it—the horrible scene between her parents.

"But you're not part of our family. And you never will be." Tessa kicked the end table and sent the lamp crashing to the floor. It shattered into pieces at Veronica's feet. "I was Daddy's little girl. Then Mama died and he married Barbara. And he forgot all about Mama. Then Barbara gave him sons. Sons!

"It was bad enough I had to share Daddy with Gerald, then that snotty-nosed brat, Sonny, came along. He thought he was Daddy's favorite. But he wasn't." Tessa was out of control. Veronica froze, afraid to say anything to add to her anger. "I was Daddy's favorite. I should have all his money. Not Gerald or Sonny. And certainly not you—you're his illegitimate baby."

"I know I'm not part of your family," Veronica said, fighting her own emotions. "I never—"

"Shut up!" Tessa screamed. "You were there. You heard what your mama said. You saw Daddy, too, and he would have taken you and then I would have had to share everything with you. And Daddy would have forgotten all about me like he did my mother."

"Tessa, I don't know what you mean." But Veronica did know. It was all coming back to her. The fight between her parents had started when Eli burst in.

Eli was her father.

A shudder racked through her at the realization. That was the reason her parents had fought.

She could see her father crying. "What do you mean she's not my baby?" he'd asked in disbelief.

Her mother had sobbed, "I was pregnant when we got married."

"With my baby," Eli had said. Then Eli had raged at her mother. "Why didn't you tell me you were pregnant?"

Her mother had broken down again. "Because you were running for senator. Your mother threatened me. She didn't want me to ruin your career."

"I don't believe that," Eli had yelled.

The whole time her father had stood in disbelief. And she'd hidden in the corner and watched her family fall apart. Her father had accused her mother of lying to him. Her mother had cried and sobbed until she couldn't talk. Eli had been furious. He had said he'd just found out the truth and wanted to claim Veronica as his own. Her mother had yelled that he would never get custody of her. Her father had threatened to leave her mother.

Then Eli had stormed out. But her parents had still been alive when Eli had left.

She glanced at Tessa, and the memory of her sneaking into the house came back vividly. Tessa had been young and beautiful, but the evil she'd possessed had caused her to attack Veronica's mother. She'd run in, yelling that she wanted to see Veronica. But her mother had told Tessa to leave. In a wild rage, Tessa had somehow grabbed the kitchen knife and fought with her mother. Her mother had been trying to protect Veronica, to keep Tessa from finding her. Then Tessa had stabbed her mother, and her mother had fallen to the floor with a scream. Her father had rushed in, and Tessa had spun around and lunged at him with the knife.

The blood had spouted out, and even as a child she'd been amazed at Tessa's strength. Then Tessa, all wild-eyed, had come looking for her. Veronica had hidden under the bed and watched, holding her breath, knowing she was going to be next.

Just like now.

"Tessa, I didn't remember," Veronica said. "All this time, I didn't know Eli was...was—"

"Was your father!" Tessa spat the words at her and brought the knife up over her head. "Well, you remember now. I can see it on your face. That night I heard Dad arguing with Barbara. He had just found out about you, and Barbara was upset he'd had a mistress. Daddy said he was going after you, that you should be a Jones, but Barbara said your mother was a cheap whore and you weren't coming to our house!''

A shudder coursed through Veronica as Tessa moved toward her, her eyes crazed. ''I'm going to get rid of you once and for all,'' Tessa screamed.

She pounced and slashed the knife at Veronica.

Chapter Sixteen

Veronica quickly backed away. She had to stall. "Tessa, I don't want your father's money. I don't want anything—"

"Be quiet!" Tessa barked wildly. "You think I've gone to all this trouble for nothing? When Daddy first learned he had cancer—"

"Eli has cancer?" Veronica felt the shock to her system as if she'd been physically punched.

"Yes. That's when he changed his will to include you. And you came back to town. Don't tell me you didn't know!"

"But...but I didn't," Veronica stammered. Why hadn't Eli told her?

"Then he started inviting you over, wanting us to get to know you. He pretended you were his goddaughter when all along I knew the truth and I hated you."

Veronica swiped at a tear streaming down her cheek. This was too much. Eli was her father. She barely knew how she felt about that, and now she'd learned he might be dying.

"How long does Eli have?"

"That's none of your business," Tessa snapped, taking a step forward.

Veronica tensed. She had to stall a little longer, try to talk some sense into Tessa. "So you shot Nathan."

"That bullet was meant for you. Just like the knife."

"You broke into my apartment and tried to kill me. And

all along I thought it was a man who tried to stab me.'' *I even suspected Eli.*

"Of course. All it took was a little padding. And a little help from my friend. She kept drugging your tea.''

"What friend?''

"Louise.'' A sickening smile lit Tessa's face.

The tea Louise kept making for her. Veronica felt dizzy. How easy it had been for Tessa. "So Louise was helping you? Why, for money?''

Tessa laughed, a hideous sound that turned Veronica's stomach. Tessa truly was psychotic. "You idiot. I didn't have to pay Louise. All I did was blackmail her.''

Snatches of small things flitted back to Veronica. She remembered Nathan saying Louise had a shaky history, but she'd never suspected Louise was involved with Tessa. She'd thought the connection was Gerald.

"I see. And she took my keys from the office. That's how you kept getting in.''

Tessa looked triumphant. "It was a great plan. Louise was so afraid someone would find out about her past and she'd have to leave. She loved this stupid small town.'' Tessa laughed. "I thought we'd succeed in making you go nuts before I had to kill you, but I guess you're stronger than I thought.''

You've got that right, Veronica thought, digging her nails into the side of her purse. If she could get the gun, maybe she could ward off Tessa.

"When Louise drugged your tea at the office before our lunch, I was hoping you'd fall asleep at the wheel.''

"But instead I showed up for our lunch meeting and got sick.''

"Right.'' Tessa waved the knife around, laughing.

"And the red jacket and pin? The fire at my office?''

"That was Louise's idea. She got nervous, wanted to cover her own tracks.''

"And that detective, Ford?''

Tessa giggled. "He got in the way." She narrowed her eyes. "And you—you're going to die just like your parents."

Veronica sucked in a harsh breath. Ironic, everyone had thought she was the crazy one, when Tessa had obviously been unstable all her life. She would not let Tessa kill her. She would see her rot in jail or a mental ward. Tessa licked her lips like a predator coming in for the kill, and Veronica knew the time had come to defend herself. She reached inside and pulled out the gun just as Tessa lunged for her.

"HURRY!" Nathan bellowed as Eli raced down the road. He used Eli's car phone to call for backup. He'd wanted to explain his suspicions to Eli, but he'd decided to wait. Maybe he was wrong about Gerald. He could always hope.

"Are you sure she'll be here?"

"No, but it's our best guess. She's been coming here to try and regain her memory."

When they turned the corner to the old homestead, a black customized Cadillac sat in the drive.

"Gerald's car?" Eli said. "What the hell?"

Eli barreled into the drive and Nathan leaped out with Eli on his heels, his bandaged arm pressed against his side. Nathan stopped by the car for his gun and quickly checked the glove compartment. It was gone. He prayed Veronica had taken it. Putting a finger to his lips, he motioned for Eli to be quiet as they padded up to the porch. Just as they made the last step, Nathan heard a scream. Then a gunshot.

Veronica.

He bolted through the door, sending a fresh wave of pain jolting through his shoulder. He'd probably undone his stitches, but he didn't care. He had to save Veronica from Gerald. He quickly scanned the den, but saw nothing. Then he heard sounds from the back. He raced through the hall toward Veronica's parents' room. Eli hurried behind him. The sounds of scuffling brought another surge of panic. He hoped he was in time! Bracing his good arm against the door, he inched into the doorway.

Only it wasn't Gerald who was fighting with Veronica. Veronica was struggling with Tessa. Their heavy breathing filled the air. Tessa knocked the gun from Veronica's hand, and it fell to the floor. Then Tessa pushed Veronica down and climbed over her, raising the knife to Veronica's neck.

Eli ran in behind him. Nathan kicked the gun aside, then grabbed Tessa's arm and tried to drag her off Veronica. Tessa struggled, clawing at him with one hand while arcing the hand with the knife above Veronica. Veronica bucked upward, trying to dislodge Tessa.

"Tessa, stop!" Eli shouted. Eli grabbed Tessa's hand and pried her fingers from the knife. Tessa stared at him as if she didn't recognize him, her face etched with fury. Veronica pushed Tessa away and Eli managed to drag Tessa to the corner. She kicked and screamed. "No, she has to die. She has to."

"Tessa, my God, what are you doing?" Eli said, choking on his emotions.

Tessa broke into hysterical sobs, and Eli took her in his arms and rocked her back and forth. Nathan rushed to Veronica and crushed her to him, prodding her body with his hands to check for injuries. Veronica clung to him, her breath erratic. He felt her heart pounding as he hugged her. "Are you hurt?"

"I'm okay," Veronica whispered.

He spotted blood on her blouse. "But you're bleeding. Tell me where you're hurt!"

A soft nervous laugh escaped Veronica. "It's not me. It's you." Her voice broke on a sob. "You undid your stitches."

Nathan looked down and realized blood was seeping through his bandage. His shoulder and arm throbbed, but it didn't matter. Veronica was safe. And the whole nightmare was over. All his prior reservations about marriage and his job faded when he looked into her eyes. He wouldn't be able to do his job if he wasn't with her. Nothing mattered without Veronica. He kissed her hair, her face, her mouth, her fingers. His voice cracked as he said, "Dammit, why did you come here by yourself? I might not have made it in time."

"You're here now, that's all that matters," Veronica said in a strangled whisper. He hugged her to him and braced her face with his hands to kiss her again.

"Eli's my father," Veronica said when he finally relaxed against her. "I...I didn't know."

Nathan stroked her hair. "I know, sweetheart. I know."

As soon as the police arrived, Tessa was taken into custody. Her frantic, hysterical sobs had died, and she looked like a shattered, injured animal. Veronica almost felt sorry for her. Almost.

"I'll be there with you," Eli told Tessa. "We'll get you some help."

"We'll wait for you in the car." Lieutenant Stevens escorted a handcuffed and subdued Tessa outside.

Eli's eyes were red and swollen and his expression wary as he approached Veronica. Nathan sat beside her on the old couch, holding her hand. She was still trembling from shock. The memories that had flooded back were painful, yet in the background of her mind, occasionally a sweet memory surfaced. She hoped in time she would recall completely the precious little time she'd had with her parents. And no matter what Eli or Tessa said, her mother and *father* were dead.

"I'm so sorry, Veronica," Eli said, kneeling in front of her. He ran a hand through his disheveled gray hair.

"I remember everything," Veronica said, squeezing Nathan's hand for support. "I remember all about that night. You and my mom...and dad."

Eli lowered his face. "I...I didn't know Tessa was there." He shook his head sadly. "I swear I didn't. When I left that night, your parents were so upset, I honestly believed what Scroggins said."

"You didn't know Tessa was disturbed?" Nathan asked.

Eli cleared his throat, his voice husky with emotions. "She had problems as a child, emotional ones after her mother died. But I never knew it was this bad. And I never realized my transgressions hurt her so badly." He wiped a tear from his cheek. "I covered up her problems. She got in trouble with the law a few times, but Scroggins always helped me cover it up. And lately…"

"Lately what?" Nathan asked.

"Lately I thought she was doing better." He sighed. "I know I made some mistakes, Veronica. I hope you can forgive me."

Veronica's throat tightened. "You didn't know my mother was pregnant when you broke up with her?"

"No. I was young and ambitious and foolish. I had no idea."

"And you didn't know your mother threatened her?"

"No. I was caught up in the campaign. I allowed Mother to run my life. Then when I found out about you…" He paused and squeezed her hand. Veronica stiffened, unsure how to respond. "I wanted you. But your parents didn't want to make it public. We argued. And I left." He paused again, then cleared his throat. "Then after they died, I wanted to come for you. But your grandmother was there. And when I saw how traumatized you were, I was afraid if you remembered, you'd blame me. I didn't think I could live with that."

"Then I didn't remember," Veronica said.

Eli wiped tears from his cheeks. "I decided that was for the best. I was so afraid you'd hate me."

The sincerity in Eli's voice tugged at Veronica's heart. She remembered Tessa saying Eli was ill. "Was Tessa telling the truth about your illness?"

Eli nodded. "When I discovered my illness, I knew I had to make up for lost time with you. Then you moved back, and I couldn't stay away from you."

Veronica felt Nathan's arm tighten around her. She pressed her hand over his and squeezed it, thanking him for his silent support.

Lieutenant Stevens poked his head in. "We're ready to go." He nodded toward Nathan. "They picked Louise Falk up a few minutes ago."

Eli stood. "I'd like to see you again, Veronica."

Veronica hesitated. "Give me some time, Eli."

He bent and kissed her cheek. "I'll be waiting."

"What about the rest of your family?"

Eli smiled. "They'll have to understand. It's about time I took charge of things." Then he left to take care of Tessa.

Veronica turned to Nathan and saw the blood still soaking his bandage. He must be in pain, but he hadn't complained. "We need to get you back to the hospital." She started to rise, but he pulled her back against him.

"Not until we settle something."

"What?"

Nathan cupped her face in his hands. "I love you, Veronica. I want you to marry me."

Veronica's emotions ranged from surprise to joy to fear. "I can't."

He winced as if she'd hurt him. "Why not?"

Veronica bit her lip and moved across the room, distancing herself from him. "I love you, Nathan. But…but I cause people to die."

Nathan grabbed her with his uninjured arm and lowered his mouth to hers. "I'm still here."

Veronica gazed into his eyes.

"Ah, darling, you've given me back my life. Don't you know, you're the very reason I want to live." Then he crushed her in his embrace and there was nothing else for her to say except "Yes."

Epilogue

Veronica slipped her hand into the crook of Eli's arm, and he escorted her down the aisle. She couldn't control the smile on her face. The wedding was set in the small chapel in Oakland, and beautiful azaleas flanked the front lawn. Tulips and wild-flowers lined the walkway outside, and gorgeous white dog-wood blossoms filled the trees. Inside she'd asked for pots of pansies so she could take them home and plant them in her yard—the one she and Nathan would share—the one where their children would run and play.

Church organ music drummed softly, and she hugged Eli's arm, grateful she'd made peace with her past and with him. Then she looked up and saw a wicked, sexy gleam in Nathan's amber eyes, and couldn't wait for her honeymoon.

At the end of the aisle, Eli kissed her and handed her over to Nathan.

"Hi, beautiful," he whispered.

"Hi." She pulled him close and whispered in his ear, "I had another vision."

A serious expression replaced Nathan's smile. He'd been so kind and understanding during the last month while she'd sorted out her past and her feelings about Eli. And while she'd dealt with a host of memories that constantly grew. Dr. Sandler had helped her understand that she'd blamed herself for her parents' deaths because they'd been arguing about her.

They'd also talked about Ford's death and how they would handle Nathan's job.

Veronica smiled. "It's a vision of our future. With lots of little Dawson babies in it."

"Don't scare me like that." Nathan dragged her into his arms and kissed her. "You're going to make a wonderful mother."

Veronica smiled. With Nathan's love and support, she felt confident she would. "I love you," she whispered.

"I love you back." He pressed his mouth to hers again.

The judge cleared his throat. "We haven't gotten to that part yet."

Laughter erupted in the church, and Veronica clung to Nathan's hand, ready to take the vows that would last for the rest of her life.

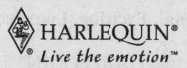

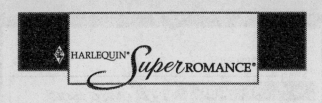

…there's more to the story!

Superromance.
A *big* satisfying read about unforgettable
characters. Each month we offer *six* very different
stories that range from family drama to adventure
and mystery, from highly emotional stories to
romantic comedies—and much more! Stories
about people you'll believe in and care about.
Stories too compelling to put down….

Our authors are among today's *best* romance
writers. You'll find familiar names and talented
newcomers. Many of them are award winners—
and you'll see why!

If you want the biggest and best
in romance fiction, you'll get it
from Superromance!

Emotional, Exciting, Unexpected…

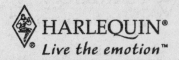

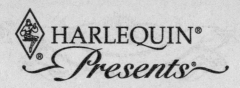

HARLEQUIN®
Presents®

The world's bestselling romance series...
The series that brings you your favorite authors,
month after month:

Helen Bianchin...Emma Darcy
Lynne Graham...Penny Jordan
Miranda Lee...Sandra Marton
Anne Mather...Carole Mortimer
Susan Napier...Michelle Reid

and many more uniquely talented authors!

Wealthy, powerful, gorgeous men...
Women who have feelings just like your own...
The stories you love, set in exotic, glamorous locations...

HARLEQUIN®
Presents®

Seduction and Passion Guaranteed!

Harlequin Historicals®
Historical Romantic Adventure!

From rugged lawmen and valiant knights to defiant heiresses and spirited frontierswomen, Harlequin Historicals will capture your imagination with their dramatic scope, passion and adventure.

*Harlequin Historicals...
they're too good to miss!*